Books by H

Shado

Best Kept Lies
Price of Freedom
Splendid Isolation
The Truth about the Liar
Counterfeit Conscience
Tipping Point

Surface Tension

Twice Upon a Blue Moon
A Smile as Sweet as Poison
The Face of Scandal

Sexy Snax

In the Presence of Mine Enemy

What's His Passion?

Fistful of Lies

Anthologies

Wild Angels
Wild After Dark
Racing Hearts

Single Titles

A Touch of Spice
Courting Treason

Bliss

ISBN # 978-1-78651-905-4

©Copyright Helena Maeve 2016

Cover Art by Posh Gosh ©Copyright 2016

Interior text design by Claire Siemaszkiewicz

Totally Bound Publishing

Printed and bound in Great Britain by Clays Ltd, St Ives plc

1

BLISS

HELENA MAEVE

Chapter One

Even once Allegra understood that the fireflies dancing above her head were fluorescent lights, she still had a hard time forcing them to stillness. She made to snatch at their fluttering wings only to realize that she couldn't reach that far up. She blinked once, twice, her vision gradually adjusting to the distant glow of electric lamps and the firm, unmoving stretch of wall beyond them.

Cinderblock and steel trapped her on five sides, with a floor-to-ceiling mirror at the far end of the room reflecting her predicament. It took Allegra a moment to recognize herself in the blonde figure stretched out on the metal cot. Her skin was ashen, like the cloudy run-off from a laundromat. A bruise that she couldn't recall bloomed high on her left cheek. Bleached silver-blonde hair hung limp despite the frankly lethal quantities of product she had sprayed into it just last night.

At least she *thought* it had been last night.

Time was a mutable thing these days. Going from trip to trip often meant whole stretches passed without her knowledge.

She righted herself slowly. Mercifully, the concrete stayed still beneath her feet. It was a start—not enough to keep panic from kindling in her chest, but a definite indication that she wasn't dreaming or dry. She would have known if she was dry. That particular brand of hallucination usually brought with it a fairly specific bite.

Allegra watched her reflection lick its cinnamon-tinted lips. She couldn't taste the familiar bittersweet tang of Bliss, but the stain confirmed it. Maybe she had taken a tainted batch. With cops making the rounds, she remembered having to go way out of her usual haunts to find anyone selling.

Times like these, dealers tried to push more conventional drugs, things like crack and meth, that would only net them a couple of nights in jail if were they ever arrested. No one wanted to cross the PharmaCorps. The guy who'd finally come through for Allegra had been a little antsy, a little shaky, but she had been too desperate for a fix to play the discerning customer.

Hindsight revealed that as a less than stellar call.

She had taken the Bliss without a second thought, only to wind up in a room with no windows and no memory of how she got there. *A day in the life of*, she thought, determined to keep panic at bay.

Allegra ran her hands down the length of her body, checking for tags or empty pockets. Everything from the credit chip at her belt to the leather boots she'd filched from a shop window just last week seemed in place — everything except her custom-fitted carbon steel switchblades. Those things had cost her a fortune at the ice market two months back. They were easily the most expensive things she owned.

Whoever had fished her off the streets must not have been keen to get stabbed for their efforts. Rumor had it junkies like her were all kinds of dangerous. The smiling, computer-generated faces on the news said as much, and everyone in the Docklands knew that the squeaky clean crowd — with their fancy hovercars and portable camcords — would never make shit up for the sake of ratings. Why come to her aid in the first place?

The perfunctory inspection helped to restore some sense of awareness, but it sure as hell didn't bring Allegra any closer to figuring out where she was or how to get out. A robber would've taken her clothes and money, and left her to dry up in a ditch. On the other hand, if rippers had taken her, she'd have a lot worse to contend with than the bruise darkening on her cheek.

If it wasn't one and it wasn't the other, that only left—

"Aw, shit." Allegra bounded off the cot. The room swayed around her, sharp edges blurring fast.

She had heard the talk on the news, but junkies weren't an APU problem. They weren't a state problem, either. Crime stats only counted them if they had an active hand in dealing the narcotics that kept them going. No one bothered trying to get them off the streets when the prisons were already overcrowded with fraudsters and tech-terrorists. Arcadia's government just didn't have the money.

The hiss of pistons at the far end of the room brought Allegra up short. She recoiled a step, the backs of her knees hitting the cot as a door in the mirrored wall slid open, offering a brief, confirming glimpse of the hectic coffee-and-donuts realm on the other side.

That fleeting glimpse was all Allegra got before a stern, martial figure stepped into view. If she was a cop, then she sure as hell didn't look like any cop Allegra had ever seen before. The woman could have been anywhere from twenty-five to fifty, her uniform dark and her copper-red hair pulled back severely. Ambition oozed from her every pore. Her voice, when she spoke, was full-on urbane Arcadian.

"Ms. Avenson," said the cop, "please sit down."

Five words and Allegra knew she was in trouble.

"Why?" she shot back, balling her hands into fists. "So you can tell me what a bad girl I've been? Thanks, but no thanks. I know my rights, and you can't keep me locked in here for more than twenty-four hours." Not unless they charged her with something, then it was 'goodbye, Docklands' and 'hello, Warden'.

Her uniformed visitor nodded crisply. "True enough, but you have only been with us for twelve."

"Swell," Allegra drawled, folding her arms across her chest. "So to what do I owe the pleasure? Am I being accused of something?"

9

She watched as the cop arched her perfectly sculpted eyebrows in a textbook simulacrum of astonishment. "Have you committed any crimes lately?"

Allegra scoffed. It was like asking if a dog had dug up any bones. There was one way to survive in the Docklands and one way only. People who tried to walk the straight and narrow soon learned that that path led nowhere.

Her new friend went on, "As far as the APU is aware, you've been clean and virtuous for a year. You have a fixed home address, a caseworker. Even a steady job." The woman's smile turned razor-sharp. "Of course, your caseworker hasn't seen you for fifteen weeks, your home is a derelict warehouse listed for demolition and your job… Well. When you have nothing else, I expect trading your body must seem like a solution."

Allegra shifted her weight from one leg to the other. She wasn't going to retreat or apologize for the choices she had been forced to make. "Is there a point to all of this? 'Cause I'm not hearing a lot of reasons for why I'm sleeping in a jail cell here…"

"Aren't you?" There it was, in the cop's amber-black eyes, the image of a predator about to lunge for the throat. "I think we both know that being clean holds another meaning for *your* kind, Ms. Avenson."

The contemptuous slant of a smile on rouged lips confirmed Allegra's worst fears. The cop had her record — the real one, the one that didn't make a secret of her larger predicament.

"Now, now," the woman said, "do sit down, Ms. Avenson. I dislike having to repeat myself. We both know you're not simple."

Allegra didn't refuse this time. Although thin and a little uneven, the cot was still preferable to sprawling on the cold cement floor. She could feel the shadow of a threat hanging over her like the sword of Damocles. It had a woman's tapered curves.

"Ms. Avenson, my name is Mallory Osker. I am Deputy

Commissioner for the APU's Homicide Division. It is my job to keep Arcadian streets from devolving into chaos, to make sure our cold case archives don't spawn new threads."

With the city being a run by crime syndicates who dubbed themselves respectable legal entities, Allegra bit back the urge to suggest a career change. Mallory Osker wasn't talking about *her* city. She was talking about those parts of Arcadia where people roamed in hovercars and hid themselves behind the tall walls of fortress homes — the Arcadia of those who had made their fortunes selling Bliss to people like her before taking the drug off the market and forcing the trade into dank back alleys peopled by mean-looking thugs.

Her addled mind caught up to another salient detail. Osker hadn't claimed that she worked for Narcotics. Whatever this was about, it wasn't the handful of pills Allegra had scored on the sly last night — it *was* last night. She remembered that much.

Allegra couldn't shake the niggling suspicion that she had landed smack in a trap, but she kept her mouth shut for a change. Better to let Osker show her hand before she made any attempts at bribery.

' "You may have read about some…recent troubles over the past couple of months. Unfortunately our censors can't control every outlet," said the deputy commissioner, clearing her throat as if to dislodge that unpleasant bit of truth. "You see, a string of murders has captivated the public's imagination. It's nothing to write home about, except it appears all the victims are loosely connected to the illegal and highly pernicious trade of Bliss." Osker narrowed her eyes. "You wouldn't know anything about that, would you?"

"Are you shitting me?" Allegra snorted. There was no flinch of outrage that could dislodge the smug anticipation on the cop's face. Allegra felt her heart skip a beat. "I haven't killed anyone!" She gripped the steel edge of the cot. "If you're trying to set me up, lady —"

Exasperation spilling from her in waves, Osker shook her head. "I'm not in the business of accusing innocent women, Ms. Avenson, and I don't appreciate you implying otherwise."

"Then you'd best ask someone else. I don't know shit," Allegra insisted. "I'll swear it on every god you please. Here—I'll take a polygraph, whatever." *Just let me go.* She smothered the plea for fear of giving Osker even more power over her. She'd had Allegra plucked off the streets and brought here for a reason. Allegra wasn't sure she wanted to find out what that might be, and yet she was sure Osker meant to tell her anyway. She had the look of a woman who liked to play to an audience—even a captive one.

Allegra had no power in this cold, blinding room. Her rights were no more a shield than a puff of smoke. The Geneva Conventions had gone out of fashion sometime around the early twenty-first century. It was hard to pinpoint the precise moment—and Allegra lacked the schooling to make an educated guess—but it had happened long before Bliss was even a speck of an idea on the mind of some enterprising lab coat.

Cops had leeway like never before. Prosecution was as good as conviction—unless you had the cash for a hotshot lawyer. Allegra did not.

Mallory Osker didn't prolong her misery by much. "We know you're an empath, Ms. Avenson. There is no need to pretend."

Allegra blanched. She didn't dare say a word. To confirm was to end up in a lab, strapped to a table and foaming at the mouth. To deny it was pointless. Osker knew. Those records were supposed to be sealed—the judge had promised Allegra as much when she'd stopped charging him.

She was suddenly very glad that she had agreed to sit down.

"You've been tested?" Osker asked primly. The click of

heels on bare cement floors made for a strange and awful counterpoint to the brutal hammering of Allegra's heart. Osker had read the file. She already knew the answer to that question, but she pressed anyway, twisting the knife in the wound because she could. "You've taken the Walleran Assessment, haven't you? Acute Empatheia Nervosa is such a rare condition…" Allegra's silence drew a sigh. "Ms. Avenson, you might as well be honest with me. I am on your side."

That is the single greatest lie you've told so far. Certainty sank into her belly like a block of cement. It was too late to capitalize on her talents now. What she knew, she knew thanks to her strange and terrible gift.

"Why?" Panic-choked, she managed to ask that much. They were in a jail cell. This wasn't group therapy. No one ever brought up her condition unless they meant to use it to their own ends.

The deputy commissioner smiled thinly. "Because I too need your help—and in exchange, I am prepared to be generous. I'm well aware that the Walleran Assessment is used to determine whether an empath's condition presents an immediate risk to him or herself, or to others. I also know that based on the results, our medical boards decide whether to treat the disease or attempt corrective surgery. You're ranked seven, Ms. Avenson. That's more than enough to merit intervention."

"No shit," Allegra gritted out. Qualifying for the op hadn't been a problem. Cash flow was a different story. Ever since the medical boards had been privatized, the only way to get on the list was to pay up or know someone high enough on the totem pole to cover the expense.

Allegra's best attempts had netted her an intern with a wealth of student loans, a rigid sense of filial piety and no interest in doing a favor for a friend in need, however good the sex. She knew she wasn't high-end escort material, and there were few surgeons who liked to slum it with a piece of ass from the wrong side of the tracks. Of those who did, none were interested in going back for seconds.

If Allegra had cared for their good opinion, she might have been insulted.

"Then this is your lucky day, Ms. Avenson. The APU would be glad to sponsor you—in exchange for your help with this case." Osker folded her arms across her chest, the picture of selfless charity. "What do you say?"

Every fiber of her being was willing her to escape this steel-and-concrete prison, but Allegra knew her options were limited. She swallowed hard. "What kind of help?" Whatever it was, she knew it would be a bad deal.

Informants had a way of becoming very popular very fast in the Docklands—and of ending up bloated and blue in the East River. Mallory Osker's aura of authority sure as hell didn't mean she'd risk her agents for Allegra's sake. As long as she was just the junkie who occasionally sold her hand or her mouth, nobody knew her name and she could go about her business unmolested. If Allegra agreed, she'd be on her own. No amount of sweet talk could convince her otherwise.

If? Allegra ran a hand through her bleached-blonde hair. Even reeling from the information overload, she knew full well she couldn't refuse. "What kind of help do you expect? I'm not in with the Triad, no one important ever put faith in me..."

"You can tell when someone's lying, can't you? Read their mood?"

Allegra nodded. *You mean, like I can tell you're not being entirely truthful right now?* She hated revealing that part of herself. As a kid, she'd gotten into trouble for skewering myths and school-fed propaganda, not to mention the hundred and one other lies adults peddled, purportedly for the sake of kindness.

No wonder she got beat up all the time.

"Then you're precisely what we need. You'll go over taped interrogations, assist in weeding out discrepancies in witness statements. We'll arrange for you to meet with your handler outside the precinct to avoid drawing attention. Once you've completed the assignment and the Bliss Slayer is behind bars, I will personally assist in scheduling your operation."

"The Bliss Slayer?"

The corners of Osker's mouth twitched up, a smile giving her face an almost human quality. It didn't last. "That's what the whisper sheets have taken to calling him. Personally, I would prefer 'dead' or 'behind bars'." She shrugged. "I would also like an answer."

"What, I don't get time to mull it over?"

"I'm afraid not." Mallory Osker didn't seem like she'd be afraid of much. Allegra doubted she lacked a stick in case the carrot didn't do it. She didn't want to know what that entailed.

Gods, she could've done with another shot of Bliss. It was sure to help make her mind up, to clear her head. She wanted, more than anything, to not need Bliss in the first place. There was only one way she'd ever get to fulfill that wish.

"And if I say no?"

"If you say no," Osker sighed, "which, for your sake, I hope you don't. Then you will be charged with possession of illegal narcotics with the intent to distribute. You will be found guilty and serve a three month sentence in a medium-security penitentiary."

What she didn't have to add was that with the same corporations in charge of both prison and the pharmaceutical industry, her access to Bliss would dry up fast. If Allegra went inside, she would have to quit cold turkey. A cold shiver rippled down Allegra's spine at the thought, like icy fingertips stroking up and down her back. The last time she'd tried to go without Bliss for longer than a couple of days, she had almost punctured her skull with her uncle's electric drill.

"Shit. Fine," she breathed. "Fine, I'll do it."

Chapter Two

The girl had a mouth on her, if not much else. She resembled a coatrack topped with a mop of silver-blonde feathers, her legs so skinny under those faux-leather pants that they might have been prosthetics. How she hadn't died of anemia yet, Darius didn't know and didn't want to ask.

"The file doesn't cite any diseases," muttered mousy-haired Jasme as she flipped her tablet shut, "but there's no reason to suppose she hasn't caught some autoimmune bug with that lifestyle..."

Darius frowned. "She has. It's called poverty." The rest just flowed from that, like a riverbed broadened by the pitiless cascade of its waters.

He knew he should have waited for the deputy commissioner to call him in before he entered, but she already had Avenson's okay. The odds of getting more out of the girl were slim. Besides, Darius had work to do.

"Commissioner?"

Osker turned too quickly to notice the prisoner's flinch but Darius saw it clearly. There was no faking that kind of instinctive recoil. He wondered if he truly looked so awful, if his trench coat and ill-fitting suit were so dreadful as to make a grown woman quail. He pushed the thought aside.

"Ma'am, if we're done here, I have a witness to interrogate..."

The deputy commissioner fixed him with a slow, level stare, the kind that usually told him he was in trouble. "Ms. Avenson, meet your handler. Detective Leon Darius."

They'd warned him when he joined the unit that Osker's punishment was swift and sudden. No one had said it was also completely, off the charts irrational.

He balked. "Ma'am, you can't be serious—"

"Perfectly serious, Detective." And her tone implied that questioning her orders was both unwise and unwelcome. "You have been working this case since the beginning. You know what we're searching for, what we're dealing with. Whenever possible, you have highlighted a lack of resources. Consider this a reward for all your hard work. With Ms. Avenson's help, you may actually stand a chance of catching the perpetrator sometime this decade." It was insult couched in flattery. Osker really was good at the politics of the job.

Darius let out a long, measured breath and fought to keep his cool. "Ma'am, may I have a word—in private?" They made it as far as the other side of the glass door before he rounded on her, aggravation bubbling under his skin like an overfilling cauldron. "Respectfully, this is a terrible idea. I don't have time to babysit a junkie with a—"

"This is not a request, Detective."

"I understand, ma'am," Darius insisted, "but I'm telling you, she can't be trusted. Bliss addicts don't think beyond their next fix. She'll tell me whatever she thinks I want to hear and jeopardize the investigation." Nothing against the kid, but Avenson was clearly unreliable.

"Then that should make it easier to secure her cooperation." Osker canted her head toward the prisoner ensconced beyond the one-way glass.

Darius followed her gaze. On the other side, Avenson was scrubbing viciously at her eyes. No doubt she was trying to force her Bliss-soaked brain to compute what was happening. Was the deputy commissioner actually suggesting that Darius use Bliss to temper the girl's sharp edges? Coercive methods were not so unusual, but giving an empath what they craved was a double-edged sword. Darius had a pretty good idea which end he would be holding.

"Ma'am—"

"Take her along for the interrogation," advised the deputy commissioner. Her tone brooked no argument. "If you can't keep a junkie under control, Detective, I'll have to rethink putting you up for a promotion. Consider this your first and final warning."

Darius bit his tongue against saying more. There was the wisdom of lodging a complaint, and there was the sad reality of his situation. He'd been a detective for six years. Most of his Academy peers had gone on to work for the DA, for the government. The lucky ones had joined the lucrative ranks of PrivaSec corporations, tasked with guaranteeing the safety of Arcadia's wealthiest. They were making nine figures a year and planning their retirement in seaside resort towns far from Arcadia's septic back alleys.

Only Darius was left in the APU—the bottom rung of Arcadian law enforcement—and he knew full well he wouldn't be going anywhere for another year. Not unless he got a few big name cases under his belt and put his name in the papers. His salary was a joke, his rent was absurdly high and he hadn't worked a real case in years.

It pained him to be so cynical, but his mother's care home bills weren't getting any easier to cover every month. He couldn't afford to be principled about this. He forced himself to silence.

The deputy commissioner seemed to take his reluctant acquiescence as a personal victory. She smiled and patted his shoulder. "Don't let me down, Detective."

Darius watched her go, every punch of heel against the tile putting that much more distance between him and any chance of being heard. He couldn't shake the feeling that he'd been scammed. "Jasme—"

His rookie partner materialized at his side like a wood sprite. Had she been there all along?

"Yes, boss?"

"Let Mr.—what's his name again? Lucan?—yeah, let him know I'll be right in."

Jasme bobbed her head into a nod. "Sure thing."

Darius filled his lungs with a deep, calming breath and stepped back into the cell. He needed to take care of business first, then he could proceed with his day as though he still had some control over the investigation. "Ms. Avenson, if you'd be so kind…"

"It's Allegra, actually," the kid said, scratching at her blonde scalp.

"I'm sorry?"

Avenson arched a pierced eyebrow. "My name. It's Allegra."

"All right. Allegra. I have a —"

" — witness to interrogate," the junkie finished for him. "Yeah, I heard. You know, with the door open, you can hear pretty much everything that goes on out there."

"Right." Darius cleared his throat. The objections he'd raised were perfectly valid. That they didn't even begin to express why this forced collaboration was doomed to failure was another matter. One look at Allegra was enough to confirm that she wasn't so much police consultant as she was a volatile element best kept far away from anything flammable.

To think that Darius' future with the APU rested on Allegra Avenson's skinny shoulders wasn't just laughable — it was downright depressing.

He led them out of the cell, past the now-empty observation room where he'd witnessed the deputy commissioner's tour de force, and into the bowels of the APU's headquarters. More than one head turned as they passed, mostly seasoned desk cops keen to spot a new face. No wonder they all stared at Allegra as she passed. She caught the eye.

Only sixty-year-old Veland, on the brink of retirement ever since Darius had first joined the APU, took it as far as commentary. "Someone order us a little R&R?" Veland adjusted the headset he had clasped between ear and collarbone, reaching out a hand to grasp at Allegra's many dangling chains.

Why it was that kids her age decked themselves out like Christmas trees, Darius couldn't say. They were all big on leather and metal, two elements so cold one might think the Docklands were a steaming sauna and not an icy hellhole north of the city.

Darius opened his mouth to tell Veland to shut his, but didn't get the chance. Allegra anticipated him. "You couldn't afford it," she taunted. "'sides, I don't do small dicks, lover."

It was just as well that Veland's caller, whoever it was, chose that moment to require his input. Darius was glad. The last thing he needed was a cockfight in the bullpen. He stopped by his desk to doff his trench coat and hat and pick up the file Jasme had painstakingly crafted on his behalf. It was good, solid paper, despite her constant grumbling.

"That wasn't very —"

"—nice?" Allegra snorted. "If this is the part where you tell me not to antagonize the pigs, save it. I wasn't born yesterday." She folded her scrawny arms across her chest, defensiveness writ in the slant of her shoulders as if bold retorts were something Allegra knew she should dread.

It wasn't hard to imagine why. As lanky as she was, Allegra didn't look like the kind of girl who could stand much knocking about.

Darius sucked in his cheeks to conceal a wry smile. "I was going to say it wasn't very imaginative." He shrugged at the surprise that flashed in Allegra's pale eyes. "I wasn't born yesterday either, kid."

Allegra almost seemed taken aback, as if she hadn't seen approval in a long, long while. Darius knew the type—dead mother, deadbeat father, siblings likely gone into the flesh trade if they even survived past infancy. No one to answer to, no one to disappoint. Most level seven empaths were institutionalized if there wasn't enough cash to get them lobotomized—or near enough. Allegra had somehow avoided that unpleasant fate. *Good for her. Not so good for everybody else.*

People in the Docklands lived on the fringes of society for a reason.

"So what's this Lucan guy done?" Allegra asked, following after Darius like a puppy dog. "You think he's the killer?"

There was something gleeful in Allegra's voice when she spoke, as if she relished the possibility of meeting a real-life serial killer. Not surprising—the regular kind must have been pretty run-of-the-mill for a kid born and raised in the Docklands.

"He found the latest victim," Darius told her with forced nonchalance. He had a hard time keeping disappointment out of his voice. It would have been easier if the butler had done it, but life didn't often play out like a novel. "Now here's what I want you to do. You go into the other room, sit down and keep quiet. When I'm finished, I'll come over to your side and you can tell me if you got any kind of... vibe from the witness." He felt his skin prickle. "Think you can do that?"

Allegra smirked. "Maybe you should say it slower. Smaller words, you know, like you'd do for my kind?"

Oh good, she's a comic, too.

Darius opened the door and gestured Allegra inside. The interrogation room beyond the one-way window was nicer than the one she'd been held in before. There was no bed, no appearance of being locked inside a tomb, only a table and two chairs, one of which was occupied by a middle-aged man with a receding hairline and big, beefy fists. Preferential treatment was given to those who paid taxes— the so-called contributing members of society—regardless of whether or not they had broken the law. The bias wasn't overt, but it was undeniable.

Darius took a deep, fortifying breath and stepped into the interrogation room. "Mr. Lucan, hello. Sorry to keep you waiting."

The man rose to shake Darius' hand. "I thought you got all you needed from me the last time I was here. But I liked Ms. Grey. I'm happy to do everything in my power to help you catch the bastard who hurt her."

"We certainly appreciate your cooperation," Darius said as they took their seats. "Turns out there was a problem with the recording equipment the last time you were here. The statement we have is incomplete." His mouth twisted into a moue of contrition. "Would it be too much to run through the events that led you to discover the victim?"

Some of Lucan's cheer seemed to curdle at the request. It was understandable—he had worked for the Greys most of his life and to find the youngest daughter dead in the family garage must have been all kinds of traumatic. But Lucan was also a man of his word, and he unraveled his skein with little additional prompting. "Every Thursday morning, I set the robots to mow the lawn, trim the hedge, clean the driveway—as you do."

"Right," Darius echoed, though he hadn't had a driveway to clean since he was a boy living in the suburbs and his cleaning robot was a third generation tin-wreck that cost a hell of a lot more to run than it was worth.

"Then I go into the house, get the other batch of cleaning droids going upstairs," Lucan went on. "Around nine, I go to the garage to check the cars. Only that morning, Mr. Grey left me a note saying the X19 had a strange squeak, like it used to after they first bought it, and could I check the pressure valves first thing. So I went in...around eight, maybe? And there she was." Lucan shook his head and peered down at his veined, broad hands folded together over the table. "At first I thought she'd OD'd... Like you hear. Only there was a nasty line of purple going around her throat." He drew his index finger from ear to ear by way of illustration.

"And what did you do then?"

"I called the APU," Lucan said, shrugging. "What else could I have done? She wasn't breathing. Her eyes were open but she wasn't blinking..." He looked over Darius' shoulder to the one-way window. "Just eighteen years old. Had her whole life ahead of her."

"It's a tragedy," Darius agreed, putting the thought of cleaning bots out of his mind. "Was murder your first assumption?"

The housekeeper narrowed his eyes. "Couldn't have been anything else," he answered definitively. "Trina was a good girl, she always made her parents proud, always did as she was told. Her older sisters were another story, but I watched her grow up and there wasn't anything that girl did that didn't make us proud. Someone broke in, I'm telling you."

"We have to consider every possible scenario. We found no sign of forced entry." Darius deliberately glanced away, making as if to jot something down on his notepad. "Did Ms. Grey have any — unsavory friends?"

The media loved princess-and-pauper stories, particularly if they ended in scandal and disgrace for the princess. There was no juicier headline than a girl from the right side of the tracks winding up dead at the hands of her plebeian boyfriend.

Lucan shook his head vehemently.

"No unsavory friends? That's a first," Darius drawled, smiling crookedly.

It had the desired effect. Lucan bristled, furrowing his bushy eyebrows. "I'm not sure I like your tone, Detective. I won't sit here and let you malign Ms. Grey's character —"

Darius softened his voice. "You know as well as I do that young people can sometimes slip from under their parents' thumb. Even the best-behaved debutante falls off the wagon at some point. It's not even their fault — they're raised in a world of constant pressure, they're expected to be the best students, daughters, wives, CEOs... And do it all while trussed up in tiny corsets and killer heels." He huffed out a mirthless chuckle. "There's not a day goes by I'm not glad I wasn't born to the life. But the fact remains that Ms. Grey consumed several Bliss tablets before she died. She *was* high."

The toxicology report had confirmed that she'd been

using the night of the murder, but it couldn't say if she was an addict or if she had been coerced into taking the pills. Bliss left little to no trace in the blood after forty-eight hours. No one knew it better than the blonde spectator on the other side of the one-way glass.

Lucan could beat his chest about angelic debutantes all he wanted. As far as Darius was concerned, there was nothing unique in dabbling in illegality, and if her death hadn't attracted a criminal investigation, it was entirely possible Trina Grey would never have taken any heat for her taste in narcotics.

But she had died, and the Bliss found in her system was relevant to the case, not least because it was the chief medication for people diagnosed with Acute Empatheia Nervosa.

"I assure you, character assassination is not the point of this interview," Darius said. "Ms. Grey is our third Bliss-addicted victim in as many months. We couldn't save her, but we can try to save another family from losing a son or daughter." Or, as in the case of Jamal Reid, a breadwinner with aspirations for public office. The deputy commissioner had been especially displeased that they had no answer to offer his backers, never mind his well heeled family.

The housekeeper weighed his answer meditatively for a long, protracted moment before nodding his assent. "Anything," he said, sighing. "Anything I can do to help."

Something about his resignation had Darius thinking of Allegra. He could almost feel the empath's eyes on him, watching, assessing, and laying bare Darius' every secret. He shivered at the thought. The sooner he was rid of his would-be partner, the better. Empaths were ticking time bombs waiting to go off.

Darius would know. He'd been married to one.

Chapter Three

"Well?" Detective Darius filled the doorway, a broad-shouldered behemoth radiating exasperation.

Allegra kicked away from the wall. "Well, what?" She had thrust her hands into her pockets because she felt so gods-damned cold, but instinct told her to get her fists free in case she needed to use them. Police had taken every other weapon at her disposal, but she could still break noses with her knuckles if need be. She had done it before.

If he noticed the unsubtle shift in her posture, the detective didn't let on. "Is he telling the truth?" he pressed, his brow furrowing. "Weren't you listening?"

"Was I supposed to?" The thought had come to Allegra halfway through the interview. She'd promised to play along, but she hadn't said she'd make it easy on her would-be handler. A girl had to find some kind of entertainment in a place like this.

"Don't play games," Darius growled, halfway between an order and a plea. "If you're not going to help me, then you'd best be on your way. I don't have time to—"

"—babysit some junkie?"

"You need to stop finishing my sentences for me."

"Why?" Allegra quipped. "It's what you were going to say. Or close enough. 'Allegra Avenson is not to be trusted, yada-yada...'" She waved a lackadaisical hand. "You *really* hate being saddled with me, don't you?" She watched as a muscle in the detective's jaw tensed sharply, ire flashing in his charcoal-black eyes.

Maybe, if she pushed hard enough, she could make the good detective lose patience and send her on her way.

Osker could hardly blame her if one of her own people tore up their arrangement. *And what about the surgery?*

"You're not giving me any reason to feel otherwise. If we're done here, I have actual work to do." Darius made to walk away. That right there was Allegra's opening, her long-awaited escape—she could probably make it about half a block, maybe three-quarters, before Deputy Commissioner Osker heard that she'd bailed on their deal. If Allegra kept walking, she might even get out of Arcadia before Osker put out an APB and had her thrown back into that cell, this time for a few excruciatingly painful months instead of a few hours.

They would catch Allegra in the end. They always did. There wasn't a hole deep enough to hide her if the entire police force and their less than lawful bounty-hunting peers caught her scent. Sooner or later, she'd end up serving those long months in prison, with no Bliss to tide her over, and no guarantee of life-altering surgery to spare her the indignity of living out her days as a slave to other people's mood swings.

"He wasn't lying," Allegra called out from the depths of the observation room.

Detective Darius halted. He turned fractionally toward Allegra with an unspoken *I'm listening*. He wasn't going to make this easy on her.

"He wasn't lying." Allegra clarified, "Not about everything." She'd always felt like a circus act when she had to explain to strangers that she knew things she couldn't explain. Using her powers for the benefit of the law made no difference whatsoever.

"What wasn't true?" Darius asked, quietly enough that his exasperation barely showed.

Allegra licked her lips, wishing she could still taste the bittersweet tang of Bliss. It used to calm her, knowing she had a way to keep the noise in her head under control. She'd once calibrated the frequency of her regimen by the taste that lingered on her lips—that had been her best method of keeping the dosage under control until she could no longer discern the difference between a high and the quick, painful drop that followed.

Right now, her lips tasted of salt and metal, usually a sign that she was about to go dry. *Definitely a bad batch last night.*

"The crime scene," she said. "Lucan said he thought she'd OD'd right off the bat...or that she'd been murdered. That's bullshit. Think he worried it might have been suicide because she'd tried it before."

"There's no record of any past attempts," Detective Darius protested mildly.

Allegra rolled his eyes. "Yeah, like her folks would make that public." Allegra didn't need fancy schooling in Arcadia's academies to know that the rich and powerful didn't air their dirty laundry in public. The world turned on deception and bribes. In the Docklands, that meant anything went as long as you remembered to pay the interested parties—Triad, cops, mobsters. It wasn't so different for the wealthy. They just called it 'managing the truth' instead of flat-out lying.

"That's...actually a good point." Darius beckoned Allegra over with a hand. "Come on, I want to show you something."

"Knock yourself out, but I've probably seen bigger."

The quip fell on deaf ears. Detective Darius had a nasty habit of not letting her bait him. He hadn't even threatened to have Allegra tossed into jail for another night if she didn't cooperate. That was out of line. Most cops played the game, like the asshole who had tried to cop a feel earlier. There was nothing honorable about their uniforms and badges— they were in the same quid pro quo business as the hookers they harassed and the street thugs who paid tithe so they'd be left alone.

But Darius acted as if he were made of Teflon or something. He didn't even touch Allegra, only gestured her to a chair and rolled her into place behind a shitty desk piled high with paperwork. He was all business about it, too.

"This is a recording of my last interview with Mr. Lucan,"

he explained. "As far as I recall there's no discrepancy in the statements, but you can tell me if the same hesitation is there when he's talking about finding Trina Grey. Today could've been a fluke. A false positive."

Allegra knitted her eyebrows. "I thought the first recording was glitchy?"

"I lied." Twin waves of smugness and shame rolled off Darius with the confession, contradicting his nonchalant shrug. How he lived with that kind of cognitive dissonance Allegra couldn't imagine and didn't ask. She reminded herself that she didn't care.

She was more worried that she'd failed to pick up on the falsehood when the detective first dished it out.

At Darius' request, Allegra tuned the holoscreen and settled to watch and listen. She stuck earpieces in to block out the steady hum of voices from the bullpen. The shimmering image of the recording played out much like the interview she'd just witnessed — all she could see of Darius was the back of his head and the curve of his left arm. Over his shoulder, Lucan seemed about as grim-faced as he'd been minutes ago. He had this habit of rubbing his hands together over and over again as he talked that Allegra found unbelievably distracting, but his voice didn't catch when he mentioned Trina Grey, or the way in which he'd found her. His pitch only crept a little higher when he spoke of her parents — *upstanding, fair, decent people*, according to Lucan.

Allegra slid her fingers over the tablet's surface and rewound that segment as she tried to block out Darius' presence at her side. Bliss drowned out most of the daily racket, but when people were in her personal bubble, she had a hard time turning a deaf ear to their emotions. For some reason Darius distracted her more than the usual white noise.

It took Allegra a few tries, the recording playing in fits and starts with every slide of her fingertips across the tablet, before eventually she came down to an opinion.

"I'm not sure," she sighed, prying out the ear buds. "Maybe."

The detective pinched the bridge of his nose. That wasn't the answer he'd been hoping for. *Tough luck.* Acute Empatheia Nervosa wasn't a card trick that once learned could be repeated ad nauseam. There were no mechanics, no guarantees of success and Allegra was having a pretty stressful day.

Darius leaned against the desk, thrusting his hands into his pockets. "You can't tell if he's lying?"

"I can tell he's stressed out. Nervous."

"No kidding," Darius scoffed, as though it was obvious. "He's giving a statement about finding his employers' youngest murdered in the family garage. Can you blame him?"

She didn't, not particularly. Sure, it was sad, but it didn't register as unusual. Then again, perhaps that was something people were supposed to find shocking in Arcadia. Everyone knew that kids died all the time in the Docklands and no one squirmed with discomfort or regret, not even the locals.

Allegra held the detective's gaze. He had pretty eyes, for a cop. Under the unflattering neon, they seemed very dark, almost obsidian. His lashes were long, too, and inky like the hair that was creeping down to meet his shirt collar. He needed a haircut. Maybe even a shower. The Docklands were reserved for the poorest of the poor, but Detective Leon Darius didn't look exactly loaded himself. "I mean," Allegra shot back, drawing out the word, "he's feeling remorseful. Don't know if it's the girl or the family or the crime scene."

Darius took her answer at face value, nodding. "Okay, but... How do you know?"

"Something in his voice..." Allegra hitched up her shoulders. "How do you know a gun fired a bullet? A puff of smoke? A bullet casing? A loud bang?" She waved a hand as nonchalantly as she could, as if she didn't feel more exposed with every word.

There was a reason she never bothered telling anyone how her condition worked. It sounded ridiculous to normal folks, no more tangible than air.

"That's what I hear when he talks." Guilt was the most common vibe she got around born-and-bred Arcadians. The second emotion Allegra had learned to ignore in the heart of town was envy. After that came the greed and hate and lust that permeated the city like chemical fumes. And people still wondered why she took meds to drown out the pollution.

"Am I done?"

There was a brief hesitation, a moment of – and Allegra knew she'd misread it because it almost felt like – fear, then Darius was breaking eye contact and shaking his head. "Not by a long shot. There's six more interviews where that came from. Family, friends... I want you to go through them and mark down discrepancies between what the witnesses' mouths are saying and what you can pick up with your... thing." He paused, pursed his lips. "I'm going to assume you can write..."

"Only Cyrillic," Allegra said. "And kanji."

"That's fine. I read both."

Before she could come up with an appropriate response – she needed to temper her bad jokes in this kind of company – Darius was already pushing away from the desk. "I'm going to talk to the coroner again. You want coffee or water, there's a machine in the break room. Or you can ask Jasme when she gets back."

Jasme, Allegra surmised, had to be the curly-haired rookie whose hand seemed surgically attached to a tablet. Or maybe the other way around. In any effect, Allegra had no intention of asking her anything. The fewer people she talked to, the better her chances of being forgotten when she got out of there.

"I hope it's not something I said," she drawled, tipping back in Darius' seat. She didn't know what possessed her to speak up, stupidity or the self-sabotaging impulse to kick the ball out of the park while she still had it underfoot.

Darius flashed her a look. Not fear, this time, but definitely wariness. "There's only so many things a guy can lie about when it comes to a murder. I want to know if we didn't miss something. Get to work."

"Right," Allegra murmured, watching as the detective cut a path between desks packed high with holoscreens and carry-tablets. Only he seemed to be hoarding paper like an old-fashioned bookworm.

If Allegra had been in the business of selling information, she might have been tempted to filch a couple of those manila folders and sell the information on the black market. There was bound to be someone—even a few someones— with a brother in jail who'd pay a pretty penny for the leverage to get him out. But Allegra wasn't stupid. The minute she crossed the APU, she'd have a ticket right back into that windowless room.

Mallory Osker would see to it personally. She had all but promised as much. Besides, Allegra was just starting to enjoy being the thorn in Detective Darius' flank.

He was so easy to rile up that it almost counted as entertainment.

* * * *

Going through the batch of recorded statements was easy work. Even running on Bliss fumes, Allegra could draw out the threads of truth and falsehood, pin each witness like an insect in amber—this one was horrified, that one was merely uncomfortable and another couple were trying to conceal their excitement and doing a lousy job of it.

She could hear her stomach rumbling by the time she returned to the first file, too weary to play any of the others to their conclusion. There was just something about Lucan and his fretful hands. He reminded her of a junkie craving his fix.

When asked if Ms. Grey had any enemies, Lucan said *no*, but also nodded his head. His voice did a weird choking thing that Allegra almost thought was a glitch of the recording equipment until she heard it again, this time when Lucan denied any knowledge of Ms. Grey's drug habit, but allowed that it was possible she'd been self-medicating through her excruciatingly hard finals at the Academy.

"She wasn't a Bliss addict," Darius said, washed out and indistinct through the haze of the holoscreen. His voice was as low as a whisper. It took Allegra a moment to realize she was still wearing the earpieces.

"Sorry, what?"

"Grey wasn't taking Bliss regularly," the detective repeated. "Toxicology report came back on the pills we found in her room. We jumped to conclusions. They *looked* like Bliss, but they weren't."

Allegra pushed back her chair—the detective's chair, actually, but she had appropriated it with all the shame of someone who squatted in a warehouse she didn't own— and gave it a spin. "Let me guess. Amphetamines?"

"How did you know?" Darius arched an eyebrow.

"Please, they'll go as far as passing sea grapes off as Bliss around the academies. You can make a pretty penny off the younger crowd, if you package it right. Amphs are cheap. You get caught, it's—what? Forty-eight hours to a two week stint…"

Darius actually seemed surprised. He didn't work the narcotics division, so it was little wonder he didn't know. Allegra still fluffed up her feathers, but her smugness was short-lived. "You didn't write anything down," Darius said, jerking his chin toward her empty notepad.

"I lied about knowing Cyrillic." The lie just rolled off her tongue, quick to chase the truth.

"That's a shame. The kanji, too?"

Allegra nodded, faithful to the cliché that once she was in for a penny, she might as well be in for the whole damn deficit. "I'm right about the amphetamines, though. Not a lot of labeling going on in the drug trade." Most big PharmaCorps hadn't cared for years what petty tradespeople got up to as long as there was no Bliss being sold off the books, without the lion's share of the profits going to the folks in charge. Ever since the laws grew more stringent and Bliss disappeared off the shelves, the crackdown had become witch-hunt.

Only upper class Arcadian chicks would believe dealers could come into the heart of Arcadia armed with real Bliss. "However she got her fix," Allegra said, "I'm willing to bet my right hand it was a mix-up."

The detective shook his head. "In my day, we did booze and cigarettes. And that was before they lowered the drinking age."

"Wow, so you're like...really old."

"Ancient." Something almost like a smile twitched at the detective's mouth. Resignation flowed from him in faint, watery eddies. "You get anything from the files?"

The sudden, embarrassing growling of her stomach cut Allegra off before she could speak. Her cheeks flamed—a first in recent history. Hunger was a generalized condition in the Docklands, as familiar to its residents as the gunshots that routinely rang out in the dead of night. She hadn't been ashamed of it since she was thirteen.

Darius noticed, though, and Allegra felt the warm glow of his concern like a lit furnace. "How long since you last ate, kid?"

We're doing pet names again? "Don't know," she shot back with a shrug. It had the virtue of being the truth. "Your boss said you had me locked up in that zoo cage for twelve hours. You do the math." She hadn't eaten before she'd had her fix, either, for reasons to do with a pounding headache and her stomach rebelling just because it could, to say nothing of limited funds. It was no secret that if she had money to spare, Allegra would sooner spend it on a vial of Bliss—pills or diluted essence, even powder—than a hot meal.

"Okay," Darius said, "get up."

"Why?" Allegra asked, but got up anyway. If she was going to play the monkey, she'd do it to the end.

Darius wouldn't meet her eyes as he shrugged on his trench coat with both hands already stuck through the sleeves. He only narrowly avoided whacking himself over the head. "I'm taking you out for lunch before you faint all over my desk."

That was a surprising one-eighty from the guy who'd done his best to get her tossed back out into the street. *What gives?* Allegra folded her arms across her chest and decided to give defiance a shot. Maybe, since they were in public, Darius wouldn't get too violent if pushed.

"It's the middle of the night," she protested. It wasn't the only objection to be made to the idea, only the first one to come to mind. The last time Allegra had shared a meal with a cop, she'd gotten paid up front, just in case the guy had turned out to be into anything weird—he had been.

The detective shot a surprised glance at the darkened windows. "Oh. How about that. Dinner, then?" Either he didn't see the absurdity of going out with someone of Allegra's caste or he simply didn't care.

He cared. Allegra could sense it even through the peaceful mire of Bliss.

The whole area around the APU's headquarters was mostly cop territory. Even the small, cramped train-car diner across the street was peopled with uniformed men and women ringing in another shift with a mug of cheap coffee and a bowl of watery udon. There was no room left at the counter, so the Darius and Allegra slid into a vinyl booth at the back of the diner, near the kitchen with its revolving doors and perpetual whiff of fried onions.

Darius went for eggs and bacon, pretty traditional cop fare—or what Allegra imagined cop fare to be like, going by decades-old flicks—up until he said he wanted a side dish of salad dressing. "I like the taste," he explained in the face of Allegra's querying glance. "Got a problem with that?"

Allegra said she didn't. There were only a couple thousand Ds left on her credit chip, though, and peering at the menu had her keenly aware that she couldn't afford anything more than a cup of coffee. So she went for that, staring the waiter down until he lowered his gaze from the obviously stuffed push-up and the leather choker with its silver D-ring.

"You're kidding me, right?" Darius glared. "She'll have what I'm having," he told the waiter, "only hold the dressing. What's with the impromptu Ramadan, kid?"

Allegra glared back. She had it in her. Questionable choices were her specialty. "I look like I eat out a lot?"

Before she'd gone off searching for Bliss last night, she'd had sixteen hundred thousand in her private account, but with the APU's crackdown on the trade and supplies dwindling, the price of the meds had gone up. Over fifteen hundred K for a single batch of Bliss was astronomically high. Worse yet, Allegra didn't have another fifteen to get her next fix. The thought had her setting surliness aside quickly enough.

"Osker didn't say how I was going to get paid for my services... Are you about to slide over a credit chip any time soon? 'Cause I've got to say, the opportunity cost of sitting here with you is—"

"Equivalent to going to prison?" Darius suggested blithely.

"I was going to say steep, but that works, too." It didn't, not really, but anxiety was getting the better of Allegra. "Look, man, if I don't get another shot of Bliss in the next forty-eight hours, you can kiss my help goodbye. That's not a warning, it's just plain fact. I can't function when I'm off the meds." Allegra settled her elbows on the table, inching forward. "From what you told Madame Osker in there, it sounded like you understood how my thing works."

Darius sank back into the booth. "I know you're an

addict—"

"Well spotted."

"—and you can't think beyond your next fix." There was no hesitation in his saying as much, but what Allegra got clearest from him by way of sentiment was discomfort.

Good Detective Darius was fearful of her addiction.

Allegra wondered if she'd misread the signals before, if it wasn't understanding and experience, but good old-fashioned fearmongering that had gotten to the peacekeeper. He wouldn't be the first to assume a junkie went from zero to stark raving mad in a matter of seconds if deprived of their fix. That could work in her favor. There were worse things in life than a Bliss batch guaranteed by the APU's own laboratory techs.

The question was how Allegra could possibly get her hands on it when the expression on the detective's face said it all—revulsion and fear made for a terrible combination.

"I'll talk to the deputy commissioner," Darius hedged after a moment, glancing away. "See what we can do to accommodate you. Until then, patience is a virtue."

Allegra snorted with forced levity. *You try to be patient when you feel like everyone's screaming at you.* This was a matter of life and death for her, and here was Darius telling her to be patient while he worked his case and caught bad guys—real, important work. Nothing she'd know about, seeing how she was just another reject from the Docklands. Allegra had to dig deep to keep from lunging across the table. "What do you know, I feel better already. You got a cigarette?"

"I quit."

"Christ, you don't smoke, you don't believe in self-medicating... If the next words out of your mouth are abstinence and sobriety, I'm going to borrow your gun and shoot myself."

The same twitch at the corners of Darius' lips threatened without quite materializing into a smile. "I don't always carry a sidearm."

"But you are carrying one now." Allegra had seen its shape under the detective's rumpled jacket. She couldn't discern the make, but it was probably standard issue, worn in an underarm holster rather than the traditional hip holster so many cops preferred for faster draw. The smart ones had figured out that faster draw wasn't always synonymous with the owner being the one to do it—more than one cop killer had used a cop's own gun.

Darius was spared having to give a straight answer as their meal was brought out. Allegra's breath caught in her throat.

The waiter balanced two identical plates on a round tray, with a side dish of salad dressing, and Allegra promptly forgot that she'd asked a question at the sight of glistening, sweet-smelling bacon and eggs—probably just protein and frozen sludge, but nothing at all like what she was used to grabbing from questionable street vendors in the Docklands. The food here tasted as good in real life as it looked on the billboards, all sizzling fat and golden yolk. Her mouth watered at the sight.

She was almost afraid to sink her fork into the greasy landscape for fear it might fizzle out like a mirage.

It didn't.

"So tell me about the others," Darius invited as he picked up his own cutlery. "Any of them lying?"

"What," Allegra asked around a mouthful of egg and toast, "now?" She felt too ravenous to stop eating for the sake of conversation.

There could be no mistaking the quizzical tremor of Darius' mouth. "Maybe when you're done. Doesn't look like it'll take you long."

Allegra swallowed. "All of them."

"I'm sorry?"

"You asked if any of the witnesses you interviewed were lying," Allegra said, gaily helping herself to a sip of coffee and chasing the salty bacon with that bitter, oaky blend. She enjoyed the kaleidoscope of flavors nearly as much as she relished the outright confusion on the detective's careworn face. "They all are."

* * * *

The train dropped her off the on the outskirts of town, far enough to be out of Arcadia proper but not far enough that she didn't have to trudge home in near pitch-black darkness, through streets that had once been thoroughfares for heavy trucks bearing merchandise to and from the harbor. These days, the only traffic was in the pale and ebony bodies lining the Red Light—just about the only club where an honest drink could be had without fear of cyanide poisoning.

Allegra squeezed herself through the door when the bouncer wasn't paying attention. Sometimes it paid to be skinny and it certainly helped that she knew her way around the bar, around the stage, to the back rooms where the squeak of mattresses and fake moans could be heard through the dyed rice paper screens.

She could've gone straight home, kept her head down, but digesting the past twelve hours on her own was likely to send her into a panic attack.

This was the only other coping mechanism she knew.

A heavy palm landed on her shoulder. "Hey! Where do you think you're going?"

Allegra whipped around, snarling. "I'm late for my shift, you dick. Let go before I tell Big John you've been touching his girls." It worked a treat. The bouncer recoiled as if struck, holding both hands aloft.

"Crazy bitch…"

The slur was preferable to being tossed out on the street. It would be another ten or fifteen minutes before he realized she was wearing the wrong shoes to be part of the evening entertainment, but by then Allegra hoped she'd be gone.

She slipped into the dressing room with heart pounding a juddering tattoo. Several pairs of heavily made-up eyes widened at the sight of her. Mild surprise was the strongest sentiment any of the feather-wearing dancers could muster. One of them even yawned pointedly.

"At ease, ladies and gentlemen… I'm looking for Aaron?"

"Back here, ladybug," he called out, sliding back his chair. Aaron was Allegra's best friend—her only friend, these days—and one of the few people who neither judged her for her trade nor coveted her clients. He had his own. His hair was done up today, a shock of blue dye in an otherwise inky fringe. Kohl rimmed his eyes. "To what do I owe the pleasure?"

Allegra held up her doggy bag. She hadn't been able to finish her second order of fries, much less the burger that had come with, so Darius had suggested she take it along for tomorrow morning. It probably counted as a premium on the debt she already owed him, but Allegra didn't care.

Judging by how quickly Aaron bounded from his chair, neither did he.

"My place okay?"

"Terrific," he gushed, attention fused to the paper bag.

They emerged out into the customary Docklands stench with shoulders brushing. They were nearly of a height— Aaron was just slightly taller in his work stilettos—and the folds of his purple robe brushed Allegra's calves as they bolted down the block. Allegra led the way past the heavy metal door of the warehouse, listening for human sounds over the skittering of rats before she dared flip the switch on the electric neon.

Nothing happened.

"Forget to pay the bills again?" Aaron teased.

"Bite me." A dangerous thing to suggest, knowing him, but for once Aaron was on his best behavior. The two of them stumbled along until Allegra could snag a glow stick from her stash and crack it.

A flare of reddish light spilled around them, carving out about twenty feet of light in the thick shadows of the warehouse. It wasn't much, but for the next ten minutes, they would be able to look at each other and feel like they were living large. Allegra held out the bag. "This is for you."

"What do I have to do to earn it?"

She rolled her eyes. "Nothing, twit. Just—I owe you for the Bliss the other night, don't I?" And if not for that, then for every other time Aaron had come through on her behalf, or rescued her from asshole clients—or kept her company when the shakes got so bad that she couldn't handle being on her own. It had been Aaron's recommendation that she steer clear of the normal routes that landed her in Mallory Osker's jail, but he couldn't have known.

"So you got your fix?" Aaron pressed his lips into a thin line. "When I didn't hear from you, I thought... I don't know. That you'd run off with the dealer."

He collapsed on her mattress with no invitation and Allegra plopped down beside him, knees brushing. "Eat your burger." They could talk afterward.

Aaron wolfed down his burger in fewer than half a dozen bites. It must have cooled since they'd fixed it up at the diner, but his pleased moans made it sound as if he was tasting ambrosia. He started on the fries as soon as he was done, choking a little in his rush.

Allegra laughed, patting him on the back with a lazy hand. "Easy there. You don't want to be sick all over Big John's stage, do you?"

"I'm not on stage tonight," Aaron said between bouts of coughing. "I'm working the back rooms."

That was never ideal, but it was a living.

"Oh. Well, at least you don't have to dress up like a peacock..." Allegra curled her fingers into the back of his robe. "You wouldn't believe the day I've had."

"Yeah?" Aaron asked, still sucking the grease off his fingers. "Want to tell me all about it while I make you feel better?" He had soulful black eyes—like Darius—and his dimpled smile had brought many a client to their knees.

"You don't have to," Allegra started to refuse, because she hadn't brought him supper as a down payment, but

Aaron was already sliding between her legs with a slow, sinuous motion. Allegra felt the air in her lungs evaporate as she splayed her thighs that much wider. She knew how to be accommodating, just like Aaron knew how to seduce her out of her pants. "There's not going to be much talking if this is the way you want to play it," she muttered—a jumbled objection, because Aaron was lowering her zipper with his teeth and toying with her nipple with one hand, which was a sure-fire way to curtail her protests.

It comforted her to know Aaron could read her body like his own. Maybe on some level it helped him to know that when she sank a hand into his hair, she wouldn't pull too harshly. They didn't have much time to waste on foreplay. Even so, Allegra refused to rush. Aaron tugged her pants off in his own time and knelt between her legs at his leisure.

And only when he was ready did he nuzzle her bare cunt with lips and tongue, parting her folds with talented fingers.

Allegra dropped her head back to the mattress and allowed pleasure to suffuse her limbs. She could feel his self-satisfaction as she moaned. She knew he liked that. For all that most of his clients these days were men, Allegra had a feeling he still enjoyed being with women.

She didn't dare think it was just her—that he liked her—because that way lay messy things like jealousy and hurt feelings, both too costly for the likes of them.

Aaron glanced up with lips shiny and red, grinning. "You want to fuck?"

"Such a romantic," Allegra snorted. But she nodded all the same.

While he pried off his robe and kicked off his shoes, Allegra reached for the strip of condoms she hid under the mattress for easy access. They were a necessity in their profession.

She waited until Aaron's cock was fully sheathed in latex before pushing him down to the mattress and straddling his hips.

"Feeling power-trippy tonight, huh?" Aaron laughed, two spots of color blooming high on his cheeks.

Allegra practically growled. "You have no idea." Just the thought of that cold, noiseless cell was enough to light a fire in her belly. She eased herself down with a sigh, flexing around Aaron's length as he slid in deep.

They had done this before. It didn't matter that there was no novelty, no mystery left in the act. Allegra could do with a little bit of familiarity. "Feels good?" she asked teasingly as she raked her short, bitten fingernails down Aaron's chest. "You like that?"

He glared. "You know I do." Aaron could be sweet — she had seen him in bed with other people, clients who paid upfront and didn't ask for anything too weird — but with Allegra he was very much himself. He pinned his feet against the mattress and thrust up when she would've baited him for a while longer, triggering a sharp noise of pleasure. He was good at this. He had to be.

Allegra let her eyes drop shut as she felt him trace the inside of her thighs with a purposeful touch. "Fuck, that's it..." Aaron pressed his thumb over her clit and it was everything she needed, if not quite the way she wanted it.

It didn't take long. Allegra pursued her climax with dogged determination, gasping and whimpering whenever Aaron did something that felt particularly right. She came hard, screwing her eyes shut as tremors wracked her body like a minor earthquake.

Aaron wasn't far behind, but Allegra hardly even heard him. She was elsewhere, wondering what it might be like — if she had the guts to find out — to take that surly APU detective to bed instead.

Would he bruise her thighs as he came? Arch his pretty neck like Aaron did?

Allegra bent forward to suck a bite just under Aaron's pectoral, feeling both guilty and aroused by the thought of Darius gasping and moaning beneath her, entirely at her mercy.

Chapter Four

The sun had been up some six hours already, but Darius didn't realize it until he checked his wristwatch. There was already a low-priority call on his answering machine, waiting to be picked up once he got off work. Darius had set up the device to avoid any interruptions when he needed to focus on things like catching crooks and examining crime scene footage. Low-priority meant not his mother's care home, which was all he needed to know after spending eighteen hours at the station.

He wasn't the only one, truth be told.

"How long have you been here, Jasme?" he asked, knuckling sleep out of his eyes.

She glanced up with a frown. "Boss?" Her desk was parallel to his, facing the perpetually gurgling water fountain, so it was no great effort to see the bruises under her eyes.

"When's the last time you saw the inside of your apartment?" Darius clarified. "You were already here when I got in. You're still here now."

"Yeah."

"And a day's passed in the meantime."

Jasme nodded. "Want me to clear out?"

"Desperately."

"We still have another file to get through. A full fifteen hundred pages of Trina Grey's public records..." Jasme grinned. "I just got to the part where she quit lacrosse and took up Swahili."

"Go home," Darius groaned, pushing away from the desk. "This is getting us nowhere." It was just busywork at this point, but he had no other leads. Avenson's input had him doubting every interview he'd conducted on any of the cases, possibly for the full extent of his law enforcement career. What good was a cop's intuition against an empath's clear-cut insights?

Jasme tossed her head with a cheery laugh. Even after eighteen hours, she could still smile and make it seem genuine. Stamina like that could take her far, to say nothing of her acting skills. "Sure thing. Only if you're heading home, too, though."

"We're negotiating now, rookie?"

"We are," she said, unperturbed by his last-ditch attempt at pulling rank. "You look like you just spent the night on a park bench. No wonder Allegra was in such a hurry to get out of here. You probably scared her half to death. Get a shower, get some sleep, and I'll see you bright and early here in—what, eight hours?"

"Make it six," Darius countered. In all likelihood, it would be more like four. He always had trouble sleeping when he was working a case. His brain couldn't seem to disconnect from the horrors it dealt with during waking hours. There was no R&R, no taking time off and letting his brain unwind. Some people got nightmares, others were fine until they came down with a nasty case of PTSD and quit the force in disgrace. Darius got insomnia.

He was glad he'd had the foresight to hide a pair of sunglasses in his desk drawer a couple of days back. A bright sun was glaring down as he stepped out through the sliding station doors.

Arcadia wasn't meant for sunny weather. It was a city of hard concrete and ugly, square buildings—the poorer tenements erected in the image of their more luxurious counterparts, both equally lacking in taste—and its people were similarly hardened.

Allegra was right. He was turning cantankerous and difficult in his old age, a sure sign that the sooner he retired from the force, the better. The sight of so many carefree citizens shambling along the sidewalks as if they were all on drugs had Darius thinking of the empath. He'd watched her wolf down her dinner – and finish off half of his – as if she was starving. He didn't think he still had the capacity for pity, but he'd be lying if he claimed that watching her eat had left him cold.

He tried not to wonder if he'd ever see her again. The Docklands were a secretive, unpredictable place. It birthed people who were both unreliable and highly paranoid. By contrast, Trina Grey's life seemed like a series of appropriate pastimes and normal friends, notable academic success and quaint extracurriculars. She was the perfect example of Arcadian achievement – until it turned out she was self-medicating to keep up.

Jostled by the morning swarm of commuters scurrying to their places of employment, Darius carved out a space for himself on the train and leaned back against the plastic seat. He had long since mastered the art of staring into thin air and letting his brain grind away, independent of his body.

Pity did indeed come with some difficulty, but he could recognize that there were more hurdles in the high society circuit than ever before. He wondered vaguely how many other smiling madonnas were taking pills by the handful. Was Veland's kid, who had only had her coming out party a couple of months back? Was Jasme?

Or were they still too poor living just under the threshold of wealth to feel the pressure? He knew his mother hadn't danced to that drumbeat. Neither had his sisters. They were all too fond of the cult du jour to need another opiate. It didn't make them any less unhappy.

The bullet train dropped him off half a block from his apartment, near the parking lot where he usually left his APU-assigned sedan. It was scenery pockmarked with kids riding old-fashioned bicycles down the street and old men sitting in rickety folding chairs playing chess on the curb.

Immigrant neighborhoods like his marked the dividing line between the inner city manors and the Docklands.

If Darius stood on the rooftop of his apartment building and looked north, he'd be able to see the smokestacks of factories long since gone out of business.

To the south, back the way he'd come, the city stretched into skyscrapers and splendid hydroponic gardens. Darius didn't think to glance over his shoulder as he reached his building. He knew what lay behind him.

He didn't keep this apartment because he was fond of living so far from the precinct.

The front door of his ancient brownstone still needed fixing—its glass pane shattered last May by kids playing soccer. He kept saying he'd do it one weekend if the owners association couldn't get around to it, but since he was rarely home, it was nothing more than a pipe dream. *Maybe this time, after he caught the Bliss Slayer.*

Maybe not.

He took the stairs to the fifth floor because the hiss and shake of the elevator gave him the creeps and emerged after three flights of steps onto a landing pockmarked with bullet holes. Once upon a time, this borough had been the favorite haunt of drug dealers and other persons of ill repute. The APU had cleared them out so landlords could drive up their leases. Darius had been a rookie back then, a kid born in the suburbs and raised on clean air and well water.

He'd never expected to end up living within the city limits.

And here you are, with a deed to your name and a four-door gas guzzler rusting in the sun just a few yards away. Congratulations, you've made it.

The thought didn't bring him an excess of comfort as he fit his thumb to the fingerprint scanner built into the door. There was always more to aspire to. Better living. A nicer car.

A spouse who wouldn't run out on him.

Darius let the door slide shut and latch automatically behind him. The place was so foreign he couldn't believe he'd only been gone a matter of hours.

The front room wasn't so bad. He had all the basic necessities—a holoscreen, a mountain of old paperbacks he still liked to thumb through when his eyes got too tired for backlit tablets. There was even a massage chair. The kitchen had its own garbage disposal unit, capable of transforming any solid produce into a murky, green-tinged liquid that could be washed down the drain, and a high-power microwave. Everything ran on solar energy, too, which helped with the bills.

His cleaning bot still needed to be charged manually, which explained why there were dust bunnies twirling in every corner.

Darius had solved the dirty dishes problem early in his adult life by replacing ceramics and silverware with paper and plastic—not the most sustainable way to live, but he had eco credits enough in his pocket by virtue of his job that he could suffer the expense. It was easily the one uncommon luxury he afforded himself—that and the tinted windows that blocked out the sunlight at the single stroke of a button. Almost instantly, the front room was plunged into semi-darkness.

In the shadows, he felt at home.

Darius plucked off his sunglasses and doffed his trench coat. He studiously avoided his reflection in the wardrobe mirror, not wanting to confront just how bad he looked after a day's worth of chasing fine print across a page. The deputy commissioner had made things no easier on him when she'd saddled him with Avenson. She wasn't blind, she could see the kid had problems well beyond a predilection for illegal drugs.

It was both cruel and borderline felonious, Darius thought, to be dangling surgery in front of Allegra's nose when Osker knew full well the commissioner would never agree to funding the procedure.

The reasonable thing to do would've been to cut the girl loose with a warning.

So why hadn't he? He fixed his reflection in the bathroom mirror with an accusing glare.

Because I need her.

He would've liked to claim otherwise, but truthfully, he was stuck. Any idea, however outlandish, was worth more than the walls he seemed to have surrounded himself with — particularly now that such a media-friendly victim had joined the roster and the case was about to attract more attention than ever from the whisper sheets.

A knock on his front door startled Darius out of his thoughts. He'd barely managed to loosen his tie, never mind get to bed.

Neighbors usually knew better than to call on him. He was never home, and when he was, he seldom did anything more interesting than sleep in or watch old 2Ds. There was never any sugar in his pantry.

A quick glance through the peephole dispelled any sense of mystery. Darius pulled open the door.

"How the fuck did you find me?"

On the other side, Allegra had the good grace to mitigate her smile with a sheepish shrug. She was going to have to try a lot harder to conceal her smugness. "You think it's that hard to follow a guy home?" she quipped. "Or do you think only uniforms can do it?" The kid rolled her eyes, rocking back on her sneakered heels. "Aren't you going to invite me in?"

"I'm really not."

Allegra made a face. "C'mon, man. It's blazing hot out there." Midday scorchers were the worst, the kid wasn't wrong about that, but going from commiseration to opening his door to a junkie from the Docklands took a big leap of faith.

Darius hadn't asked to be tailed. He pointed that out only to have Allegra hitch up her shoulders in a slow, rolling shrug. "Can you at least spare a glass of water?"

No, Darius thought. He didn't have the heart to say it, so in the end he only warned Allegra not to touch anything.

"Wait here," he shot over his shoulder, feeling as if he was skidding on thin ice.

It was basic kindness, a thirsty man asking for water, a starving man asking for food—Darius had been raised a Jesuit, but he wasn't completely unrepentant. All he needed was to get over his fight or flight instinct and he could even pull off feeling as if he was doing Allegra a favor instead of playing into her hands.

He left the door open for Allegra as he moved to snatch a bottled water from the fridge.

The girl caught it easily, bemused.

"You break off the cap, put the bottle to your mouth and swallow," Darius instructed archly, trying not to let his mind wander. "Not an exact science, so lose that 'alien in a strange new land' thing you've got going."

"I'm not—" Allegra crinkled her brow. It was a short-lived thing, but she actually seemed perplexed for a fraction of a second. Angry, too, though that came later, on the cusp of a sneering barb. "I just forget you people buy your water. Guess dysentery's a Docklands problem, too." Like the junkies and crime rates no one talked about—she didn't have to say that part aloud for Darius to hear the follow-up.

She wasn't wrong. The Docklands suffered every consequence of poverty there was, from delinquency to illiteracy and disease. No one cared to fix that part of town, though, because there was no profit to be made from it.

There was enough space between them that Darius should have felt comfortable standing there, watching Allegra's throat bob steadily as she swallowed big gulps of purified, vitamin-enriched water. As far as he knew, empaths could only pick up surface emotions, nothing more, not without skin-to-skin contact.

He was probably safe.

His pulse sped up anyway when Allegra lowered the bottle, its contents already half gone. Cinnamon-tinted lips curved into a smile. "You don't like me very much."

"Do you care about that?"

Allegra nodded pensively. "I do if you're supposed to be my meal ticket until Osker gets this Slayer. She seemed pretty adamant I wasn't going to get out of our bargain any other way." Her voice had dipped to a low, sultry purr. Darius recognized the cadence, the electric thrum of desire that loitered beneath loathsome, onerous words.

To Allegra, this would be normal. She was, after all, in the business of trading her body for drugs or credits. Why should it matter that she was trading it for safe haven from the wrath of the deputy commissioner? If their circumstances had been reversed, Darius could see himself making a similar calculation.

The difference was that Allegra was just a girl. Darius had a hard time putting that out of his mind. Bad enough that he could feel the stirrings of want in the pit of his stomach. He didn't need to fan it into a steady flame.

"You've got the wrong idea," Darius tried to counter, clenching his fists. "I'm not part of your deal. I just follow orders. She puts you at my disposal, I've got to make use of you whether I like it or not." He regretted saying as much as soon as the words registered. "I don't mean—" But it was already too late. Allegra had set the bottle down on the coffee table. She was looking at him through lowered lashes.

No coaster, Darius thought belatedly as he watched condensation drip onto the faux-mahogany. *That will leave a stain.*

Allegra was suddenly standing very close, her green-gray eyes gone black in the low light. "So why don't you make use of me now?" she asked, looping a hand around the joint of Darius' shoulder. "I can be likeable, Detective. And sweet. And obedient, if you're into that." She ran her free hand down the length of Darius' tie, all the way down to his belt buckle. She didn't stop there.

Darius caught her wrist just as Allegra made to cup him through his pants.

"Not interested," he gritted out.

"Sure about that?" Allegra's tongue lapped at her Bliss-stained lips, wetting them. It was a nervous tick, common among addicts enamored of that particular substance. Darius had seen it before. Hard though the memory bit into his flesh, he still had a hard time tearing his gaze away from her mouth.

He shoved Allegra away. "I don't fuck whores."

Indignation, verbal sneers—even violence were the reactions Darius anticipated after that vicious barb. He'd gotten into it with more than one prostitute when he was working his beat on the streets—he knew what they were made of.

He didn't expect to hear Allegra give a shallow burst of laughter. "Bullshit. I've seen you cruising around the Docklands in your fancy car, window rolled down, eyeballing the merchandise... I'd buy that you're not into junkies, but c'mon, a mouth's a mouth, right?"

"Someone should wash yours out with soap," Darius shot back, marching to the door on quivering knees. "You've had the water, now get the hell out. I don't give a shit what you think you know—"

"I know you want me," Allegra purred sweetly.

It was what Darius had been dreading—their hands had touched, if only for a moment. Allegra could read him like a book. Darius had never met an empath more powerful than a paltry level three, and those could usually pry into his dreams as if it was a walk in the park.

A level seven, like Allegra, was extremely rare in the wild. There was a reason for that.

"You don't know shit," Darius said, and grabbed Allegra by a mercifully clothed shoulder. "I said get out."

Basic training taught every rookie how to dodge a frontal attack, but Darius was distracted. He never even saw it coming. By the time he registered the pressure of Allegra's lips against his, it was already too late. She was soft and lanky, bones fragile in his fists. He didn't dare squeeze down too tightly for fear of breaking her.

Tendrils of want spread through Darius like the insidious caress of a hand stroking skin. Desire pooled in his gut, summoned by a force far beyond reason or sheer lust. Darius found himself clutching Allegra to him instead of pushing her away. It had been so long since he'd embraced someone.

The empath moaned, tilting her head just so and opening her mouth to Darius' kiss. She wanted this, too. She was gagging for it.

"I can't," Darius ground out, mashing the words against Allegra's pale cheek. Yet even as he protested, he was busy scrabbling to undo her snakeskin belt—it was too complicated, his fingers too big and too clumsy, and the buckle wouldn't come loose. In a fit of frustration, he grasped Allegra by the hips instead, hoisting her into his arms as he backed them violently into the door. It swung closed under their combined weight, latch sliding automatically into place.

"I shouldn't," Darius tried again, with even less conviction. He could feel his resolve slipping, tension clenching his fingers into Allegra's flesh.

Allegra kissed as if she was trying to mimic fucking with her mouth. She moaned unreservedly, sucking at Darius' tongue and shamelessly wrapping herself around his body as if she couldn't stand an inch of distance. He felt her fingernails scratch runes into his shoulders and when their hips met in a sloppy, reckless thrust, she broke away with a wild, throaty cry.

A small, distant part of Darius was aware that he was going against everything he'd said and breaking every rule in the book. He knew it was wrong, but the roiling maelstrom of want pulsing in his belly was too overwhelming to be ignored. He rolled his hips forward and up, into the slope of Allegra's pelvis, and felt her try to hitch her legs higher around his thighs. Darius caught on quickly and slid his— *shaking, sweating*—palms under her knees, splaying her as best he could against the door.

He knew his knees would pay the price for that extravagance later, but in that moment he couldn't think beyond the friction of his body moving against Allegra's, of the empath's lips nipping at his jaw and neck and collarbones.

He heard rather than felt the popping of buttons as Allegra wrenched his shirt open. Cool fingertips stroked down his chest, seizing the peaked nub of a dusky nipple and twisting. Darius moaned and rutted even harder. He could feel the wet drag of cotton against his cock, the bruising thump of heels digging into his ass—it wasn't enough to stop and reassess. Rational thought had been abandoned some time ago.

He didn't last long. When he came, it was with Allegra rolling that clever tongue of hers around and around his nipple, his erection still trapped in his slacks. Darius jerked once, twice, then stilled abruptly as he sullied his clothes.

He wound down slowly, watching through half-lidded eyes as Allegra struggled to work a hand under her waistband and finish herself off with a few furtive strokes.

Darius knew he shouldn't have watched. He did it anyway.

For her part, Allegra barely made any noise. She climaxed quickly, stealthily, her head bowed against her sternum and a hand braced on Darius' shoulder. She kept her eyes closed as if to savor every precious second. A fine sheen of sweat burnished her skin gold. She looked ethereal. Sublime.

She looked a picture of decadence. And the sounds she made—

Darius didn't mean to keep holding her up once they finished, but Allegra took her sweet time getting her feet back down on the floor, and even then she seemed wobbly and weak-kneed, as if she needed a little help. That duty fell to Darius—it wasn't much of a duty, truth be told.

He steadied them both with a hand against the door and his heart thudding madly. It was too dark to see his sweaty palm print, but he could feel the clamminess on his skin and he breathed in the unmistakable smell of sex as it hung heavy and pungent in the air.

Slowly, his better judgment crept timidly back into the room.

Had he actually just slept with an informant—with an unwilling, dangerous prisoner? The haze of post-coital bliss faded—a puff of smoke evaporating into thin air. It left Darius to grapple with the harrowing reality of his actions.

And with Allegra, who was still mouthing lazily at his neck, tiny shudders rattling through her in the afterglow.

Chapter Five

Darius allowed her the use of his bathroom, which was plenty welcome. The vast majority of Allegra's clients usually wanted her to get lost as soon as they got off. Some of their haste was probably born of guilt, but the rest, in Allegra's opinion, was really just bad manners. Would it kill them to give her a chance to catch her breath?

True, Darius' home wasn't exactly a five star hotel, but it had a working neon lamp over the bathroom sink and the water that came out of the tap was clean and scalding hot. There were no rust stains on the enamel sink and the toilet paper was as soft as velvet. Much as she might have wanted to linger, Allegra tried not to outstay her welcome. She stepped out after a perfunctory washdown and a piss, sighing wistfully.

Maybe if she played nice with Osker, she could have a bathroom as nice as that someday.

Yeah, and maybe pigs will fly.

"Thanks," she said, returning to the living room with her pants still undone. Some clients were willing to go for doubles if given a little time to recover. Allegra was seldom adverse — another round meant double the credits in her pocket.

She found Darius on the couch, holding his head in his hands. *Okay, awkward.* Apparently he had gone right past conflicting emotions to embrace guilt in all its useless drudgery. Swell. It was precisely what Allegra had been hoping to avoid.

"So, uh… You want me to stick around, or…?" She felt like an intruder for the first time since she'd worked up the nerve to knock on his door. "I mean, I can go if that's what you want, but I can help with the headache, too…" She could play dumb when it suited her, but Darius didn't seem to have heard her. Allegra shuffled her feet, scraping her sneakered toes into the rug. "Uh, do you just want to meet tomorrow, then?

The plan was to meet at St. Michael's and ride to the station together. There was a real risk that being seen heading into the APU headquarters on her own could get Allegra into trouble — for values of trouble that had to do with severed horse heads being deposited into beds, that kind of thing. But that had been their understanding before Darius had a change of heart and took frottage to a whole other level right there against his front door.

Allegra could still feel the clasp of his strong hands around her thighs. It hurt just enough for a reminder that she could take home with her and finger while she got herself off. She couldn't help but think this was one romp she'd want to revisit again and again, if only in her fantasies. Detective Darius might appear past his prime, but he fucked like a man half his age. Allegra almost regretted not taking proceedings one step further.

Maybe next time.

"What did you do to me?" she heard, the words a mumble, at first, but slowly gaining strength. Darius tilted his head up. "What the fuck did you do?"

So much for enjoying the blissful afterglow.

Darius was livid and stony-eyed, his earlier passion contained behind a high wall of ire and fear.

Allegra was suddenly hit with the urge to recoil. She didn't. She still had a small shred of pride left. "Do to you? What are you talking about?"

"I told you *no*," Darius said, his voice shaking. "And suddenly you were kissing me and fondling me and —" He shook his head, folding his fingers together as if in prayer.

What right did he have to be play the victim? Allegra glared back, her own anger stirring like a cornered beast.

"Hang on. You had me pinned against the gods-damned door! I didn't do anything to you. Except maybe get you off. No need to thank me, by the way, for the free service. Asshole. You sure as hell didn't look like you minded my expertise a minute ago…"

Clients freaked out all the time about screwing a whore — and a junkie, at that — but that usually happened when Allegra reminded them of her fee. It was a whole new experience to be stared at the way Darius was staring at her now, all scandalized and wounded and incredulous, as if Allegra had forced herself onto him. As if she even could.

"You're lying," Darius said, inexplicably sure of himself. "Get out."

"With pleasure." If there was hurt, Allegra did her level best to conceal it. She had no desire to appear needy in front of any man, never mind a cop.

She even slammed the door behind her with a gratifying thump on the way out. It rang out into the corridor like a gunshot but did nothing to dispel the image of Darius sitting there on the couch, despondent and lost.

* * * *

Allegra raked a hand through her sweaty hair as she took the stairs two by two. She hadn't forced anyone into bed with her before, not ever. This was just — buyer's remorse.

Yeah, that's right, Allegra told herself. He's worried he'll catch something from me. He wouldn't be the first to accuse her of being diseased.

Maybe Darius wasn't used to picking up skin in the Docklands after all. Appearances could be deceiving, and not all pigs were the same. It did nothing to temper the lightning bolt of annoyance still sparking in her breast. He had some nerve.

Allegra clambered down to ground level. Already the rising temperatures were beginning to get to her, sticking her cheap synthetic clothes to damp skin however much she tried to keep to the shade of the stairwell.

The blissful chill of Darius' swanky bathroom was swiftly undone by the time Allegra hit the lobby. Not a soul was around. The locals had wisely retreated to air-conditioned interiors as soon as the midday scorcher hit. Only homeless folks ambled about at this hour.

Well, the homeless and the insane. And, lucky me, I tick both boxes.

In the Docklands, risk-taking was par for the course. Sooner or later, every junkie did a few midday runs when he or she ran out of drops or pills — or whatever they used to get high. She knew the cost too well to attempt it too often, but desperation made men do foolish things.

Allegra hovered uselessly in the hallway. The heat was spilling in through the broken door, driving up the mercury by another five or six degrees. She could feel the air in her lungs turn to soup as she tried to wipe the sweat from her brow.

At least she wasn't jonesing for her next hit this time. Thank the gods for small mercies, she thought, smacking her chapped, bitten lips together. She didn't have a watch to tell the time, but the scorcher could last anywhere from half an hour to two. Then the big blue marble turned just enough that the daily heatwave no longer affected Arcadia directly and the city could go about its business.

The ancients couldn't have foreseen this or they would've built their town some place farther inland, away from the polluted, boiling seas.

With nothing to do but think, Allegra tried to retrace her steps. She must've been in Darius' apartment some ten, maybe fifteen minutes — time in which she'd probably ruined a good thing before it even began. She had anywhere between another fifteen minutes and three times as long to wait until the weatherman said it was safe to venture outside.

Fuck that, Allegra told herself and resolutely shouldered past the front door.

She wasn't afraid of a little sunstroke.

The blistering sun was already glaring down hard as Allegra slipped out into the deserted streets of Darius' verdant neighborhood. Her sneakers sank into the soft pavement, the imprint of her footsteps denting the asphalt like paw prints on a muddy forest floor.

All those government warnings banning folks from braving the scorchers? Not really propaganda, as it turned out.

Allegra had only made it a few steps before the buildings around her began to tilt and sway, their outlines turning watery in the midday blaze. The sweat that had begun seeping through her pores evaporated just as quickly in the blistering hot sun, doing next to nothing to help cool her down. Every inhale seemed warm enough to singe the inside of her throat. When she opened her mouth to yell for help, there was only a pitiful, zombie-like noise, a mute *blurgh* of ridiculous proportions.

She tried to steady himself against a bare brick wall — graffiti was absent in these parts and she could just about make-believe that the same fetid air didn't traverse the city from the northern Docklands, bearing with it the same airborne viruses — only to trip when her foot caught on a raised cement divot.

Allegra closed her eyes as her knees buckled. There were worse ways to die. At least her end would be warm, a pleasant little prelude for the fiery damnation that awaited whether she wound up in her uncle's fire-and-brimstone version of hell or her soul was forever devoured by a creature with the head of a crocodile and the body of a leopard, like in stories.

Darius would be so cheesed off. It might even ruin his day, to think he'd endangered a life. He really had that 'protect and serve' air about him. Few cops did. Allegra could only hope. She had to be a lot more delirious to think a cop — hell, a mark — could give a shit if someone like her dropped dead on their doorstep.

"Well, ain't you in a bad way," she heard a voice say above her.

The sound seemed to come from the sun itself, no doubt a sign that Allegra was slowly but steadily losing what little sanity she had left. She thought she felt something grasp her arm, but since her body no longer felt as if it had a physical dimension, she couldn't bring herself to care.

"Easy now," the voice said. "I've got you."

It was a woman's voice, Allegra told herself. She felt bird claws catch in her clothes, then something silky and cool enveloped her like a shroud. The air smelled of plastic under the cloth, but somehow it was easier to breathe.

"Let's get you inside, sweetheart..."

Allegra didn't think to object. She couldn't if she'd wanted to—which she didn't, for obvious reasons. She could barely hold herself upright.

Dimly, she thought she heard another voice calling her name. She recognized the familiar cadences echoing dimly under the rush of blood pounding against her eardrums, but she couldn't crane her neck to see.

She felt her eyes droop shut, scorching heat and bone-deep fatigue conspiring to jettison Allegra into blissful oblivion.

* * * *

When she awoke an hour or a day later, Allegra discovered that the shadows were slow to give way. She could make out the shape of her hands in the semi-darkness, as well as the outline of a bed. The rest of her surroundings resolved into sight more sluggishly—a table here, an armoire there, nothing Allegra recognized from personal experience or temple myth.

This wasn't hell. It lacked the scent of scorched flesh and the promised screams.

It wasn't prison, either, that much Allegra knew from the first whiff of lavender and almond bread. The bed sheets she was lying on were too soft, to boot, and the bed too wide. The room she'd been brought to smelled clean and felt warm, but lacked that familiar tang of antiseptic used in hospitals and holding cells alike to prevent vermin of her ilk from spreading their maladies. But if it wasn't prison, where the hell was she?

Allegra righted herself slowly. She needed to stop passing out and winding up in strange places. One of these days, she'd wind up in a flesh mill, one of many doped-up bodies to be turned into the sludge of black market protein used in the fertilizing of crops and the making of packaged meals alike.

Her head was swimming, a dormant fanfare rousing to remind her of her foolish attempt to brave the elements. As if she could forget. It had backfired quickly enough.

At least she still had the clothes on her back, though oddly enough her shoes seemed to have vanished. She had already lost her blades to the APU, a loss felt keenly as she tried to make sense of her predicament.

It wouldn't hurt to have a weapon at hand, in case she needed the extra deterrent against whatever creep had dragged her in off the streets.

Only two kinds of people selflessly took in strays — bleeding hearts bent on saving junkies from themselves in the name of this or that god, and folks with a knight in shining armor complex who sooner or later expected some kind of payment, usually delivered through sex.

Neither of those thrilled her, but she knew how to deal with both. Hard not to learn, being a woman, alive and a native of the Docklands all at once. There were also Good Samaritans whose purposes were a touch more nefarious — Allegra didn't think about those if she could help it. She'd been weaned on horror stories about cannibals and slaver's rings from a young age.

The fact of the matter was that she was unarmed in a stranger's house. The only thing that mattered was finding a way to get the hell out — of the house, of Arcadia, possibly even the country, if she wanted to survive Darius' ire.

Allegra padded out of bed on socked feet, trying to ignore the lush bristles of the carpet underfoot. Her eyes had adjusted enough to the darkness by now that she could pick out two doors set into the far wall. One was white and presumably led into another palatial bathroom, like the one Allegra had visited and mooned over at Darius' apartment. The other she could only assume to be a way out. It was the one she reached for, testing the knob with a careful little twist.

"Leaving so soon?"

The click of a lamp preceded the piercing glare of a single yellow bulb. Allegra spun around, blinking the rainbow cobwebs out of her eyes to see a woman seated in a chair by the bed, the shaved pate of her skull gleaming ebony-black.

"Pity," the woman drawled. "Thought you and I could have a chat..."

Allegra steeled himself against the cold grip of panic. "If you're expecting a thank you..."

"Please," the woman scoffed. "You were probably trying to kill yourself anyway. Going to start bitching at me for interrupting."

"I wasn't," Allegra started, aborting the denial when she caught sight of a semi-automatic lying sidelong in the woman's lap. "I was just... Doesn't matter. Who are you?"

"Name's Ley," came the slow, throaty answer. "But you can call me Mrs. Ley, if you don't think a little respect for your elders will kill you. And this here's just a bit of insurance," she added, hefting the gun in a bony fist. "Nothing to be scared of."

Allegra didn't fall for that. She had seen enough guns to know they were only ever used as one thing — leverage against those without one of their own. "Insurance against what? Me?"

Stupid question, she realized half a beat later. As strange as it seemed that anyone should be afraid of her, any lone Arcadian woman in her right mind would keep well clear of Docklands scum. That this Mrs. Ley had apparently dragged Allegra all the way into her home rather than let her sizzle in the open road was all kinds of perplexing, but it didn't preclude the taking of precautions.

"You were running from the police, weren't you?" Mrs. Ley asked testily. "Had me an argument with that boy across the street, but he went home quick enough when I introduced him to Alma here."

"Alma?" Allegra repeated, disbelieving. Her hostess only patted the gun propped against her bony knees. "Oh." She had named her pistol.

And they say folks in the Docklands are missing a few screws...

"Well, he hasn't broken down my door yet," said Mrs. Ley, "so maybe he won't be giving us any more trouble. You want something to eat? Drink?" She was slow in getting to her feet, a ragged sum of bones held together by veined, wrinkled skin and a flowery print dress.

"Um..."

Mrs. Ley snorted. "Quit your gawking, girl. Haven't you seen old folk before?"

"Sure." Allegra wetted her lips. "I mean—no, not really." Not recently, anyway.

Once upon a time, she'd had a mother and a father—one who stayed, not like other men. And though her folks hadn't been old when they'd had Allegra, the years had worn them down fast, sapping strength like marrow from a bone. Soon there was nothing left but aches and pains and fast-piling medical bills they had no way of paying.

All Allegra remembered of her folks now was two pairs of black-ringed, sunken eyes and pale lips thinned with permanent exhaustion. Eventually her mama had just gone to sleep and never woken up again.

Her father had filled his pockets with rocks and had gone to find his rest with the fishes in the East River. They'd asked her to identify the body, later, when it had washed ashore. What was left of it, anyway.

Allegra must have been thirteen.

Some remnant of seldom-used good manners crawled into Allegra's throat to keep her grief company. "I'm fine. Thanks."

"Ain't no trouble," Mrs. Ley shot back. She was steady on her feet once she was out of the chair. It took Allegra a moment to realize she was working one of those pricey mechanical braces. The glint of metal exoskeleton peeked out from beneath her hemline like a particularly dazzling fashion accessory — *modern medicine meets robo-chic* — but it was the hiss of pistons as loud as constant sighing in the silent apartment that revealed the machinery for what it was.

Mrs. Ley was too frail to walk unaided. In an era when gene transplants were a dime a dozen for the people who could afford them, that said a lot about her condition.

No wonder she kept a gun.

Allegra followed her out of the bedroom and into a patterned living room that had clearly seen better days. Everything was chintz, from the sprawling, ornate couch to the peeling wallpaper and frayed carpet. Embroidered lace doilies decorated every available surface, from the windowsill to the cathode ray tube television — a big-ticket antique that might have allowed Mrs. Ley to get her spinal problems checked out if she'd been in the business of making an honest buck.

Potted pockets of leafy azaleas and prickly Japanese roses lined the windowsill like a miniature jungle. Allegra scented lavender, too, but she couldn't make out the whorls of purple blossoms in the shadows of the room.

Yet even though the place seemed in bad need of refurbishment, it was clean — too clean for the likes of Allegra. She felt awkward standing idle by the couch, an interloper in someone's home. At least Darius' place had been bachelor-bare and uninviting. This was lived-in.

This was sacred.

She was still contemplating escape when Mrs. Ley returned from the kitchen with her gun in one hand and a tray of bite-sized cakes in the other. "You ought to eat more. Ain't nothing but skin and bones... Though I suppose when you're running from the cops, it's only common sense to keep trim. I never managed it. Sit, you're giving me a complex."

"I wasn't running," Allegra lied, thrusting her hands into the tiny pockets sewn into her leather pants. It was all she could do to curb the urge to grab a miniature slice of cake.

It didn't help that the snacks looked spongy and soft, or that they seemed to be filled with some kind of pink cream. Allegra's mouth watered the more she side-eyed the colorful stacks. This was how they got you — kindness and promises — before they sprang Jesus on you out of nowhere. Either that, or this was some Hansel and Gretel shit. She fought off temptation with a gruff snort. "We had a disagreement."

"About your fee?" asked her hostess.

Allegra cut her eyes to hers, momentarily thrown for a loop.

Mrs. Ley chuckled thickly. "Doesn't take a genius to know you don't belong here." She sat herself down onto the couch with another hydraulic suspiration. Just walking a few steps seemed to pain her, which begged the question of what she'd been doing outside in that scorcher in the first place. "Now, it might not be any of my business..."

"It's not," Allegra answered, more curtly than she'd meant to.

Mrs. Ley pressed on, undeterred. "Be that as it may, you could take some fattening up. Eat."

She was too weak-willed to resist a second invitation. With a forlorn glance at the shuttered windows, Allegra helped herself to a piece of sugary cake. She'd been right to fear — the spongy sweet tasted divine. Almost as good as the bacon and eggs she'd had for dinner, courtesy of her new partnership with the police. Courtesy of Darius, who had paid for her to eat.

Mrs. Ley explained that Allegra wasn't to get her hopes

up. "It's one of those straight out of the box mixes, nothing special. You caught me at a bad time. I was going shopping, when I saw you. Not suicidal, my ass!"

Allegra ignored the barb, her mouth already full. "You go shopping in this weather?"

"Why shouldn't I?" Mrs. Ley asked, affronted. "I'm old, not comatose. Doesn't hurt that most folks stay away 'cause they're scared of a little tan. I can take as long as I want in the aisles, no one to tap their foot or scoff at me for being' too slow." She explained that she wore an insulation suit to protect herself from the lethal heat and the malignant UVs that rained down for a couple of hours each day, decking herself out like road workers and traffic police — neither of whom stopped working because the weather was inopportune.

"Quietest time of the day," Mrs. Ley said, "or it used to be, before we started getting cock-eyed youths ambling about in the neighborhood…"

"I could leave," Allegra suggested, biting into another cake. "I'm not from around here, anyway."

"Do and I ain't fishing you back in again. That cop friend of yours might… Tough to get rid of, that one. I'm surprised you even made it out the door with him chasin' you."

"You know him?" It shouldn't have surprised Allegra. Even a town as big as Arcadia had its fair share of gossiping biddies. A cop was bound to attract interest, especially in a sleepy little neighborhood like this one.

Mrs. Ley nodded. "He's a hardass. Very stubborn."

Allegra clenched her jaw. "I'm not afraid of him."

"Yeah, you're all invincible, you are. Word has it he was married," Mrs. Ley put in, a glimmer in her eye. "Wouldn't know nothing about that, would you?"

"No, ma'am." Between the fuck and the freak-out that had followed quickly on its heels, there hadn't been much time for conversation. It wasn't outside the realm of possibility — normal people got married, had two point five kids and a picket fence. The works. They weren't all slave to a disease they'd been born with and couldn't control except through illegal narcotics.

"Hmm," said Mrs. Ley, pressing her lips into a stiff line. "Bad business, that was. I remember when he tossed my Harlan out. My boy was an empath, too, you know. Just like you."

Allegra did a double take. "Your Harlan?" Of all she'd heard, that was the least objectionable bit, but knee-jerk disavowals were slow this afternoon. Surprise took the upper hand.

"Oh yes." Her hostess smiled, shark-like and plainly self-satisfied. "Didn't I say, child? I'm the mother-in-law."

Chapter Six

Allegra wasn't going to show up. Darius was more or less certain of it by now. She wasn't going to show up, and the consequences would be dire when the deputy commissioner found out. Worse, Darius hadn't slept since yesterday afternoon, courtesy of that thoughtless romp, and his nerves were shot to hell. He didn't know how long he'd be able to cover for her.

What if Allegra was already dead? He didn't trust Mrs. L. not to throw her back out again as a kind of message for Darius. Resentment made people do strange things and Mrs. L. had never been shy about thinking him a fraud. But maybe she was too weak in her old age to drag a body all the way to Darius' front door. Maybe she'd leave Allegra on the sun-baked pavement outside. That would work just as well.

He never should have left Allegra behind, gun or no gun. It wouldn't be the first time he'd taken a bullet in the line of duty.

Darius started badly when the car door opened with a hard jerk. Allegra slunk in wearing ripped jeans and a shirt that had likely been black once upon a time, but was now a mid-range gray, splotchy from one too many stints in the tumble-dryer. It also hung a little low in the shoulders and the long sleeves all but covered Allegra's painted fingertips. The word 'fuck' was emblazoned like fading graffiti in chipped neon yellow across the front of the shirt.

For a girl like Allegra, this likely rated as conservative.

On a normal day her choice of apparel might have warranted a quip, but all Darius could manage was a shallow "Hello" as his brain slowly caught up. Allegra was in his car. Not dead on the sidewalk, not sleeping by the train tracks on the edge of the city — she was here. She had even dressed down for their rendezvous. *How thoughtful.*

"Are you going to start the car any time soon?" she drawled, glancing out of the window at the tall bell tower of St. Michael's cathedral. Her gaze wandered restlessly, focusing on the dusty interior of the sedan, the deserted sidewalk outside — anywhere but at Darius.

He watched the bony fingers of her right hand worry a loose thread in her jeans and felt oddly bereft without the usual mockery. In a matter of hours, he had come to regard her quips as the norm. Their absence gnawed at him.

"Sure," Darius said, but made no move to start the engine. "You make it back to the Docklands okay last night?"

"What's it to you?"

The vitriol was to be expected. Darius had thrown Allegra out after taking his pleasure like a callow boy, all on the basis of unfounded accusations. That he'd felt sure of himself at the time didn't matter now. He'd made a mistake. There was no other word for it. Allegra was just a girl. She had offered herself to him because it was the only thing she understood — and Darius hadn't refused.

"Look," he started. "I'm sorry about what I—"

"Start the damn car," Allegra interjected. She clearly didn't want to hear it.

And why should she? Darius was her keeper as much as she was his ball and chain. They were both trapped in this arrangement.

This time Darius obeyed, albeit with heavy heart. He drove the Mustang into non-existent traffic, intent on ignoring his passenger's stubborn moue of displeasure. They left St. Michael's behind and made it as far as the wide lanes of Hangman's Court before Darius abandoned his resolve. The silence was beginning to wear on his already frayed nerves. He'd never been good at letting conflict fester.

"You clean up nice, you know. I, uh, like that shirt..." *A teenager's brand of flattery and every bit as awkward.*

"What," Allegra taunted, "for a kid from the Docklands?"

"No. Just—in general." It didn't come out as smooth and effortless as he'd hoped, but at least he had her talking again. Her silence would only make him wonder if she was reading him like an open book, prying into his head and pulling out the secrets.

She must have felt his discomfort, his remorse. If she did, though, she didn't care enough to assuage the unease. She snorted derisively. "Conversation skills like that, no wonder you got divorced…" She did glance at him then, much to Darius' dismay.

For a kid determined to hold a grudge, Allegra seemed a trifle shamefaced to discover the jibe had slipped through her teeth.

He hadn't slept much. It took him a moment to realize why she suddenly lost her verve. *Oh. That.* "Mrs. L.'s been talking, huh?" Allegra seemed about to respond, likely with some cheap shot about Darius having no say in the company she chose, so he anticipated her. "Here—your thirty pieces of silver," he said and pried a thin, unmarked vial out of his trench coat pocket.

Three pills, easily recognizable by their shape and color, clinked inside the clear plastic bottle. If he hadn't known better, Darius might have mistaken them for candy. It was strange to think that something so small, so innocuous, was capable of inducing the wildest trip or blurring the third eye, depending on the need. No wonder PharmaCorps had taken them off the market.

"I didn't know if you preferred the injectable stuff or…" Darius trailed off. Allegra had already snatched the vial from his grasp.

There was nothing fanciful in the way she battled the pressure cap with shaking hands. Darius recognized the frenzy.

She only took one. No doubt she was saving the rest for a rainy day—classic behavior for an addict with no guarantee of a next fix. This was the woman Darius had accused of playing with his head. She could barely go twenty-four hours without a shot of Bliss. She was no Machiavellian foe with designs on his honor. Hell, the backs of her hands were still pink from her last brush with danger.

There was something twisted and nonsensical about trying to reassure a junkie, but Darius couldn't help himself. "I realize this might not mean much, but as long as you work for me—"

"Attention all units," blared from the car radio. "Ongoing four-five-nine at the corner of Fletcher and May." The crackling request came again, and a third time.

Darius was already leaning on the accelerator.

"Get your seat belt on," he said, changing gears.

For once, Allegra didn't quibble. "What's a four-five-nine?" she asked.

"Robbery." The APU usually only heard about those after all was said and done, money gone and not enough clues to dig up the culprits. Darius felt his heart skip a beat as the Mustang sped through the streets with an awful racket. He worked Homicide—which meant that he was often in the business of finding more bodies than perpetrators. He was ready for a change of pace.

Fletcher Avenue was behind them, two blocks west from the cathedral. Darius did a U-turn at the first intersection, tires squealing as they skidded on the asphalt.

"Wait, we're going in?" Allegra asked, her voice cracking.

"I am. You're staying in the car."

"Can't you just drop me off?"

Out of the corner of his eye, Darius caught sight of her stricken expression. She was scared—and rightly so. Most people ran away from danger, never toward it.

"You'll be fine," Darius said. He had a duty to Arcadia. He had sworn an oath.

He couldn't just sit this one out.

"This is a terrible idea," Allegra gritted out. "I want you to know that."

Darius touched her elbow, which between the radio in his hand and having to keep an eye on the road was hard to do, and gave it a squeeze. "You'll be fine. I promise."

He didn't have to wonder what a cop's promise might be worth to someone like Allegra. The answer was obvious in her incredulous, wide-eyed stare as they came to a sudden stop. "Lock the doors behind me," Darius advised and leaped from his seat with his pistol already drawn. It didn't occur to him to tell her to call for backup.

It was a cool morning and the pavement beneath his feet was still damp with run-off from last night's icy showers. This was his neighborhood. His turf. The blocky constructions all the way down Fletcher Avenue were nothing worth writing home about, just the usual chrome and concrete monstrosities pockmarked by garishly bright billboards. Only the jewelry shop on the corner of May Street stood out.

Darius noted the smashed window, the broken lock on the door. No getaway car was idling by the curb, though, so the bastards must've been hoping to run out the back way. Not a bad plan, but Darius knew his way around these parts.

He gingerly stepped over the shattered glass in the entryway, trying to avoid giving away his position. The roar of blood whooshing against his eardrums was making it hard enough to make out sound in the depths of the store. With the blinds drawn, the whole place was delivered to shadow and stale, musty air.

The last time he'd come here, it had been to pawn his wedding band.

A flash of movement in the darkness caught his eye. "Stop! Police!" Darius hefted his pistol, aimed, and pressed the trigger before he could think the better of it.

The shot went wide, barely grazing the perp's cheek. Darius fired again, his ears ringing, but it was already too late. A broad-shouldered figure rammed into him, sending him sprawling to the ground.

He hit the floor hard and felt the gun slip from his fist.

It fetched up against a glass-walled display, too far from him to reach without straining. He thought better of it as he put his elbows up to fend off a punch—a useless defense against a pistol shot, but from the way he'd been tackled, he didn't think the robber had brought anything more explosive than a bat.

The first smack of a boot against his ribcage lent truth to the assumption.

Darius curled in on himself to mitigate the sharp stab of pain and thrust out a hand to snatch at his assailant's ankle. He'd been a wrestler in high school and hand-to-hand had always come easy to him, but he had also just turned forty and his days in the gym were history.

Another kick caught him across the face, sent his head flying ninety degrees to the right. It was like whiplash— one sudden pull, then the cold grip of disorienting panic. *Get up. Get up, you have to get up.*

His body wasn't responding, the link between his brain and his muscles temporarily severed.

Darius hoped it was temporary.

He saw a gloved hand snag his pistol off the ground and through the haze of panic a single thought resolved itself into being— *Allegra's going to think I was lying*. That was all that registered before the robber brought the butt of the pistol down hard on Darius' temple. It was as if someone had flipped a switch.

The whole world promptly went dark.

* * * *

Darius came to with the distinct impression that someone was smacking him across the mouth. And not a perfunctory swat, either. The whole left side of his face stung bitterly— which didn't make it as nerve-wracking as the fact that the right was numbed by a dull ache.

He went from the dull fog of blackout to waking in the space of a few blinks. An open palm was swinging toward his face, fingers splayed out and tipped with scuffed black polish. Darius caught it just before it made impact.

"Oh, thank the gods," Allegra gasped. Her silver-blonde hair resolved into view before her green-gray eyes and flushed cheeks. "I thought you were dead, you fuck!"

"I'm not," Darius grunted. Not unless the afterlife took after the city he was paid to defend. "What happened?"

"You got hit over the head like a moron. I told you I had a bad feeling about this! No, don't move. Paramedics are on their way."

Allegra must've called them. *Clever girl.*

"Thanks," Darius breathed, his voice thick with gratitude. He still hadn't released her wrist, but since Allegra didn't seem to have noticed, he didn't give more than a passing thought to unclasping his fingers. He needed the anchor. "Did he see you?"

"The robber?" Allegra shook her head. "You put him down."

"I did what?"

She canted her head, hair spilling across one shoulder in a shiny waterfall. "You must've clocked him one. He's out."

Darius followed her gaze to the figure slumped a mere ten feet from the door. There was a pool of dark, viscous red spreading around him. "He's more than out..." And Darius had no memory of shooting him, though he must've done.

His sidearm lay beside him, harmless-looking and lethal, like a vial of Bliss.

It wasn't long before the ambulance arrived. Jasme was with them, moving briskly between the beat cops cordoning off the scene and the forensics team snapping stills of the victim.

"Seems like an open and shut case, boss. You okay?"

From the height of the gurney on which the paramedics had insisted on hoisting him, Darius grimaced. "I'm swell. He's dead?"

Jasme nodded, drawing her bottom lip between her teeth.

"I wouldn't worry about it. Anyone can see it was self-defense." She meant the deputy commissioner. Mallory Osker didn't think much of police shootings, but this was an election year and Darius wasn't so sure she'd tolerate the incident. "You'll have to give a statement," Jasme added, shifting her weight at his side. "You remember what happened, don't you, boss?"

Darius craned his neck. Allegra had moved out of his field of vision, taking a step back from what must have been her worst nightmare—a plethora of uniforms and badges, all empowered to stop and frisk and bring her in for questioning.

"Yeah," he said. "Sure I do. Can you do me a favor?"

He was still gazing at Allegra when Veland hobbled over to his side. "She's a pretty one," he drawled. Darius scowled, but Veland wasn't wrong. Even chewing her nails like a squirrel with an acorn, there was still something captivating about Allegra. If Darius had put more stock on New Age-y mumbo-jumbo, he might have said it was her aura. He didn't. He knew he was just a dirty old man lusting after a woman he should've stayed far away from.

It wasn't Allegra's aura that'd had him jumping her bones back at the apartment.

"What are you doing out in the field?" he asked Veland, deflecting.

Veland snorted, his gut hitching up. "I was in the neighborhood, heard we had a man down. Got me curious to see what idiot got his ass handed to him by a petty crook. Figured it'd be you, sweet cheeks."

Darius flipped him off.

"You remember what happened?" Veland asked.

"There a reason everyone assumes I'm going senile? Course I remember." He had already lied once, to his partner. The only way forward was to keep peddling the same story until it became the truth.

"Cool it, cowboy. You know it's just procedure. Walk me through what happened so we can both get out of here? I haven't had my second coffee yet."

Of all the people who could've been tasked with taking his statement, there was no one more interested in getting everything wrapped up nice and tight than Veland. He liked his desk job — he worked cold cases, for the most part, that didn't involve any running around. He didn't think much of Darius.

By the time they were finished, Darius had almost managed to convince himself of the order of events. There really was only one way this could've played out. Allegra had been cowering in the car and there were no other witnesses. Adrenaline must have done for Darius what he himself could not.

The paramedics proved harder to shake.

"They want to do some tests," he told Jasme when she and Allegra approached, the former more valiantly than the latter. "You'll have to get back to the precinct without me. You okay with that?"

Jasme rolled her eyes. "Think I still know the way, boss."

"Will you be okay?" Allegra asked, her voice small.

"He'll be fine," said one of the paramedics. He did a double take when Allegra's cinnamon-dark lips registered. "Are you — ?"

"She's with me," Jasme cut in. "There a problem?"

The APU seldom collaborated with empaths — everyone agreed that they were too volatile to be trustworthy — but Darius had forgotten that there was a very real prejudice against their kind in the wider population. It wasn't so long ago that laws had been proposed to have them all rounded up and confined to special compounds.

Common folk didn't, as a rule, think much of having their minds read. Darius knew it well. He'd rejected Allegra's advances for that same reason — but only after he'd got off.

"Head back to the precinct," he told Jasme. Allegra would be all right there.

The paramedic had already moved on, but the specter of his presence lingered. Darius reached out a hand. "Thank you," he said again, to Allegra. Whatever had happened, she had called for help on his behalf. "I owe you one."

"Don't mention it," said Allegra. Her hand was very small in his grasp, but her grip was firm. He could still feel its pressure long after she'd pulled free.

Chapter Seven

"You okay?" Jasme asked, shattering the silence.

"Yeah."

Monosyllabic answers must not have been to her taste, because Darius' partner tried again. "I mean, it's okay if you aren't. It's been a busy twenty-four hours."

"You don't know the half of it," Allegra murmured. If she kept her eyes on the window and not on her companion, she could almost pretend she didn't feel twin eddies of concern and protectiveness rolling off Detective Sarli. It reminded her of the camera crews who used to stop by the Docklands in search of a good story — something about teenage pregnancy, perhaps, or rampant drug use. Except Detective Jasme Sarli also radiated pride.

"He'll be all right," she said after a beat. "Darius. He's hardy, that one. Been on the force six years. It'll take more than a robber to put him down. Lucky you were there, though. Think you saved his life."

A more perfect picture of the man behind the badge was beginning to take shape, despite Allegra's best efforts to deny any interest. "Doubt that's how he feels," she muttered. It would've been rude to keep quiet when Jasme was trying so hard to make conversation. "Did you know his husband?"

Jasme shook her head. "He was married?"

"Yeah..." And if he hadn't shared that fact with his partner, he probably wanted it kept private. Allegra bit the inside of her cheek. "Long time ago. You should probably forget I mentioned it."

"He's not big on talking about his personal life," Jasme

said, hitching up her shoulders into a shrug. "How did you find out?"

His mother-in-law told me, Allegra thought. She bit back the arch reply—it would've been one more revelation. "Intuition."

"Oh. You mean your empathy thing?" Jasme glanced over as they idled at a stop light. "That's cool. I've never actually met an empath before. What's it like?"

It should have been a harmless question, easily deflected, but after the night she'd had, and realizing she knew the paramedic who was attending to Darius, Allegra's snark was in short supply. "Like having twenty-twenty hearing in a world where everyone's deaf," she said. "Trust me, you're better off not knowing."

Jasme was sharp. She puzzled out the finality of her reply and said nothing else for the rest of the journey.

The silence didn't last—as soon as they were inside the precinct, the din of ringing telephones and overlapping voices cleaved through the tension building between them. That many people in room should've given Allegra a headache, but she had gotten her fix an hour earlier. She was ready to work.

"Don't look up now," Jasme said, setting a plastic cup on the desk before her, "but the Wicked Witch is making the rounds. Also, I didn't know how you took your coffee, so here's, like, ten packets of sugar." She upended her pockets onto her partner's desk with an apologetic smile.

Allegra furrowed her eyebrows. "You didn't have to do that." There was no such thing as handouts in the Docklands and she had long discovered that the only way to avoid debt was never to trust in other people's kindness. But Jasme was already retreating to her own desk, waving a hand as if gratitude was irrelevant. It might have been, if she was expecting Allegra to pay her back in some other fashion.

No surprise there—this whole arrangement was predicated on quid pro quo, not free rides. Allegra twisted her chair around and glanced down the narrow aisles of the bullpen.

The deputy commissioner was indeed strolling through, stopping occasionally to talk to this or that underling. Allegra couldn't make out what was being said—lip reading had never been a strength—but she could feel Osker's pique like the scratch of sandpaper against the inside of her skull. Bliss filtered out the noise. It didn't make her deaf to powerful emotions.

"I hear you were something of a hero this morning," Osker said, once she'd made her meandering journey over. She towered over her in a smart, black suit and skirt, her stockings as black as her shiny shoes.

"The radio was on," Allegra demurred. "I just picked up and shouted for help. No need to give me a medal."

"Don't worry, we won't," said the deputy commissioner. But her gaze lingered on Allegra, as penetrating as it was fearless.

You know I can read you like an open book, Allegra found herself musing. *You don't care.*

Or worse, she got off on confronting Allegra with the weight of her innermost sentiments. An empath, after all, couldn't tease out specific information. They were a magnifying glass for flimsy twitches of human behavior, grimaces that body language experts might have otherwise puzzled over in an attempt to decode.

Empaths suffered other people's feelings. They couldn't turn that part of their brains off. Not ever. And Mallory Osker understood this.

It made Allegra wonder what else she knew—about what happened this afternoon, about Allegra's past.

"Any word on Leon?" she asked, addressing Jasme, but still looming over Allegra like a rain cloud.

"They took him away for tests, ma'am. He should be back tomorrow morning."

"He'll be back sooner than that, if I know him at all." Osker flashed them a smile. "Well, carry on. I'm sure you'll be fine on your own for a few hours, two brave young women helping to keep Arcadia safe... It's like something from the vidreels."

Allegra said nothing and Jasme's smile seemed more than a little frosty.

"She gives me the creeps," Jasme muttered once the deputy commissioner had stalked off out of earshot, a predator combing the tall grass for easy prey.

"Me too," Allegra echoed. Not for the first time, she had the distinctly uncomfortable feeling that what she'd been co-opted into went beyond a few high profile victims.

Mallory Osker hadn't shown her hand yet.

Allegra smothered a shiver and slid her ear buds back in. She had recordings to go through. She still needed that surgery.

* * * *

The day went by quickly enough without Darius constantly peering over her shoulder. Allegra spent three hours with the ear buds in and the physical world reduced to white noise in her peripheral vision, until Jasme placed a plastic-wrapped sandwich on the desk before her.

Allegra considered refusing, but food was hard to come by in the Docklands, and constant hunger won out over her misplaced sense of pride. She ate as she worked, tethered to the sight of family and friends talking about finding their loved ones dead. By no means was Trina Grey the only victim. The other two—a would-be politician and a recluse—had both been older. They were all strangled and all three had expired while high on Bliss.

Not a bad way to go, for normal folks.

Trina Grey had preferred pills to injections or snorting powder. The other two victims were fonder of the syringe. There was no sign that any of them had known each other or had common interests, friends, ambitions. The only thing that united them was a certain level of financial prosperity, which explained how they'd been able to elude the police for so long.

The APU didn't need to go knocking on doors in the fortress-boroughs of the city when it could send a pair of plain clothes into the Docklands and fill up half a minimum-security prison—which on occasion was done, when the forced labor camps ran low on manpower.

By the end of the day, Allegra had a more perfect understanding of the case, but no leads to give Darius, no flashes of genius to justify her presence at the precinct.

She pushed her empty sandwich wrapper into the trash bin and folded her arms over the wooden desk between two perilously high stacks of papers.

"No joy?" Jasme asked, on the cusp of a yawn.

Allegra groaned something that she judged close enough to a *no* to suffice by way of answer.

"You should head home. They probably gave Darius something to sleep off his bruises. He'll be back tomorrow, don't you worry. You need a ride?"

As tempting as it was to jump at the opportunity, Jasme—whom Allegra found herself referring to more and more by first name instead of rank—had done enough for her already. She shook her head. "I'll take the train." Not having credits enough for a ticket had never stopped her before. Public transport was essentially free transport for those born in the Docklands—the government just didn't know it.

"Okay," Jasme said with a beaming grin. "See you tomorrow, then."

It took Allegra a moment to realize that she was being left alone inside the precinct. She jerked upright. The station never really emptied out, but the bullpen was lacking in warm bodies. Only Veland was left, tap-tapping idly at his tablet as a plastic cup steamed on his desk. The lights in the deputy commissioner's office were still on.

A lump of panic seized in Allegra's throat. She wasn't supposed to be here—bad enough that she'd felt remotely comfortable in Jasme's presence. Had she forgotten where she came from?

She felt her knees quake as she stood. It was a symptom of atrophy, nothing more. A few long strides and she was past the last remaining cops, through the durasteel barriers. The cool evening air buffeted her cheeks as she stepped out of the building with heart hammering against her ribcage and palms sweating. Of all the things to be panicked about, this made the least sense.

"Heading home?" a voice asked.

Allegra spun around to find Darius climbing slowly out of his Mustang. His tie hung loosely around his neck, the top button on his poly-blend shirt undone. There was a splotch of blood on his collar that she knew was his.

"Sorry," Darius said, "didn't mean to startle you."

"You didn't." Lies just rolled off the tongue whenever Allegra opened her mouth. She couldn't help herself. "Okay," she said, backtracking, "maybe a little. How... How are you feeling?" He looked rough, as if his stay in hospital had been less than restorative.

"Clean bill of health. They cleared me for work. Seems I should've gone home, though. Jasme left?"

Allegra nodded. It was coming up on ten o'clock, but yesterday had proved to her that Darius didn't give much thought to work-life balance. Mrs. L. wouldn't tell Allegra why her son's marriage had ended in divorce. She didn't have to. What kind of self-respecting Arcadian would put up with being second best?

Darius twirled the car keys around his index finger. "Guess I should head off, too... You want a ride?"

It was the same offer Jasme had made. Allegra didn't dismiss it so quickly the second time around. "Should you be driving?"

"Technically?" Darius shook his head. "I can drop you off at the nearest subway stop."

"Yeah, okay." Allegra rounded the Mustang, trailing her fingers around the solar panels mounted on the rusty hood.

Both ride and rider had seen better days.

Watching Darius put the car into gear and pull away from the curb brought with it a powerful sense of déjà vu. Yet unlike this morning, Allegra couldn't bring herself to resent his very existence. Maybe seeing him sprawled on cold tarmac, his gun in someone else's hand, was enough to put things into perspective. She tried not to dwell.

"There's a stop by your place," she said, pulling her knees up to her chest. "You can drop me off there."

"You sure?" Darius didn't look it. He stole a glance at her, though, and Allegra saw his eyebrows furrow. Apprehension radiated like a furnace in infrared. "There's one just over on—"

"I don't trust you not to crash if you go joyriding," Allegra interjected snippily. "You're about to keel over."

She wasn't exaggerating. Maybe the white coats should have spent less time reading their charts and more time observing their patient. Darius wasn't well. She could feel his exhaustion, his resignation. Dark circles ringed his eyes. She smothered any sense of guilt that might have kindled at the sight of him.

Everything she had done she'd done because she had no other choice.

"How did it go today?" Darius asked as they turned into his lane.

"Don't worry, I didn't crack the case without you," Allegra said, the best and easiest way she could think of to tell him his input was still invaluable. It came out a little more acerbic than intended.

"That's not... I don't expect you to do my work for me." He sighed as though the very assumption made him feel wary.

Allegra rolled her eyes. "Don't take everything I say so literally."

"How else am I supposed to take it? You don't come with an instruction manual."

That, at least, restored Allegra's righteous indignation and did away with her regrets. "Says the guy who can't decide if he wants to fuck me or lock me up," she shot back. It was just as well they had reached the car park, because the look Darius turned on her then was too long, too hefty to allow for multitasking.

It had been a low blow. It wasn't the first or the last in her repertoire — short folks aimed where they could.

The moment passed gradually, silence stretching between them like an elastic band pulled taut. Without the car engine and the din of traffic muffled by blast-proof windows, there was nothing to distract Allegra from the stubborn *sorry* that nearly crept past her lips.

"Jasme's nice," she said, at length.

"She's a good kid," Darius agreed.

"Kid? She's thirty-three." A fact Allegra only knew with such a degree of certainty because she had helped herself to the other woman's wallet while Jasme was in the restroom. She had taken no credit chips, though she'd been tempted. Somehow stealing from the woman who had made her coffee and bought her lunch just didn't gel with whatever scraps of ethics Allegra had left.

She watched as Darius tilted back his head, a shallow smile tilting up the corners of his lips. "I'm an old geezer, what do you expect?"

"To cut the bullshit? I bet you think I'm eighteen or something, don't you?"

"I've read your file," Darius pointed out.

"Hasn't helped you much, has it?" He had let her into his apartment — he had put his faith in her. Allegra glanced away. "We should get you upstairs. Wouldn't want someone calling the cops because they think you're soliciting." There was only so much a guy like Darius could have to say to a woman like her. She gave the car door a light shove, taking her frustrations out on inanimate objects. At least they couldn't fight back.

"*We?*" Darius asked, emerging from the Mustang on his side. "What, you think I need a babysitter now?"

"You needed one this morning," Allegra shot back. So much for handling him with care because he'd had a rough day. Care wasn't in her repertoire. On the other hand, she had always excelled at verbal tennis.

Darius must have been tired indeed because he didn't offer much resistance. Together they stumbled up the stairs of his ancient brownstone, mindful to keep at least ten inches of space between them at all times.

His apartment was unchanged—a vast and impersonal space that seemed no more lived-in now than the last time Allegra had stopped by. The blinds were down in the living room and the air smelled of musk and cloying heat. Even so, it was better than anything Allegra had ever called home.

"If you want something to drink," Darius sighed, "kitchen's through there. I just need to sit down for a minute." He'd been breathing hard as they'd crept up the final flight of stairs. Allegra had wondered if he was going to have a heart attack, but true to Jasme's predictions, Darius was hardy. He pulled through.

Allegra eased the door shut behind them. "I'm all right." People kept trying to feed her, buy her drinks. It was messing with her head, too, because they didn't seem to remember to ask for anything in return.

That was why yesterday had been so easy—she'd learned to use her body as currency a long, long time ago. Only Arcadians would feel shame for something so banal as surviving at all cost.

"What are you—?"

"Helping you out of your coat," Allegra shot back. "What's it look like, geometry? Gods, you'd think you were afraid of me or something…"

She wanted Darius to acknowledge how ridiculous that was. She wanted to see him roll his eyes.

"You have your moments," he said instead, dutifully moving his arms to allow her to pry off his trench coat. His suit was rumpled underneath, his tie askew.

Allegra decided against sticking pins. Darius really wasn't

fit for sparring. "You got something stronger than water in the kitchen?"

"Bourbon behind the sink." An alcoholic's quirk.

Or maybe just a coping mechanism for a lonely guy. Allegra had no room to judge. She shook out his coat before folding it over the back of an armchair, and fetched the bottle out of the kitchen. It was some foul-smelling stuff, but most hard flavors — liquor or otherwise — failed to crank her engine. 'Once you taste Bliss', the old tag line went, 'you won't want to go back'. For once the ad men were right.

She filled two plastic cups she had rinsed out in Darius' sink, under a tap that actually gushed with clear water, and pushed one within his reach.

"To not getting killed... You stupid jerk." She'd seen people toast in a movie once. She had some idea that this was the way to do it and the uncertainty made her feel just a little more hostile than was necessary.

She didn't know what to do with Darius smiling wryly as he held up his glass. He peeled it off in one swig. "Another."

Allegra had barely put her lips to the glass rim.

"Is this you falling off the wagon?"

"What wagon would that be?" Darius asked, vividly playing up his ignorance. "I just spent the day getting poked and prodded by lab coats, my back's killing me. And the psycho I'm supposed to stop is probably zeroing in on his next victim as we speak. Pour me another."

He made a compelling case. Allegra tilted the bottle in a steady hand.

"Still reckon I'm a liability?" she asked, leaning back in her armchair.

"Not right this minute, no."

Drunken testimony wasn't likely to count for much, but Allegra couldn't stop herself. She was curious. No one had ever been afraid of her before. Dubious, sure. Hostile, often.

Never scared.

She tugged a longish slice of hair between her lips, like she used to do as a girl. It didn't go far in gagging her. "You're really so sure I can't be a contributing member of society?"

Darius arched his eyebrows, raising reddened eyes to meet her gaze. "Does it matter what I think?"

No. He was nobody. Just some guy she'd been saddled with as part of her probation deal. Allegra bristled. "I don't ask every guy I fuck for feedback, if that's what you're asking."

"It wasn't." For a moment, she thought Darius might choose to leave it there. He had every reason to—Allegra had invited herself into his apartment again, and she was lingering when he likely wanted her gone. But Darius went on, "I don't think a level seven is compatible with living around other sentient beings. Not for our sake and not for yours."

"Right," Allegra snorted. "You're all so fucking concerned with our wellbeing."

Darius fixed her with a look that said more than words ever could. "Am I wrong?"

The hot flush of shame rarely crept onto Allegra's cheeks. She had no use for it, no time to waste on worrying whether or not she'd made a faux pas. But Darius was asking her to deny something she objectively knew to be true by simultaneously agreeing she was a danger to herself and others.

Wasn't that what Osker had promised to correct?

"You catch this Bliss killer—"

"Slayer," Darius corrected softly.

"—and it sounds like I won't be anybody's problem anymore." Allegra pursed her lips. "That is, if you think Osker's going to keep her end of the bargain."

Darius held her gaze so unflinchingly that she couldn't help feel he was trying very hard to appear truthful. "I do."

She didn't have to strain an inch to feel the tidal wave of guilt that rose up with the breathy answer. He was lying through his teeth. "Awesome," she beamed blithely. "Then you're stuck with me for a while longer. Hey, you mind if I use your shower? Mine's busted." Or, as the case might have been, non-existent.

"Knock yourself out," Darius said.

"Awesome." Allegra bounded from the armchair, her nonchalance an undisputed improvement over his amateurish attempt.

It wasn't until she'd locked the bathroom door behind her that she allowed herself to smother a wail into her fists. She should have trusted her instincts. She should have made a break for it. Now there was blood on her hands—and for what?

Chapter Eight

Allegra had a habit of grinding her teeth. Darius knew he should've found it irritating, a distraction from work more important than the presence of a skinny woman-child in his apartment, but the fact was that he had to smother his concern whenever he heard the muffled grating noise.

What was she dreaming of? Should he have roused her and sent her on her way? It was certainly against regulations to confuse the professional with the personal, but others did it, too. The letter of the law no longer meant much for the people meant to enforce it. Perhaps it never had.

Darius scrubbed a hand over his face and turned back to his notebook. He contemplated getting himself another drink, but as much as the thought appealed, he knew he'd had about as much as was wise. The last time Allegra had been in his apartment, her nails had scraped his shoulder blades raw and Darius had only been able to beg for more. He didn't want to go down that slippery slope again. Best he remained sober. Clear-headed.

In control of his wandering libido.

It didn't help that there was very little difference between the tenor of Allegra's moans as she came and the sound she made as she yawned awake. Out of the corner of his eye, Darius watched her stretch her arms and arch her spine like a cat. "Mm," she muttered. "You're up."

He hadn't slept all that much, just a couple of hours, and even that was only courtesy of his medication and the bourbon.

"Why didn't you wake me?" Allegra asked, uncoiling her legs. The furrow between her eyebrows deepened. "What time is it?"

"Eight-fifteen." Darius was almost proud—his voice hadn't cracked, he successfully avoided eye contact. Were this high school, he'd feel almost cool.

Allegra swore. "And you couldn't wake me sooner? Gods..."

"I thought sleeping in strange places was a habit of yours." It was a low blow, but Darius couldn't pull the punch. It was every man for himself and Darius had spent the past couple of hours wondering if he should wake Allegra or join her.

"Screw you," Alana said and snorted a guffaw. "You think I get picked up by the cops every day? This whole week hasn't been exactly representative of my day-to-day."

"I hear you." Whatever else, chasing crooks and sleeping with strange—beautiful, possibly insane—junkies wasn't Darius' modus operandi.

He heard Allegra sigh and push herself to her feet. "You're right. I should let you work or whatever..."

"There's a cheese sandwich in the fridge," Darius said. "And you can make the coffee."

"What?"

Despite his better judgment, Darius glanced up. He had steeled himself for derision and disbelief, but found only confusion hovering in Allegra's puffy eyes. "I still need your help. If you're willing to offer it."

He had been going about this the wrong way. Junkie or not, Allegra wasn't a resource with a highly lucrative gift. She was a person. Pointing her at a witness and expecting a miracle wasn't going to work.

"It occurs to me that you're lacking the full picture," Darius said when Allegra had returned from the kitchen with the cheese sandwich in hand. The coffeemaker's familiar gurgling served as their background music. It set the mood. "You know about Trina Grey..."

Allegra smirked, her mouth already full. "How could I forget? Little Miss Perfect with the devoted housekeeper."

"Right. But you don't know enough about the other two."
Darius pushed two manila folders across the table. "Efrenn
Weiss, professional recluse and spiritual leader. He had
some cult going, I forget what it's called."

"*Fidelis et natura*," Allegra supplied between bites.
"They're the same tech-free nutjobs who used to come to the
Docklands and try to get us to lead"—she made air quotes
with her fingers—"a more authentic existence. Whatever
the fuck that means. We ran them out of town pretty fast.
Should've seen their faces when they realized we're not all
misunderstood little lambs... What? Don't look at me like
that. We get *some* news in the Docklands. It's not another
planet."

"Right. No, of course." Darius cleared his throat, making
a valiant attempt to conceal his surprise. "Sorry." He didn't
want to admit it, but thinking of the Docklands as a place
through which information flowed as easily as the rest of
Arcadia just didn't gel with the image he had of the slum.
He tried to brush past it, for the sake of his ego. "Second
victim was Jamal Reid. Complete one-eighty from the first
case, which threw me for a loop until we found Bliss in his
bloodstream."

"What's his story?"

"Father of three, stinking rich and proud of it. Nothing at
all like Mr. Weiss."

Allegra had flipped open the manila folder and was
already peering critically at his picture. "He sounds like a
hard-ass."

"Rumor has it he was acquainted with our very own
deputy commissioner," said Darius. "Make of that what
you will."

"Acquainted? You mean like we're acquainted or...were
they having an affair?"

Darius felt a sudden rush of heat course through him.
"None of my business." His superiors' sex lives were
something he tried to stay well away from. Nothing good
came of sticking his nose in questionable couplings. "Reid

was running for office. The deputy commissioner can't come out in support of one or the other candidate. The law says—"

"The law is bullshit," Allegra interjected, finality in her tone. "And you don't have to pretend that Arcadia isn't a cesspool of corruption. Not with me."

"Why not with you?" Darius asked and just as quickly remembered the surgery, the Bliss—Osker's promise to sponsor Allegra's future if only she did her civic duty and helped with this case. "Oh."

Allegra held his gaze. "Reid was strangulated, too, right?"

"Just like Grey." A breath of relief spilled free of Darius' lungs. At least he was treading on safer ground with murder and dead bodies. He didn't have to speculate.

"Weiss, too." Allegra didn't give him a chance to answer. "What were they strangled with? A shoelace? A garrote?"

"A shoelace? What do you—?"

"I once beat up a client with a back issue of *Cosmo*. He wouldn't pay up."

Darius tried to tell himself that he had dodged a bullet, when the truth was that he felt as if it was still lodged in his sternum every time he stole a glance at Allegra. "You're leaving breadcrumbs all over the files," he pointed out.

"That's what you get for killing trees," Allegra quipped. She could be a real smartass when it suited her. Darius desperately wanted to find that infuriating.

He rose, turning his back to conceal a smile. "Weiss was killed with a belt. The Slayer used nylon cord on Reid. Best guess on Grey is her purse strap, but we're waiting on confirmation. Bag's missing." He returned from the kitchen with two mugs of coffee. Allegra didn't have to ask for sugar and milk in hers, Darius remembered from their late-night breakfast at the diner.

"So it's not the same weapon every time?"

Darius shook his head. "No, we think the Slayer uses whatever he has on hand. He probably keeps the weapons as trophies afterward. It's not uncommon among serial murderers."

"Or pack rats," Allegra mused, reaching for her cup. "Thanks."

"You're welcome." It was almost normal—the two of them sharing a modest meal in Darius' apartment, the door locked and the windows peering out over a still-silent, still-sleepy avenue as the waste trucks rolled by en route to the Docklands.

Darius tried not to let his imagination run away with him.

"Can I see the crime scene stills?" Allegra asked out of the blue. "Not to gawk at the corpses, honest... Sometimes I get vibes from places as well as people. Like there's a signature left behind." She studiously avoided his gaze as she offered the olive branch, and though Darius didn't know why, he found himself leaping at the opportunity.

"We have video. At the station."

"Oh. Right. You'll probably want to get going soon."

We don't have to hurry. He bit back the clingy, foolish lie. What, did he think Allegra wanted to be here? She must've insisted on seeing him safely into his apartment to make sure he did nothing foolish. That was all there was to it.

"Finish your sandwich first," he said instead, yearning snagging in his throat.

* * * *

They didn't talk much en route to headquarters. Darius drove while Allegra mapped out the shapes of houses—all alike in architecture—and shops—all above Darius' budget—with her fingertips dancing over the passenger side window.

An uneasy silence permeated the inside of the Mustang, thick with apologies Darius was too proud to utter. Admitting his errors had never been his strongest suit, but more than that, he was afraid to ask what else Mrs. L. had said during their one-on-one. He feared truth more than fanciful lies, because the truth was damning.

94

The truth revealed him for what he really was.

He didn't need to be friendly with Allegra, only to find a happy medium in which they could collaborate to crack this case and escape the red dot of the deputy commissioner's sights. He had given up hope for a promotion. If he did his job right, caught the so-called Bliss Slayer, he was going to opt for early retirement and do what the smart people did—go into the private sector. There had to be a firm somewhere that could benefit from his experience in spotting bad apples.

Allegra slipped through the precinct's front doors with shoulders hunched and a hangdog expression. The lack of handcuffs was conspicuous and would tip anyone off as to her real purpose there, but the kid couldn't be faulted for play-acting. She had a reputation to maintain, as did Darius.

"Back already?" Jasme said upon seeing them together. "And just when I was looking forward to taking point on Ms. Weiss... How's it going, A.?"

Darius had only been gone a day and in that time, Jasme had already made a new friend. It shouldn't have surprised him—she was painfully likeable—even if that friend was a stony-faced empath who seemed to blow hot or cold depending on what suited her best.

He tried to ignore the stab of jealousy in favor of doing his job. "Weiss is here?"

Jasme nodded.

"She's early," Darius sighed, shrugging out of his trench coat. He had been hoping to get some time to explain that case to Allegra in better detail before they began, but there was no time.

"Want me to let her know, boss?"

Darius didn't dignify the question with an answer. Ms. Weiss was a wealthy widow with a social calendar as long as Darius' arm. If she was so eager for their interview, it could only mean that she had somewhere else to be. Getting a hold of her had been difficult enough in the first place, and the last thing Darius wanted was to get on the woman's bad side. Rumor had it she played golf with the commissioner's daughter.

Everyone knows everyone in this goddamn town.

Jasme smiled wryly. "She must be dying to help. You want some coffee?"

"I'm good, thanks." He'd already had his fill of caffeine before leaving home. Yesterday's incident had forced him to acknowledge that he wasn't as young as he'd once been. The doctors had been clear — 'cut back on coffee and takeout, exercise more, or get used to spending the remainder of your active career behind a desk'. Today wasn't the day he started to heed them.

Jasme didn't press him. "Allegra?"

Allegra seemed taken aback by the question. "Uh, sure. Can I come with you? I mean, I should learn my way around here, right? Seems like I'm going to be here a while."

"It's not as dreary as it looks," Jasme told her with a conspiratorial wink. "Remind me to show you the catacombs sometime…"

Her voice faded, lost in the cacophony of sound that populated the bullpen. Phones were always ringing and calloused fingers were typing fast over sticky keyboards, the flurry of noise never dimming, never ceasing.

Darius caught Veland's eye and sighed. Some people got sent to the madhouse, others entered it voluntarily. Maybe they all should've had their heads examined.

"So what's Ms. Weiss' deal?" The coffee Jasme had fixed her up with was steaming hot in a chipped mug when Allegra returned. Her fingers were wrapped tightly around the ceramic, as though leaching off its heat. "Merry widow?"

"Not so much. Efrenn Weiss was her nephew." And never had two people been more different. By some accident of genealogy, Ms. Weiss was actually younger than the victim. She showed no interest in abandoning the material world for spiritual peace, much less taking over her nephew's sizeable following. "We've ruled her out as a suspect for lack of motive," Darius said. "From what we've been able to piece together, she's the one who held the family purse strings—and pretty tightly, at that. Efrenn wasn't a big spender, anyway. He lived like a monk, didn't believe in property or taking alms…"

"Or he had other sources of income," Allegra offered with an acerbic little grin. The coffee seemed to have restored her good mood. Darius couldn't explain why he found that to be a relief, but he did.

"What do you mean?"

Allegra pursed her lips, hitching up her shoulders into a nonchalant, defensive shrug. "He wouldn't be the first guy to put a still in his basement. Only instead of still, think more meth lab, and instead of basement, think more secondary address." She flashed Darius a smile. "There's always users and there's always sellers. If Weiss was doing Bliss, why not sell it, too? I can think of worse covers for a smuggling business…"

The ease with which she put forth the theory left Darius wishing the APU hired more in the Docklands. Up here on Arcadia's sunnier side it was taboo to even infer that the wealthy and the powerful were as fraudulent as the vermin who lived in the toxic waste of long-condemned factories. Everyone turned a blind eye to public money that went into the building of private estates or the racing of yachts. It was a way of life—perhaps not the best or the purest, but it was Arcadia's.

Efrenn Weiss had preached another. Was it all a front?

"Do me a favor and keep that theory to yourself," Darius told Allegra quietly. "We've got an interview to get through before we make guesses. Come on."

Allegra's icy smile was all the disbelief she offered. "Aye, aye, Captain. Whatever you say."

I'm going to pay for that.

They found Ms. Weiss seated in an uncomfortable plastic chair, her dress somber and her face as though carved in granite. "Good morning, Detective," she said, holding out her hand. "I understand you're hoping to clarify a few details about my nephew's passing." She didn't use the word *murder*. Darius understood, with weary resignation and steadily mounting annoyance, that it wouldn't have been proper.

He sat down, keenly aware that he didn't have the upper hand on this one. He couldn't help a glance toward the one-way mirror that separated the interview room from Allegra's gaze. The kid was probably picking her nose. Even after her questions at home, he still couldn't believe that she felt an ounce of real interest in the proceedings.

Liar, a voice whispered at the back of his mind. *You want her to be on your side. To care as much as you do.*

You need her.

"I'm sorry for the inconvenience," Darius started, only to be promptly interrupted.

"It's no trouble," Ms. Weiss said, smiling primly.

"All right. Well, then, I'll get straight to business. Could I ask you to recount how you discovered Mr. Weiss?"

"*Again?*" Ms. Weiss pursed her lips tightly, like a disapproving schoolteacher.

"I know you've already been through this with my colleagues and with me, but I'd really appreciate it if you went through the facts one more time. Sometimes it takes a few days — or weeks, in this case — for memory to settle. We're doing all we can to catch your nephew's murderer. Every detail helps." Allegra's reading of Trina Grey's housekeeper had also given him the impression that she fared better when confronted with a live testimony rather than the recorded — but that was just a guess.

Ms. Weiss reluctantly canted her head. "Well, as I told you *twice* now, I found Efrenn in his bedroom. He had stopped answering his phone a week before. He didn't come to dinner on Friday evening as we had planned..." She shrugged demurely. "I was worried."

"Did he usually keep in touch?"

"Constantly. Ours is a very close-knit family, Detective.

We don't lose track of one another for days at a time. And Efrenn... Well, I knew he'd been having some trouble."

Darius had read the file and made note of this the first time. Still, he asked, "Personal trouble?"

"He separated from his wife in the spring. His life took a turn for the worse after that." Ms. Weiss explained that her nephew had become withdrawn, solitary. He only ever left the house anymore to attend her dinner parties because, "He knew how much I enjoyed his company." Her expression remained cold and distant throughout the interview, giving Darius little to work with. He wondered if Allegra was faring any better.

She had said that all the witnesses he'd interviewed were lying. Did this count as proof?

Darius cleared his throat. "You found him in the bedroom, you said."

"Yes. At first I thought he was sleeping, but the place was a mess. Sheets half pulled off the bed, the blinds drawn tight... I didn't notice the needle and syringe until I circled around to check his pulse." Unlike Trina Grey, victim number two had taken the Bliss intravenously. It was equally illegal and no less dangerous, considering that the black market needles in question were often improperly sterilized. Strangely, that didn't seem to concern junkies overmuch.

"And you assumed he had suffered an overdose?"

Ms. Weiss nodded. "I called the emergency services as soon as I found him. They were very prompt, very efficient. I don't know what I would've done if they delayed." The memory seemed to grab hold for a moment, but she shook her head to dispel it as though uncomfortable with the distraction. "It was the paramedics," she said, "who discovered the strangulation marks. I only heard about them later, when the police returned to verify my statement. At least it wasn't suicide, they said, as if that's supposed to make it easier! The rest you know."

The autopsy had revealed that Efrenn Weiss had injected

himself—or been injected with—five milliliters of diluted liquid Bliss, enough to render a non-empath weak and limp-boned in the face of an assailant's attack. The time of death had been narrowed down to late Friday night, a fair eighteen hours or so before his aunt had let herself into his apartment. There was no sign of forced entry and the security cameras had been shut off, recordings destroyed, suggesting that whoever was with Efrenn Weiss knew what they were up to.

"The door was locked," Darius said thinly, "but you had a key. Did your nephew give it to you?"

"No, we— I was worried he might lock himself out. It's happened before, so we made duplicates of the keys and access codes. Efrenn didn't believe in retinal scans, you see. It was part of his creed. Otherwise I would've insisted he install one." Ms. Weiss pinched the bridge of her nose. "Of course, none of that matters now that he's dead. What I'd like to know is what you're doing about it, Detective."

A fine question. Unfortunately, Darius didn't have an equally fine answer to give. "Everything we can," he repeated, as though that tired old excuse comforted anyone.

* * * *

There was nothing to hold Ms. Weiss after she so graciously obliged them with a repetition of her earlier testimony, so Darius was soon forced to walk her out to the limo she had idling outside the APU headquarters.

Allegra was picking at her fingernails in the observation room when Darius went to retrieve her. Someone—possibly Jasme, though Darius had no proof—had brought in a desk chair and Allegra had taken to spinning around and around in it like a little kid. The thought had a certain level of bite, considering.

"Did you get anything?"

Allegra glanced up, as if only then realizing she wasn't alone. "You won't believe me... But I got the same thing from that broad that I got from Lucan. How's that for a pattern?"

"Similarities don't a pattern make," Darius said. "Could be a coincidence..." He could think of a dozen things Ms. Weiss might've had to hide about her cult-leading nephew. In certain circles of Arcadian society, people who stood out the way Efrenn Weiss had stood out were shunned, derided. Encouraged to disappear.

"Knew you weren't going to believe me." Allegra seemed fine with that, as though Darius was being deliberately obtuse and difficult to work with while she was doing her best to deliver on their arrangement.

Darius propped a shoulder against the cinder block wall, aching worse now that the painkillers had washed out of his system. "So Ms. Weiss is lying about the crime scene, huh?"

"The crime scene, the nephew... You're kidding yourself if you think any one of these high society suits will be telling you the truth. I'm going to get more coffee —"

"Allegra."

She arched an eyebrow. "What?"

"I do believe you." If there was one thing he knew, it was that empaths were capable of great insights into human behavior — insights that often became troubling for those doing the reading. "But these witnesses are all I've got. Well, them and inconclusive forensic evidence. The Bliss Slayer doesn't leave a calling card, only broken families."

"Oh." Allegra scratched at the back of her neck. "Right."

Darius sighed, shook his head. "I realize you have a bias going here, I do, but I need more than an inkling that someone isn't being truthful. I need evidence."

Allegra propped both hands on her hips. "What about the night of the murder? Does Ms. Weiss have herself an alibi?"

"She does."

"Oh. Is it a good one?"

"She was at a charity auction until ten p.m., after which her driver says he drove her straight home. And like I said,

101

she has no motive to kill her nephew…"

"Like the housekeeper didn't have a reason to kill his favorite chick."

Darius nodded. "Something like that."

"You still want to show me the crime scene footage?"

It was likely to do a number on her, even if she was from the Docklands and stronger than a piece of durasteel pulled taut. "Sure. Ask Jasme to hook you up. I'll get you some more coffee."

He didn't put much stock in the quality of the brew, this being the APU, but Allegra seemed to have forgotten where she was going or what she was supposed to do when she got there. She had been behaving a little strangely all morning, blowing hot and cold, making nice with Jasme and keeping her tongue when there were so many opportunities to abuse Darius. Then again, it was hard to say just what qualified as normal for a Docklands-born empath. If this was how guilt looked on her, Darius wished she'd give it a rest. The mistake had been his, anyway.

Their fingers brushed as Darius reached for the cup, but there was nothing, no spark of electricity, no simultaneously held breaths — as if he needed further proof that he had exaggerated abominably when he had accused Allegra of somehow invading his mind. Every study denied the possibility. Empaths were just listening devices. Much to the chagrin of PharmaCorps, they couldn't be used as weapons.

Allegra paused in the doorway, digging her fingernails into the wood. "Hey, Detective? That shit I said about you being divorced. I'm sorry. It was out of line."

"So were the things I said when you came to see me." Darius stopped just short of bringing up their romp. There was no telling who else was listening in on their conversations while inside the precinct walls. "I overreacted."

Allegra tilted up her lips into a smile. "Yeah, you did. But Mrs. Ley's a pretty good baker. So it worked out in the end."

No doubt that was her attempt at putting a brave face onto a badly handled situation. Darius didn't dare believe it was done for his sake. He had thrown Allegra out in a heat wave. He'd been helpless to retrieve her from Mrs. L.'s apartment – barring the calling of reinforcements, which he couldn't do for all obvious reasons.

He was determined not to bring any of it up, though a part of him wanted to find a delicate way to ask what else Mrs. L. had said about him, how she had maligned him. His throat wouldn't cooperate.

Mercifully, Allegra anticipated him. "I should get to work. Go easy on the sugar this time." She flashed him a grin. "I can't afford diabetes."

She was gone, sauntering toward his desk before Darius could think of anything to say. It was for the best. There was no hilarity in her predicament. The sooner their collaboration ended, the better it would be.

Chapter Nine

The thought came to Allegra as she was diluting coffee with soy milk—her sixth cup of the delicious concoction Jasme had shared with her earlier in the day. She nearly dropped the milk carton in her haste to get it back into the fridge.

"Darius!"

The bullpen was almost deserted, but even so a few heads turned her way, a mix of surprise and disapproval flashing across weary faces. Allegra paid them no mind. If anything, she was beginning to feel at home at the precinct. "I just had an idea," she announced.

Darius held up a meaty hand. He was on the phone, something he seemed to be doing as often as brooding over the paper files piled high on his desk. The information age hadn't caught up with the APU, it seemed, or not enough to clear out the clutter Darius loved so dearly.

Allegra scoffed. "Hear me out—"

She cut herself off when Darius glared and the hand he'd raised to stop her became a single finger brandished in warning. 'Shut up', he seemed to be saying with his murky black eyes while his mouth promised he'd be right there.

It took forever, but eventually he deigned to hang up and Allegra ventured right into the wispy silence that followed.

"So I was thinking about Lucan and Ms. Weiss. What they have in common, you know. I mean obviously they're both lying—"

"Allegra."

But Allegra wasn't listening. Her coffee-and-soy-milk cocktail nearly splashed the desk as she sat gingerly on the edge. "Then it came to me—love, right? It's like the old movies. A crime of passion—"

"Allegra, the pathologist found traces of DNA under Trina Grey's fingernails."

"Oh. That's great." It was also fairly rude of him to interrupt, but maybe Darius figured that swanky badge of his gave him a free pass. "That *is* great, right? You don't look pleased," Allegra noted.

Darius canted his head into a sideways nod. "I'm not. The DNA is a match for Jamal Reid, almost-representative of the city of Arcadia."

"Shit..." Allegra bit her bottom lip. She felt too jittery to sit still, but the carefully outlined roadmap in her mind had been blown to smithereens with that single new piece of evidence.

"That's my thinking exactly." Darius sighed, scrubbing both palms over his eyes. "I can't exactly interview a dead man. As far as we know, he didn't have anything in common with the Greys or Efrenn Weiss. And he's very much dead. I'm headed down to the lab now, see if someone can explain to me what's going on..." He shot her a weary glance. "You want to join me?"

Allegra felt her shoulders slump. So much for her theory. "Sure," she muttered, her disposition taking a nosedive.

"You'll have to leave the coffee. They're pretty strict about food and drink in the lab. You took your meds?" Darius asked, donning his trench coat. Waves of fatigue and frustration rolled off his shoulders like an endless, suffocating torrent of dashed hopes.

The last thing Allegra needed was to start feeling sorry for the guy when he couldn't even call Bliss by its name. What, did he think he'd hurt Allegra's ego? She was no Trina Grey.

I don't get you. Most tricks lashed out when they felt emasculated. They didn't recant and apologize, or handle her with kid gloves. When she'd gone to the detective's apartment, it hadn't been to end up even further indebted to the guy.

"I did. I took my pills like a good girl," she told Darius. "Don't worry, I wouldn't want to go all crazy on you."

"That's not what I meant."

Allegra elbowed him in the ribs and tried very hard not to think about pulling him into a dark alleyway and having her way with him. It would settle no debts and Darius would probably freak out.

There was only one way to spare them both. On the way out of the precinct, Allegra tossed the plastic bottle and its remaining two pills into a trashcan. It didn't take as much effort as she anticipated. Darius needed her to *see*, not do his job for him. It was the only way they'd ever be free of each other.

* * * *

The lab and its adjacent morgue were not supposed to be a cheerful place, yet someone had seen fit to cloak the walls in blinking, sprightly green emoticons.

"Part of some ad campaign," Darius explained as they pulled up in his battered sedan. "Apparently it's supposed to liven up the place."

"Livening up a morgue. How Arcadian."

For once, Darius didn't protest her bias. Arcadia was a straightforward city. The upper crust got ads and billboards, the Docklands made do with graffiti-stained shacks barely held together by duct tape and willpower.

The morgue, like Darius' apartment building, straddled the invisible line between poverty and plenty. Unlike Darius' home, the morgue also smelled quite strongly of formaldehyde. Allegra's good cheer curdled like sour milk between the rows of steel slabs and drawers labeled with numbers rather than names.

One day, if Allegra was very lucky, she'd probably end up here, one more transient occupant of death's waiting room.

"Doctor Rhodes," she heard Darius say, the sound of his voice loud enough for Allegra to tear free of her bittersweet, morbid fantasies.

The pathologist was every bit as creepy as Allegra had been hoping. He wore his hair long and limp and very black. When he held out an ungloved hand, she could see the veins criss-crossing along the skin of his skinny forearm like threads of colorful yarn.

"Detective, welcome!" he greeted cheerily. "And this is...?" The pathologist swept his bespectacled eyes over Allegra without the usual assessing quality of men who asked how much for a blow job.

"Allegra Avenson," Darius answered quickly, doing an awkward little quarter turn to glance back at Allegra. "She's a consultant, helping us with the case."

Since handshakes were the norm in this part of town, Allegra obliged. "Hi." No 'good to meet you, Doctor,' because it wasn't a particular pleasure and she saw no point pretending otherwise when there was a body lying on a cold slab between them, sheet covering all but its slim feet.

The upper crust clung to false politeness and so-called good manners, though, even in a place like this. In the Docklands, people spoke frankly, for good or ill, and knew what to expect from one another.

It shocked Allegra to realize she missed the place. That she missed sharing body heat with people who understood where she was coming from—people like Aaron. He had always been something of a safety buoy for her to cling to. It was comforting to know he'd still be there when she returned.

That she hadn't thought of him at all since she had shared Darius' bounty was another story. She didn't think Aaron would begrudge her if he knew. He was a Docklands boy, born and bred.

A tag dangled from the corpse's pale right foot. On it was written *E. Weiss*.

Allegra felt her stomach drop into her knees.

"So what are we looking at?" Darius asked.

Allegra didn't know what more he wanted. They were in a tomb filled with disparate bodies and the shiny instruments that had been used to eviscerate their insides.

Doctor Rhodes pushed his horn-rimmed glasses higher onto his oily, aquiline nose and led them to a row of tables at the far end of the room.

A glass wall separated this room from the rest of the morgue and Allegra imagined the doctor working hard with his saws and his knives as he surveyed the latest crop. She knew it was unkind. No doubt the doctor was a very nice person and there was nothing weird about his job.

Allegra, of all people, shouldn't have been throwing stones.

"I can tell you Ms. Grey definitely fought her assailant, though someone went to great effort to conceal the evidence. We had found traces of third-party DNA under her fingernails during the initial examination, but until now we'd been unable to come up with a match. It turns out they're consistent with the samples we collected from Jamal Reid." He affected a shrug. "We only just entered them into the d-base."

"Blood?"

"Skin cells," Rhodes reported brightly. "Still no fibers," he added, "synthetic or otherwise."

Allegra waited a heartbeat for an explanation that didn't follow. "What does that mean?"

"We still don't know what was used to strangle her." Darius turned back to the pathologist, pinching his lips into a pout. "Jamal Reid died eight days after Grey's body was discovered. So either the killer didn't wash his hands between jobs, used the same weapon, or…"

"Or Reid killed Trina Grey," Allegra said, catching on. She couldn't account for the sudden shiver of certainty pulsing in her veins, but she knew that it had opened her mind to a possibility previously unexamined.

"I was trying to tell you earlier," she added as she turned to Darius with dry lips and an avalanche of words trying to spill from her throat. "You know how I said I felt Weiss and the housekeeper were both lying about the crime scenes? What if they were lying about their relationships with the deceased? Everyone's being very protective—"

"I'm sorry," Doctor Rhodes interjected, his tone suggesting he was anything but apologetic. "You *felt*…?"

Allegra bit her tongue. *Shit.* Probably wasn't supposed to broadcast the fact that the APU were so desperate to solve this case they'd harangued a junkie empath into working for them. "I meant, uh…"

"Ms. Avenson is very perceptive," Darius said, effortlessly stepping in.

The doctor thinned his lips. "Uh-huh. All right. I can show you Reid's body, if that helps?"

Allegra shook her head, tasting bile on the back of her tongue. "My thing only works for the living." And right now she could tell that Doctor Rhodes was feeling uncomfortable—normal, no doubt, for a man of science. He wouldn't be the first to mistrust the vagaries of evolution as sham.

"Oh," Rhodes said, "right." Disappointment coursed from him like a brook through a riverbed. "Well, your theory has *some* merit."

"Does it?" Darius chipped in. He'd been silent too long, observing them like a hawk.

Allegra flashed him a smirk.

"Yes," the pathologist acknowledged. "There are no other bruises or lacerations, or indeed any marks consistent with a struggle. Were it not for the point of strangulation, I would've assumed the victim was alone when she died. As it stands, it's much more probable that she knew her assailant. Perhaps even trusted him."

Allegra could hear what he was implying even if Rhodes was cautious not to spell it out. Being a good girl from a good family, suicide was a better deal for Trina Grey than a reputation for loose behavior. People from the Docklands were godless and reproduced like rabbits, but here, in Arcadia's lush hills, the gated communities incubating the city's future leaders allowed no such diversion from the preordained script. Someone had hooked Trina Grey on Bliss, which had in turn led her to commit suicide.

If not that, then she had been murdered for reasons to do with jealousy or sexual perversion. Her reputation, as Lucan had so loudly defended, could not be called into question.

No way had she been seeing a man old enough to be her father.

"Thank you, Doc," Darius said. "We'll let you get back to work." He didn't have to say it aloud for Allegra to know that he believed this detour had brought them nothing. The web was simply drawing itself around them, more intricate and complex than ever. Darius was tangled in its threads—just like Allegra, just like the other suspects in this increasingly murky tapestry.

He laid a hand on her shoulder, palm broad and warm and solid. She couldn't bring herself to shake off the tentative touch. Physical comfort had always been her undoing.

A shiver snaked down her spine, lodging itself under her skin. By the time they got to the car, it had turned into a full-body shudder.

Darius noticed, too, because he put a tentative arm around her. "You okay?"

"Just cold," Allegra lied, teeth chattering. She knew what was happening, she just didn't want to acknowledge it. She had dumped the Bliss in a fit of pique. Dealing with the consequences always took a little more planning. "You know how I said... How I said I could feel things, residual emotions in various rooms where bad things have happened?"

She felt Darius nod, his chin brushing her temple as the night leached off their body heat. "Is that what you felt in there?"

"No. I couldn't feel anything." The morgue was a place where dead things went to be poked and prodded, organs weighed and bits of skin and hair and nail cataloged for further study. "I couldn't feel *anything*," Allegra breathed, tucking her face into the curve of Darius' neck. He smelled so good—like pine needles and grass and leather.

She stopped herself from licking at his skin. Some guys freaked out when she did that and Darius more than any other was likely to misunderstand her intentions.

They were in his car, at least, and therefore shielded from view. It was the best Allegra could do until the gray clouds overhead quit forecasting rain. Shielding herself from other people had never really worked.

This is the crash, she thought. *The lowest point. The only way from here is up.* That wasn't necessarily ideal. She could already feel the burn of excitement starting to creep in, overriding better judgment.

* * * *

Darius drove for a while, saying nothing. The streets were not as empty as Allegra had thought once they hit the busy downtown. Lit billboards illuminated the sidewalks where men and women ambled idly by in leopard print and gaudy, shimmering sequins. There was a vast and pressing urge to gawk whenever Darius stopped at a light, but Allegra tired of that quicker than she would've done on Bliss.

"We're taking the scenic route, huh?" she asked, when the silence got too heavy.

Part of her knew that the high bubbling in her veins was partly psychosomatic, but her treacherous reptilian brain didn't seem to care. Synapses firing, Allegra just craved an outlet. She only had the one—Darius, brooding and silent behind the wheel, the city lights reflecting in his liquid black eyes.

"What happened back there?" he retorted, a question for a question.

"I freaked out?" It should've been obvious. Allegra shrugged off his confusion. "Hey, do you want to see a show? The only cabaret down in the Docklands is this filthy little joint. Figure there's got to be something better around here, right?" She watched Darius frown, saw his hands go white-knuckled around the steering wheel. "We can play hooky for one night. I won't tell Osker if you don't." That there was probably a GPS tracker in Darius' battered old car didn't stop her fantasizing. She had spent her whole life breaking rules. She wasn't about to stop now.

"We're not stopping to see a cabaret show," Darius said.

"You're no fun."

He sighed, turning off the main roads onto a verdant avenue where the only traffic lay somewhere high up. Allegra had to press her cheek against the window to glimpse the undersides of hovercars visible through the crooked branches of synthetic linden trees.

"If you wanted fun, you shouldn't have made a deal with the devil, kid…"

"I didn't realize I was in the car with him," Allegra shot back, smirking. She didn't want to go back to the precinct. Not yet. Just the thought of delving into mountains of inconclusive evidence made her palms itch. "What's down there?" she asked, pointing to a black gate set into a brick wall. It was open and no looming mansion waited within.

Darius followed her gaze. "Community park."

"Oh, so that's what they look like in real life…" Allegra sank back into her seat. "Cool."

She could've counted down the seconds until Darius eased the Mustang to a rambling stop at the edge of the curb. "You've never seen one?"

Allegra shook her head. It wasn't a lie, not really. The only parks in the Docklands were overgrown with nettles and weeds, used as temporary housing by homeless junkies who couldn't stay sober long enough to find a shack with a roof. Allegra had been among them a couple of times. The mosquitoes were by far the biggest drawback to that lifestyle. Word had it they carried malaria.

Dour as he was, Darius still killed the engine and removed his keys with a ponderous, long-suffering sigh. "Ten minutes."

"For real?"

"We'll say it was car trouble."

"What, with this sweet, sweet ride?" Allegra darted out of the front seat, her knees practically shaking. She had never been in a neighborhood as well kept as this one. All the hedges lined up neatly and the houses on either side of the street burned with the soft halo of uninterrupted electric light. It was breathtaking.

She nearly jumped out of her skin when Darius sidled beside her. For only a moment, they were wreathed in the shadows at the edge of the park, surrounded by ivy and expertly trimmed shrubbery. Darius fumbled briefly in the folds of his trench coat, then lit up, the glow of the lighter reflected in his eyes. The cigarette perched between his lips was slim and delicate, nothing like the uneven, hand-rolled kind half-filled with sawdust that Allegra was familiar with.

"I thought you said you quit," she noted.

"Don't remind me." Smoke eddied around his careworn face when he puffed a minty breath. "You want one?"

It wasn't an unexpected offer. Darius didn't seem to understand that nothing was free, much less that Allegra despised his charity, so he made the same mistakes over and over again. He called her *kid* when she was a woman. He scowled at her with a wary, guilty frown, as though Allegra couldn't remember the flush on his face when he shoved her into the door of his apartment.

Perhaps the real trouble was that they both could remember it so well. Discounting the shouting match that had followed, Darius had actually been one of the best lovers she'd had in a long time. Allegra shook her head.

The park opened around them, all rolling hills and carefully swept paths. Flowerbeds aligned like soldiers in a firing line, slender stems crowding against fat clusters of fragrant blossoms.

It was the stillness of the place that Allegra noticed the most, though. There were no birds, no insects. No people. When the crisp evening air moved through the oak trees, it didn't stir a single creature.

This must have been what the Garden of Eden was like before all the animals, before Adam and Eve. The old stories had captivated her once. Now they were just stories. The real world didn't leave much time for daydreaming. Allegra had to seize her nirvana where she found it—be it in a diner by the APU HQ or in a public park, surrounded by silence and shadow, the scent of mint permeating her lungs.

Allegra rose on tiptoe, snagged both hands into Darius' lapels and brought their lips together in a sloppy, wet kiss. She had the upper hand for mere seconds, but it was enough to feel him tilt into her grasp, as desperate for her as she felt for him.

"What—what do you think you're doing?" he gritted out when they pulled away for breath.

"When at first you don't succeed," Allegra said, trying for levity she didn't particularly feel. Playing Darius had been easier before she found him unmoving in the debris of a ransacked jewelry store. She hesitated. "If you're going to start yelling again…"

"That's not… That was wrong of me," Darius interjected. The crease between his eyebrows had deepened, though, and he didn't look like a man who found her advances that enticing.

Allegra gathered up her pride. "Don't mention it. Shit happens, right?"

"Not like that." Darius slid a hand around her waist, his palm warm through the flimsy, threadbare fabric of her shirt. "Not like this."

"Then how?"

Seducing cops should have been easy, but the more time she spent in his company, the more Darius seemed to enjoy shattering her expectations. He did it then, by cupping her cheek with a delicate hand — as if she was something precious, to be handled with care. He kissed her softly, as though Allegra might flee if he rushed. It wasn't unwelcome, but Allegra's tolerance for tenderness was low these days.

She surged into the kiss, pressing her body flush against his without a care in the world for the open spaces around them and the odds of someone — anyone — peeping in on their tryst. *Let them look.* Darius staggered, his cigarette a blur of flying embers, as she backed him into the nearest oak tree. Shadows engulfed them, concealing their frantic kisses from indiscreet gazes.

"Is this better?" she panted. "Is it? Darius —"

But he wasn't listening, too preoccupied with nibbling at her throat. Allegra desperately hoped he'd leave a mark. He squeezed her ass, a show of initiative that she recognized from the other night. It still kindled a fervid spark in her belly, whatever the consequences for her impassioned advances the last time she made herself vulnerable to Darius.

She never did bother learning how to spare herself heartache.

They fumbled at each other's clothes with clumsy hands, wheezing for breath between bruising kisses and stolen caresses. At one point Darius had a hand under her shirt and his talented fingers rolled over her nipple until Allegra thought she'd come just from that — she'd done it before — but Darius must've misread the tenor of her moans, because he eased off, he gentled his touch.

Allegra was in no mood for soft, stuttered petting. She shimmied out of his hold and busied herself with tugging open his belt buckle. It caught under her fingers on the first try, but not on the second. By the time she had his zipper undone, Allegra was already sinking to her knees in the aesthetically pleasing lawn, smirking up at Darius with half a mouth.

"Don't worry," she said, "I don't bite." She had, a couple

of times, but the occasion had called for a little violence. This did not.

She drew Darius' length out with nimble fingers, tracing the vein on the underside of his hard shaft with her fingertip.

A breathless, husky sound escaped Darius' lungs, halfway between a moan and a heated gasp. It registered as permission. Allegra put her mouth around him tentatively, once more eager to taste and feel the ridges of his cock on her tongue rather than simply to bring him off. She would do that, too, but there was no need to rush. She had ten minutes — less now, but still enough to acquaint herself with the proud, thick column of his sex. She probably wouldn't get another chance.

"Allegra…"

Here it comes. He's going to ask me to stop. "Don't you dare," she said, pre-emptively. "Don't you — I can make you feel good." Desire itched in her veins. She needed this. She wanted to see him undone and thunderstruck for all the right reasons.

Darius swallowed hard. "Okay. I won't touch you. I just… Sorry, I —"

"That's what you want?" Allegra paused, the stream of her very sensible arguments momentarily stoppered. She watched Darius dip his head into a nod. "That's fine. I thought — never mind. This is why gentlemen finish last, you know."

She might as well have been trying to convince him to kick a puppy. It was a battle lost before it had begun, so Allegra wisely turned her attention to more realistic ends — like driving Darius to distraction with lips and tongue, squeezing her fist around the base of his cock until he had no choice but to roll his hips forward, into her grasp.

A moan tore from his throat, bordering on despair, and Allegra sealed her mouth just under the flushed, pre-cum-slick cockhead. *Come. Come for me, sweetheart.*

Darius obliged her with a hand hovering just at the hinge of her jaw and an apology bubbling out his throat. He couldn't stop himself, not with Allegra pulling out all the stops to propel him into a mind-blowing orgasm. Frankly, she would've preferred he didn't try, but that wasn't up to her. If this was real—if Darius was truly mistaken about her toying with his head—then she had no control over the moment he found rapture.

Allegra almost believed it. She told herself that what had happened at the store had been pure coincidence, an accident of fate. One crazy robber took his life and Allegra just happened to be in the vicinity when he did it. Nothing more.

She choked a little on Darius' hot seed as he came into her mouth, but it wasn't reason enough to release him. She spat out the rest into the grass, wondering dimly if the authorities considered that littering. It hardly mattered. Darius was watching her through his lashes, a fine sheen of sweat gleaming on his brow and upper lip. Allegra held his gaze as she licked him clean and tucked him into his boxers.

She snagged his smoldering cigarette, nearly burned down to the filter, and took a deep pull.

"What about you?" Darius asked, squinting against the distant glow of street lamps.

Allegra affected a nonchalant shrug. "You only said ten minutes." She didn't want to force his hand, not again, so she darted out of his grasp before Darius could try to persuade her. "Come along, stud. We got work to do."

She crushed the cigarette underfoot at the edge of the park. Nothing in this town had any business pretending to be so gods-damned pristine.

Chapter Ten

The scary thing was that Allegra was beginning to make sense. Darius didn't know what to make of that. She was spitballing half the time, sure, but not without purpose.

It had started in the morgue and continued in the car, stemming from a transparent attempt to distract her from any lingering queasiness. By the time the clock ran down the shift and the working day slipped into that all too familiar post-midnight lull at the precinct, they had covered three flip charts with spidery scrawl—Darius' doing, mostly, but also Allegra's.

Jasme had come to lend a hand, but she preferred her tablet computer and refereeing their efforts with dogged fact-checking. Bizarrely, Darius seemed to get it wrong more often than Allegra. Evidence just laid itself down at her feet, and when she had a piece of theory arranged neatly enough to satisfy Darius, she seemed to fly into an outright frenzy.

Getting her to call it a day proved more difficult than prying barnacles from the hull of a ship.

"I've got this," she insisted, tugging absently at her wispy blonde hair. "Seriously, give me another hour…"

"You said that three hours ago." Jasme yawned.

"Traitor," Allegra accused.

Jasme flipped her off good-naturedly. "Hey, I'm Switzerland. Don't piss off the Swiss or we'll withhold chocolate and… Cuckoo clocks. Gods, I'm tired. Nobody talk to me! I'm going home." She staggered to her feet without anyone's help and plucked her red-trimmed synth-wool jacket from the rack. "Night, boss. Allegra."

In the time it took them to go from circling carefully around one another, Jasme and Allegra had dropped surnames and picked up teasing each other like old friends. It helped that they were close in age, Darius imagined. Even if they belonged to completely different worlds, they must have had some things in common—attitude, mostly, and an impish sort of fondness for teasing their elders.

Jasme drove a small two-seater and rarely welcomed company. Darius didn't dare say she should drive safely. She'd only pull up her favorite gender-based statistical breakdown of traffic violations in the past ten years and point out that middle-aged men were six times more likely to crash their cars than women in her age bracket. It wouldn't be the first time. Darius had learned long ago that a woman with an uplink was ten times more dangerous than a woman behind the wheel.

Mousy-haired Jasme was no exception.

"I'll give you a ride home," Darius offered Allegra in an attempt to sweeten the pill. The kid actually seemed as if she wanted to stick around the APU to work on the case. She had outlasted Jasme, whose dogged devotion to the job was as unprecedented at HQ as it was exhausting to witness.

At this hour, only the night shift was left at the station to ensure ringing phones would be answered. Not one of them was likely to be of use.

It wasn't jealousy that prompted the judgment. Darius knew his colleagues and the kind of *company* they could provide.

Allegra shook her head. "Nah, I'll walk. Need to work off this excess energy, you know?"

Darius didn't know, but he said "Sure" anyway, and left it at that. Better manic excitement than depression—or the silent treatment. For his part, he could only think of his bed and the humming of his AC unit as it lulled him to sleep.

They separated outside the precinct doors, with Darius making for his lone Mustang in the all-but-deserted parking lot and Allegra starting off in the opposite direction. There was something different about her. Darius had noticed the change earlier in the day, but put it down to mercurial youths being mercurial. It saved him having to do any serious thinking about the amount of time he spent worrying for or about Allegra Avenson.

It didn't take a savant to know the girl was troubled — or that his attempts to constantly refer to her as a girl were hiding a deeper issue. In less than twenty-four hours, Allegra had gone from righteous indignation, to a borderline panic attack, to eager participation in police casework.

Darius turned the key in the ignition. His console let him know that the battery was fully charged, the day having been as sunny and hot as all the ones before it, not that he'd know it by the nippy evening chill. He'd barely made it out of the parking lot before the thought came to him, sneaky and insidious like a virus — he should've insisted on giving Allegra a ride back to the Docklands. Even dropping her off by St. Michael's would help cut down on the miles she'd have to walk in the freezing cold.

The Mustang rocked, jostled by a divot in the road. Darius barely felt it. The more he thought of it, the more he wondered at Allegra's shifting moods. She had been disturbingly eager to be on her own. To walk back to the Docklands in the dark. Unarmed. At best it was just foolish bravado, at worst —

"Ah, damn it." Darius slammed his palm against the steering wheel. The car lurched, zigzagging down the deserted road. Darius belatedly checked his mirrors, trying not to think of Jasme's stats. There was barely any traffic at this hour and none at ground level. The overhead glint of hovercars didn't concern him as he pulled the Mustang into a sharp turn and floored the accelerator.

Allegra needed the backup. She just didn't know it yet.

* * * *

It shouldn't have been hard to track her down.

The streets were largely barren at this hour, in this part of town, and there were only so many skinny youths stomping the pavement, their neon colored hair and acid-washed jeans thrown into sharp relief by Darius' headlights.

All the same, Allegra seemed to have vanished into the ether by the time Darius doubled back to retrieve her. Cold cement and lonely street lamps greeted Darius' search, but no sign of life. No Allegra. This close to the APU and its labyrinth of security cameras, not a whole lot of idle passers-by, either.

The network of underground and overhanging tunnels that separated pedestrians from the nuisance and pollution of motorized traffic for everyone's safety and comfort didn't help matters. Allegra could have disappeared into either and Darius wouldn't be able to follow with his lumbering wreck of a car. There was no sense abusing the steering wheel, the Mustang wasn't to blame, though Darius wanted nothing more than to beat his fists bloody against the reinforced plastic.

He should have been more careful. He should have hung onto the pills, made sure Allegra spaced out the dosage. If Osker found out about this, he'd be toast. Her patience was already running thin.

The thought came to him like a thunderclap in summer — he could always go to Allegra's place.

It was a bad idea, but a better one than letting Allegra traipse around town, high to the heavens and willing to do gods only knew what. It was particularly true of a part of Arcadia where dealers abounded. Allegra would surely seem like easy pickings. She was in no shape to fight off requests for more than the usual cash return.

Darius stepped on the gas. He remembered the address from the file Osker had retrieved when they first picked Allegra up. To say the kid didn't live in a good part of town would've been an understatement.

The scenery had already started changing by the time he

reached the Docklands Steel & Armaments manufacturing yard, once the lifeblood of Arcadia's economic boom, now just a wounded, ghostly relic pockmarked with broken windows and lewd graffiti. Beyond its grounds sprawled the river shacks that had once been trailer homes and temporary housing, and the tenements formerly touted as Arcadia's best accommodation for semi-skilled, seasonal workers.

It was hard to believe, but not so long ago, this place had been something of a modern paradise. Those days were clearly long gone.

A smattering of working street lamps were sputtering with the green fog of the lower city. In their dim glow, Darius could see here and there groups of men loitering on the sidewalk without apparent purpose. All, without fail, stopped their murmured conversations to watch him drive by, their blank faces more than slightly menacing in the flickering light.

Darius was suddenly glad that his car didn't bear any distinctive APU markings, but it was still too shiny, the paint barely scratched. The solar panels strapped across the hood were too neatly wired for the Docklands.

People would know a cop was around. They would talk.

He took a left before he hit the red light district, keen to bypass the hordes of scantily clad men and women who darkened street corners. He had worked this beat before, but it had been years since he'd last stopped by the underbelly of Arcadia.

It must have been just after his marriage failed. He'd had a notion that Harlan might have made it down to the seedy underworld. Dreadful as the final throes had been, Darius had searched for him — albeit without luck.

Maybe that didn't imply a swift, merciless OD. Maybe it only meant Harlan was too smart to let anyone strong-arm him into selling flesh for drugs.

Darius pushed the thought out of his mind.

The detour took a scant half dozen minutes out of his

journey, but though Darius caught glimpses of faces in the windows and figures disappearing around corners as he drove by, he didn't see Allegra anywhere.

Her registered address, he discovered, was traced back to a dilapidated warehouse. Darius didn't need to look it up to know that a demolition order was pending because some Arcadian donors got it into their heads the land could be used for a free clinic, or a church, or a community center — whatever played well in the PR reels. The same was true of most land holdings in the Docklands. Nothing usually came of them. No one cared to house the squatters who lived there now, or pardon the rats about to be massacred in the demolition. Charitable offenses were a dime a dozen in this town and they always struck the needy.

There was no profit in free clinics, anyway, not unless you ran a parallel drug trials business on the side.

Darius killed the engine. The Mustang stilled its rumbling, becoming one with the street and the closed storefronts on either side. Wood panels barred the windows, but it was impossible to tell if they'd been meant to hold people inside as though in some makeshift prison, or to keep intruders from breaking in. Either way, the Docklands were a veritable hell on earth.

It stank like it, too, though Darius only realized this once he'd gathered up the nerve to get out of the car.

He suppressed a shiver. It was cold, but close to the river that bordered Arcadia around the northeast, the wind was mostly mild and foul smelling. His sleeve barely served as a face mask.

"It's the sulfur," a voice said in the darkness. Darius whipped around to see a young man watching him — young, but not so young that he couldn't appreciate the risk of speaking to a stranger. He couldn't have been much older than Allegra.

He must have been crouching in the shadows when Darius got there, because there wasn't a sound, not of footsteps or breathing, as he materialized into view.

"I'm sorry?" Darius asked, his voice a little too loud in the barren street.

The boy grinned crookedly and Darius saw that one front tooth was badly chipped. "You're forgiven. I was talking about the river. Sulfur in the water," he explained. "Ironically, the least toxic thing about it. That's why it smells like a fucking sewer around here."

"Is it always like this?" A stupid question, no doubt. The putrid odor was all but making him gag. He was fiercely glad he hadn't stopped to eat anything before leaving the precinct.

The kid shrugged. "Better during daylight. Course that could just be a matter of me sleeping all day long so I don't have to inhale the bouquet." The smile turned vicious. "Don't you like it, Officer? Take a big whiff—*eau de Docklands*, straight from the source." A glint of silver pierced the night. The boy was armed.

"Hey now—"

"—and when you're finished sniffing the air, you'll get right back into your car and drive away, you understand me? Or you might just end up swimming in that soup over there."

"Do you think it's smart to be threatening a cop, kid?" No use denying it. The boy had already figured out that Darius wasn't here to admire the scenery, and fibbing now would likely only inspire the kid to start slashing. Darius really wasn't in the mood for another trip to the ER.

"You think anyone in the Docklands is scared of you?" His would-be attacker snorted mirthlessly. "You're not the law around here."

"Aaron?" Allegra's voice came from somewhere slightly to the left of Darius, before the woman herself came into view. She was a breath of fresh air. "What do you think you're doing?"

"Cleaning the streets. What's it look like?"

"Like you've lost your gods-damn mind. Put that gods-damn knife down." Slow, staggered footsteps slid across the pavement. Darius had to squint to see her approach through the thick, gray shadows. She'd been fine when they parted less than a half hour ago, but already she seemed wrung out, as if the manic parts of her had been drained and dried. "Hey," she greeted wearily, leaning one hand against the brown brick wall. "Thought you were going home to get some sleep."

Darius fought the urge to offer his shoulder. He had to remind himself that it wasn't his place and that any move he made was likely to get him knifed. "I was," he admitted. "Then I figured out why you were so chipper earlier. High before the drop?"

Shiv-wielding Aaron glanced sidelong at Allegra. "You know this guy?" Next he was going to ask *how* Allegra knew him and all their attempts at keeping her entanglements with the police secret would be for naught.

"You didn't take the Bliss I gave you," Darius interjected, saving Allegra the difficulty of lying when she was exposed like a raw nerve.

Allegra smiled, lips quivering at the corners. She was a smart woman, she could read that blatant attempt. "Thought you'd like me better clear-eyed and bushy-tailed.

"Aaron," she added, "it's fine. He's my…dealer. We've got an arrangement."

"Really."

"You calling me a liar, pipsqueak?"

A glint of silver caught Darius' eye as the knife folded shut upon itself. Aaron smirked. "Nah. You know, you don't look so good. Better ease up before you tank." Aaron shot him a sidelong glance. "You ain't a cop?"

"Does it matter?"

The kid weighed that answer, unsatisfactory as it was, and shrugged. It was that easy to get him to scram, sashaying as he vanished into the maze of darkened streets and crime-infested back alleys of the Docklands.

"Yeah," Allegra echoed.

Another second and she might have crumbled to the

grimy asphalt if not for Darius to catch her. "Whoa, there! I've got you."

Allegra howled, pushing him away. "Don't. Oh gods, don't—I can't. *Fuck*, it's too much. It's like I'm mainlining everything—you—" The garbled torrent of pleas and protests died in her throat, smothered by Darius' kiss.

If she had to feel something—and without Bliss in her system, that was a given—better it be desire and concern than whatever filthy mixture of fear and anger and despair was floating around the Docklands. Allegra fisted a hand in his lapel, tugging him closer. With the wall behind her, it was easier for Darius to hold her upright even if his own knees felt a little weak.

Allegra kissed him with newfound eagerness, licking her way past his lips and into his mouth, sucking at his tongue and greedily lapping up his moans. She was flushed and panting by the time they broke for breath. She wasn't the only one.

"Let me take you upstairs?" Darius asked, breathless and husky with want.

He knew he shouldn't. He had promised himself to respect Allegra's boundaries, to recognize that he had power over her and this was wrong, so very, very wrong. The tug of duty around his heart was all barbed with self-recriminations, but better to be a mark willingly going to Allegra's bed for cash than a cop taking advantage.

He knew which one he was and told himself that with one word from Allegra he would've pulled away—like he hadn't done in the park. He almost did so now, but then Allegra liberated a key from one of the many pockets sewn tight into her jeans and twisted open the latch.

"After you," she said, lashes fanning low over flushed cheeks.

Darius swallowed hard. "Why does that worry me?"

Probably because it sounded like an invitation into the netherworld and those seldom, in Darius' experience, worked out for the best. He took one last look at his battered old Mustang and wondered if there was any chance he'd still find it parked out front come morning. The door swung shut. It locked automatically, courtesy of hacked, black market security.

Darkness draped around them like a blanket, interspersed with only the occasional slash of light in those parts of the warehouse where moonbeams peeked through slats in the boarded-up windows.

Darius groped blindly in the shadows, seeking an anchor. "Allegra?"

"I'm right here." A warm press of bare, naked flesh against his side. Allegra was indeed right there. She was also wearing far fewer clothes.

Darius' breath caught. He knew Allegra could pick up on the thrum of arousal in his body. He tried to deflect. "What happened to going upstairs?"

"You didn't mention," Allegra murmured sweetly, "that I had to be dressed by the time we got there." She rose on tiptoe, dipping her tongue into Darius' ear and flicking at the lobe until he was sure his knees were about to buckle.

If he ended up sprawled in sawdust and dirt, he couldn't help think it'd be worth it. The things Allegra could make him feel, the depth of his desire for her — she was the sun he orbited, and he had a feeling he was about to get his fingers burned.

Allegra laughed, short and sharp. She couldn't read minds, could she?

"You're like a kaleidoscope and you're changing your shades so quickly," she said, shuddering against Darius' flank. "Take me to bed. *Now*."

Easier said than done, when Darius didn't know which way was up anymore and he could barely see the outline of ancient machinery around them. His vision was becoming cobwebbed the more he tried to squint into the darkness around Allegra's golden head. The whites of her eyes were like two beacons, just this side of eerie.

"Don't be afraid, Detective. I'm not going to let you fall..."

Allegra seized his wrists in her hands, tugging him along gently, gently. "There are steps here, lift your leg. There you go..." She still sounded drunk and not all present, but her instructions checked out.

Darius only stumbled once on the way up and that was his own fault, because he'd tried to take the steps two by two. Luckily Allegra was there to steady him—and steal another kiss as they drew apart.

"Not to criticize your home," Darius murmured over the roar of his own pulse whooshing loudly in his ears, "but are you part bat, by any chance? How can you stand to live in the darkness like this?"

"I don't..."

A flip of a wall switch and the loft was plunged into soft, buttery light.

Darius could make out a bed that was mostly mattress and a vast array of candle wax decorating the floor in splashes of red and blue and glossy white, evidence that the electric light wasn't much guaranteed.

He might have seen more—he was reasonably sure there was a flat screen concealed in the shadow of a claw-footed bathtub packed high with glow sticks—but Allegra's body suddenly fell into focus. Darius' reptilian brain took over. It was a sad thing, but whatever time he might have spent honing his fine investigative skills at the Academy, the sight of a good-looking woman could still distract him. And Allegra *was* good-looking. A little on the skinny side, perhaps, but not as stick-thin as Darius had imagined when they were pressed up against his front door and every jut of hip and rib seemed to designed to bruise.

The unearthly pallor also didn't touch all of Allegra's body—there were places where the neon light hit that Darius noticed were covered in dark spirals and swirls of ancient runes.

"Do those mean anything?" he heard himself ask, barely recognizing the haggard echo of his own voice.

Allegra smiled, glancing down. "This one says 'know

thyself' in Cyrillic." A hand covered the writing on her belly. "Just about all the Cyrillic I know... This one's the symbol Thracians used to represent their seers. And this one," she added, palming the curlicues so painstakingly drawn over her left thigh, "is Urdu for—"

Darius stole the words from her lips with a soft kiss. "They're beautiful."

"Yeah?" A breathy exhale. "What about this?"

He couldn't help it, he glanced down to see Allegra part her labia, showing herself off, all pink and glistening wetly against her skinny fingers. It made Darius' mouth water just to watch. The thought of doing more, of putting his mouth to her, was enough to make him feel acutely aware of the firm clutch of his belt.

"You can, you know," Allegra was saying. "I mean, if you want to touch. Or you can just keep staring." She grinned, her cheeks flushing prettily. "I, uh, I like it the way you look at me."

Darius knew right then that Allegra wasn't putting these thoughts into his mind. That she never had. It was all paranoia and denial because the thought of doing what he wanted was hard to swallow unless someone was forcing his hand.

"This is all wrong," he whispered, pressing the words into Allegra's temple. Better that than her warm, kiss-swollen lips.

"Why?" Allegra's voice was wrecked, her shoulders hunching under Darius' hands.

"You're not thinking straight. Bliss messes with your head, you know that..."

Allegra pulled back abruptly, retreating a few steps to put distance between them. "*This* is who I am, Darius. Without the Bliss, without any fetters...this *is* me. You can't stand there and tell me you don't want me. I can see your cock tenting in your fucking pants!"

A ripple of muted aggravation pulsed in Darius' veins, almost to the rhythm of Allegra's ragged breaths. "If you still want to sleep with me in the morning, then we'll..."

"Fuck?" Allegra added helpfully.

"Talk about it," Darius corrected. He wanted to do the other thing, too, so very badly, but he'd already messed this up once. He didn't want to make Allegra run again. He plucked a pill bottle from his trench coat. "You should take these," he said and tossed over the vial. "You're lucky I was a Boy Scout. Always keep a spare on hand, just in case."

Allegra caught the bottle easily. "You know, for a cop, you've got some game. Playing hard to get when we both know you're into me—what's that about? Aren't I good enough?"

Darius shook his head. It was definitely not that. Standards hadn't been an issue since around the first time he'd kissed Allegra and enjoyed it, but he refrained from saying as much. There were plenty of other objections—related to age difference, the wisdom of a cop sleeping with an informant, Darius' disastrous track record with managing other people's addictions—that could be raised. "It's because you're asking questions like that," he explained, shrugging.

"Questions like what?"

"You know I want you. You know I'm hard for you." Darius coughed, trying to his shift his weight as he stood there, in Allegra's derelict abode, without appearing as though he was adjusting his erection in his pants by the same token. "I'd rather fuck Allegra, not her uninhibited alter-ego. Take the Bliss. Get some sleep. I'll... I'll be right here."

"You'll lullaby me to sleep?" Allegra snorted, her gaze flinty.

"Trust me—you don't want to hear me sing."

Allegra popped open the pill bottle with a flourish. "How about a bedtime story?"

"I know one about a blonde kid who didn't take her medicine on time, would that do?" Darius couldn't keep a note of reluctant amusement out of his voice. "Is that how you sleep?"

He got exactly what he deserved by way of answer—a bark of laughter, a question for a question. "What," Allegra laughed, "you figured I was one for leopard-print pajamas?"

"I'm the last man to protest your fashion choices."

Allegra's lips tugged up into a smile as she made her way to the mattress laid out on the unvarnished floors. "So I noticed. Well, come on. I'm going to drop very soon and then I'll start shivering my tits off... Power's about to die, too, so unless you want to play Marco Polo for the rest of the night, you'd better get your ass in here."

She held up one corner of the threadbare covers for Darius. He had to admit the warehouse was arctic, probably thanks to all those gaps in the skylight windows.

He shed his trench coat and shoes before doing as told, despite Allegra's diverting little leer. "This isn't a five star hotel, I've had guys with—" She caught herself. "You'd rather I don't talk about other men, huh?"

"Is that something you picked up from my aura...? Or whatever you call it?"

"No," Allegra scoffed. "You just got the biggest frown." Her fingers crept up to stroke the furrow between Darius' eyebrows. "There, no more pit bull face."

"I can still bite," Darius challenged, mostly for want of something to say. Allegra's body pressed against his, a long line of warmth and nubile youth that should have made him feel like a pervert, but was only making him want to protect Allegra, to hold her even tighter. He didn't have to. Allegra squirmed until she was flush against him, her inked back to Darius' front, and tugged one heavy arm across her belly.

"I hope so," she murmured. "I've got a thing for boys who fight."

Darius felt a flush gain his face and was glad that Allegra couldn't see—for about a handful of seconds before he recalled that Allegra was an empath and the Bliss couldn't have kicked in yet.

Allegra took no notice of this. "Hey, Detective?"

"Yeah?"

"How come you didn't take off your holster? Isn't that going to be uncomfortable?"

It wasn't the question Darius had been expecting. "I'm not counting on sleeping," he said. Fatigue wasn't lacking, but his cop instincts were still alive and well, and the chances of relaxing while on the job were slim.

Besides, he remembered the last time he'd ventured in to a situation all cocky and out of his depth. His cheek was still bruised.

"Oh. Well, in that case you're in luck," Allegra mumbled sleepily. "I've been told I snore like a helicopter."

Chapter Eleven

Allegra woke to the heavy weight of an arm around her waist, a pressure not unwelcome and only slightly unsettling. She couldn't immediately recall if she had gone tricking after work — tricking used to *be* work, which at least suggested that the memory loss was only a few hours' worth. There was no reason why she would have done. Darius' frowns notwithstanding, the APU were willing enough to provide her with Bliss in return for her services. Surely she hadn't decided to go rogue.

Slowly, the heavy curtain of sleep peeled away and last night's events filtered back into focus. She remembered working late, turning down an offer from her would-be partner and saying she'd walk home alone.

She remembered catching the last underground train to the Docklands, watching her reflection in the scratched windows and feeling every rusty point of frustration and grief and paranoia that permeated the air like toxic smog. She also recalled seeing Darius outside her door, threatened at knifepoint. She remembered wanting and offering — and being turned down.

Careful, so as not to attract attention to herself, Allegra turned over under the tattered coverlet. Sure enough, Darius dozed quietly beside her. He still wore yesterday's clothes, minus trench coat and shoes, and his tie was askew around a pale throat. Allegra watched his pulse thrum beneath a day's growth of stubble, conscious of all he'd said yesterday, and all the ways in which she'd probably screwed things up.

She shouldn't have gone without the Bliss, whatever her

intentions. It was foolhardy.

"Darius?" Allegra murmured. "Darius, wake up..."

He came around with a jolt, coal-black eyes snapping open and breath catching in his throat. "What — oh. Shit. I must've..." Darius stiffened. He retrieved his arm as soon as he realized he was clinging.

Allegra was surprised to discover she felt bereft in its absence.

"I must've fallen asleep," Darius repeated, pinning an elbow to the mattress as he struggled to rise.

In another minute, he'd be back on his feet, all composure restored and last night's events brushed aside as a junkie's advances. They'd go on as before, with Darius chasing his serial killer and putting up with Allegra's nonsense to that sole end.

But it wasn't nonsense. Allegra slid a hand around Darius' nape and reeled him back in. Gravity was on her side. Darius could only follow, eyes widening a little before the distance between them narrowed to millimeters and their lips met in a chaste kiss.

Bliss had dulled Allegra's abilities enough that there was nothing to interfere with her own flare of longing. She heard Darius inhale sharply as they parted for breath, a slight stutter catching in his throat. Allegra swallowed hard. For once, she couldn't read Darius' reaction. That was new. Thrilling, yes, but also new and scary.

"Last night," she reminded timidly, "you said we'd... talk. In the morning."

Darius nodded. "Right. I did. That's how you talk?" He didn't seem put off by Allegra's initiative. If he was reluctant, it could have nothing to do with not wanting her. Allegra had been right on the money about that last night. Her ego swelled like a balloon about to burst.

She allowed herself a grin, cocksure and brazen. "I figured we could just pick up where we left off. I'll be old and gray before you make the first move." She knotted fingers into Darius' hair, where there were indeed a few gray strands, and tugged gingerly.

"What will it take to convince you that I'm really, really into you?"

She almost wished she hadn't asked when she felt Darius go rigid against her flank, his charcoal dark eyes scrutinizing. Allegra fought the urge to duck her head as she might have done with a client. Darius didn't want her meek and humble. He'd been a perfect gentleman last night—and not much of one after Allegra had paid him a visit unannounced at his apartment.

It was almost as if he was a complex human being, with contradictions and nuances, just like Allegra, but Allegra wasn't stoned enough to dwell on the thought.

Darius spared her. "You weren't into me the other day," he pointed out, eyebrows arched. "Things you said..."

"I was pissed off," Allegra scoffed. "You threw me out. Called me a freak." The insult had long lost all power over her, but she couldn't mistake it for an endearment. It was enough to see contrition twist at Darius' careworn face to put the abuse to rest. "Looks like you've changed your mind..."

She didn't give the detective another chance to speak, just pulled him in. This time, Darius followed bodily, his knee creeping between Allegra's bare legs as he levered himself into place.

Allegra soon discovered what it was like to have an armful of Arcadia's finest, all wool suit and massive steel belt buckle bearing down on her belly. The bulk of Darius' well-fed body nearly knocked the breath out of her. Nearly. Darius picked himself up on his elbows. "Is—is this okay?"

"Oh, gods," Allegra laughed, "shut up and kiss me."

They pulled and pushed at each other gracelessly, animated by urgency and need. Allegra groped at Darius' hips, dug bruises into his flesh as she arched into the curve of his hardening cock. "You're fine, you're—fuck, right there." She moaned and canted her head against the mattress, exposing her throat to Darius' greedy lips.

The detective was a quick study. He didn't waste a single moment in latching on with teeth and tongue. There would be love bites when he finished. Allegra relished the thought just as much as the prickle and scrape of his coarse stubble.

She almost laughed, but the sound was lost to another needy whimper as she found herself riding Darius' thigh. His clothes would be a mess when finally he went into work today, but knowing as much wasn't reason enough to stop.

Fingers grasped blindly at her shoulders, forcing her down to the mattress. A keening noise of protest crested on her tongue. It went unheard. Darius' hold was firm. *Stay*, it told her, and though Allegra growled she also obeyed, watching as Darius struggled to free himself from the tangled bed sheets. His eyes were wild and liquid, dawn reflected in two pools of gold light.

A flood of warmth coursed down Allegra's body. She was so keen to feel his bare cock nudge between her thighs that it almost scared her. Normally eagerness like that came with a price tag, but she'd blame her enthusiasm on Darius before she took ownership for how much she desired him.

She'd settle for a sloppy finger-fuck, if it came to that. Anything to feel his hands on her, to know she wasn't just a plaything to someone in this gods-damned world. Darius had other ideas.

Allegra's whole body went rigid as he took to his knees and reached for her ankles. Her body was too weak to resist, his hands too strong. She almost missed the greedy flash of tongue wetting lips, and soon it was too late to say anything, too late to move or pray or do anything except cry out because Darius' soft, lush mouth was on her cunt, a tentative lick tracing her slit from the opening of her vagina to the hardened nub of her clitoris. Allegra curled her toes into the sheets and arched her spine, nearly coming right there.

"Fuck!" she shouted. "Oh sweet gods, Darius — Darius…"

His name was a litany on Allegra's tongue, uttered in the form of a plea but wholly without purpose. She didn't know if she wanted Darius to stop, slow down or keep doing what he was doing already. It hardly mattered. Darius had a mind of his own. He proved oddly talented for a cop when he took Allegra's labia into his mouth, sucking the folds of flesh and skin until her hips rocked desperately against the mattress, rutting against the sharp point of his tongue.

You're going to kill me. Allegra curled her hands into the sheets. She wanted to thrust up and take more than anything in the world, but she'd been on the receiving end of enough callow patrons in the past to know that could be unpleasant. She forced herself to keep still.

"Just like that," she heard herself mumble, "just please don't stop."

She would beg if she had to, though Darius gave no signs of wanting to cease what he was doing. A low, humming breath vibrated over Allegra's clit. It was all she could do not to give in to the sensation, to ride it out until she careered over the edge.

Darius seemed to take that as encouragement, because he did it again, his thumb casting down in a gentle caress over the flushed, wet folds of Allegra's cunt. He pressed lightly against her anus, just toying with the tight, puckered ring — something she should've found worrying since they hadn't even brought up the possibility, and yet her first thought was *yes, please, more*.

Darius knew his way around a lover's body. Allegra only had a little trouble reconciling this skill set with what she knew of his day job. She had been so sure for so long that only whores bothered to learn how to please that the slightest bit of care was enough to make her weak in the knees.

In retrospect, that probably said a lot more about the people she'd slept with than Darius.

He'd stopped, Allegra realized, glancing down to find him stroking her lightly with the tips of his fingers, barely skimming her sensitive, glistening pussy.

"I want to make you come," he said when their eyes met.

"What—with your mouth?" It was a miracle Allegra didn't climax right then and there. She was so close already, and every wicked possibility sent an electric jolt of arousal straight into her clitoris.

Darius nodded.

"I—I can't." Allegra reached for his wrist and brought his fingers to her mouth. "Not because of you. Not with anyone. I need to, um... I usually can't unless I'm—unless you're fucking me." She didn't think it necessary to tell Darius that she could fake it if he preferred. Or that he could always fantasize about someone else while she made it up to him the way all men wanted. This wasn't the time to muddy the waters with tricks Allegra had learned in the line of duty. Darius didn't qualify. He wasn't a client. He was—she didn't know what to call him. A friend, maybe.

"Okay," Darius breathed, licking his lips like the cat that got the cream. *Not yet,* thought Allegra, *but if he keeps this up, soon.*

She gaped at the offer. "Seriously?" She didn't want to screw this up again.

"Yeah," Darius insisted and made to dip his mouth to her small breasts and hard, long nipples.

"Wait—" If he started, she knew she'd be helpless to get him to stop until it was too late. She reached under the mattress, fishing blindly until she finally touched a strip of shiny condoms, still necessary in the Docklands even if Arcadia preferred its STD-prevention done through patches and easy-to-swallow tablets. "Here. They're not flavored, but—" She felt a little apologetic offering the wrapper, which was a first for her. Of all the times she'd done it— with strangers, with people for whom this constituted an even trade, with Aaron—this was the first time she'd felt like she was admitting to some personal failing.

Darius sank back onto his haunches and kissed the inside of her knee. "Clever girl."

It was impossible to bite back a sheepish smile—all the more so when Darius tried to tear off the shiny foil with his teeth and ripped the condom by the same token. Allegra laughed, pushing herself up onto her elbows, and liberated another wrapper from his grasp.

"Haven't done this in a while, huh? How about you just watch, Detective?"

"That usually works," Darius protested.

"Where, in skin-flicks?" Allegra craned her neck to steal a kiss from his pouting lips. "Don't let it kill the mood. Things were just starting to get promising…"

"Only just?" A soft chuckle escaped Darius' kiss-swollen lips. "Right. They were." He shuffled back down, all obedient and flushed with want. He took his time stroking Allegra's thighs, circling closer and closer to her sex without ever quite giving her what she wanted. She let Darius dip his head one last time, quaking as his tongue lapped steadily against her clit, then nudged him up and out of the way.

Neither of them spoke as she rolled the condom down his length with a practiced hand. It was the first time she'd touched him since that night in the park, Allegra realized belatedly. He was heavy and hot in her fist, the shiny condom already glistening with lubricant.

"Still up for this?" he asked, voice a little choked as he removed his fingers from her pussy.

"Yeah." She hadn't changed her mind about sex since she'd done it the first time. She liked this part best.

"You're okay on your back?"

"Very okay." She was beginning to wonder if Darius was half as confident as he pretended when he settled between her legs and hitched up her leg around his waist. "*Very*— very okay," Allegra amended, in case it needed to be said.

Darius entered her slowly, just the head of his cock pressing into her, then withdrawing, then pressing in again, filling her with that delicious sensation of heat simmering just under her skin.

Take your time. Allegra struggled to clamp down on the urge to rake her nails down his spine. She carded her fingers through his hair instead, trying to be all gentle and soft, without pulling.

It seemed to take Darius a moment before he adjusted. He was beautiful like that, perched over Allegra, his biceps clenched and gorgeous beneath glistening tan skin, his lips drawn tight in a grimace of effort. He inhaled sharply when Allegra first clenched around his length, squeezing down until she heard him whimper.

"Yeah," Allegra moaned. "You like that, don't you? Look at you..." If that wasn't pleasure on Darius' face, it was the best caricature Allegra had ever seen. She dropped her heels to the mattress, the better to lift her hips and move with him, and her breaths shorted out. *So good*. She could barely believe this was happening at all, let alone here and now, with a timid sun creeping outside and crows perching on the broken windows, but then Darius' eyes fluttered open and their eyes met.

It wasn't bliss, she'd been wrong about that. Bliss dulled the edges of her awareness, washed everything out in grays and faded pastels, like a washing cycle that had run too long. This was vivid hues of red and purple, of Darius greedily biting and nibbling at her breasts as he pistoned his hips. Of Allegra peering at the broken rafters above their heads and not worrying that the roof could collapse.

She felt herself nearing the edge and thought to warn Darius, but all she managed was a hoarse moan, her words strung together without a trace of meaning. The pitch was enough to help her communicate what she was trying to say — it had to be, because in the next moment Allegra was shuddering and sobbing as she came, pulling Darius to her by the nape. Always wanting more.

Tremors rattled her bones like little earthquakes. They left her shattered.

Darius wasn't long in following suit, his thrusts jostling her against the bed until he collapsed on top of her, heavy and slick and so lovely that Allegra had to blink back tears for fear of his noticing that she had gotten sappy. If not for the condom, Darius could've spilled himself into her and over her thighs, painting her skin with his semen. The thought alone was enough to tug another brutal tremor from her limbs.

There was a waxy, latex taste to his cock when he finally pulled out and Allegra crawled down the bed to take him into her mouth. She heard his breath catch, but if he didn't mind, then neither did Allegra.

"That was so fucking..." Allegra flopped down, spent and exhausted, at a loss for words.

"Good?" Darius suggested helpfully.

She could only nod. Everything felt warm—even her sordid ruin of a home felt charmingly antique.

The brush of fingertips stroking the sloped wing of a shoulder got her attention after a while and she turned her head just as Darius was walking his digits down to the small of her back. Allegra was naked, but he still had his shirt on.

The unmistakable curve of a pistol tucked under the arm aborted any enjoyment she might have taken in the moment. "How are you still wearing your holster?"

Darius smiled wryly. "Artfully?" He hadn't taken it off last night and this morning's rush had left little room for him to tug off the restricting harness.

Allegra returned the smirk, more than eager to take the credit for his oversight.

"That's a first," she drawled, repositioning Darius' arm to reveal the holster. "Okay. I dig the leather." The bands were only visible when the suit jacket fell away to reveal the wrinkled dress shirt beneath. Allegra didn't get a chance to wonder how Darius even suffered so many layers because he was letting her unravel the tight-laced plackets of his armor, starting with the holster and ending, after a few shuffled efforts, with his socks.

Allegra couldn't help but think he seemed somewhat vulnerable once naked. His body was a far cry from the models plastered all across the billboards in their full airbrushed glory. There were scars—bullet-shaped starbursts or sketched-in slashes of sharp instruments here and there, a latticework body of proof attesting to his service to the Arcadian Police Unit—and faint discoloration where he'd gone under the knife over the course of a long career. There were bruises, too, but she had plenty of those herself. It didn't bear comparing.

She ran her fingertips down his chest, under the waistband of his briefs, and pushed his underwear past his thighs—it wasn't enough to feel him inside her. She wanted to see him. To touch him as if there was no clock to run down, no job to get to.

"You want me to return the favor?" she murmured. She could tease with the best of them, but Darius looked too good laid out on her bed like that for Allegra to concentrate.

"I think," he choked out when she seized his softening cock, "I think you already did."

Allegra tightened her hold just a fraction and watched as Darius pushed with his heels against the bed, trying to get more. "I could put my mouth on you." The power trip was heady. "Or," Allegra pressed, "you could lie there pretty while I ride your cock and get myself off."

There was no concealing the way Darius twitched at the sound of that, his whole body arching into Allegra's hand and his fist darting down to clutch at Allegra's wrist in search of an anchor. "You'd like that, huh?" Allegra had only just come and yet even she greeted the possibility with no small amount of pleasure.

And why not? It seemed unlikely that she'd get another shot at this. *Might as well make it count.*

"I'm going to make you see stars," Allegra promised, straddling Darius' hips. "You'll see. I'll be so good…."

"Hey," Darius said, "hey, look at me." He cupped Allegra's cheeks with gentle fingers, his hands smelling only faintly of latex and Allegra's own arousal. "You don't have to do it again. I'm—I like you, okay?" *Even if we don't fuck,* he might have added, but he didn't have to. Allegra understood.

"Right back at you," Allegra echoed, heart pounding. She tugged Darius' hands from her face, watching as panic and worry ebbed from his pretty eyes. She was tired enough to welcome the break, but lying there with Darius was a novel experience. "This is kind of new. Not the sex, but the…"

"For me, as well," Darius said, stroking her spine. "But I like it."

She believed him.

Chapter Twelve

"So," Darius said, tugging his shirt on, "you mind dispelling the mystery of the glow sticks?"

"Hmm?"

"In the tub," Darius added, nodding to the claw-footed basin and its myriad contents peeking out like colorful, translucent worms. "Are you a collector?"

Allegra sat up in bed, Darius' tie looped around her slender neck. There were pink marks here and there on her fair skin—Darius' doing. He should've felt a lot guiltier about that, but it was hard to do when Allegra wasn't wearing anything besides his tie, a handful of love bites and a blissed-out grin.

"You'll think it's stupid," she said.

"I won't."

"It kind of is, though."

Darius sighed, reconsidering. "If you don't want to tell me…"

"Sometimes when I drop, it helps to shine a really bright light into my eyes," Allegra interjected, "to knock me out of—whatever it is I'm feeling at the time." She shrugged her naked shoulders, glancing away. "And if I'm around here, what I'm feeling is usually panic. It's kind of like shock therapy."

It came as little surprise. As an empath, she was susceptible to the most pervasive emotions around. It made sense that in the Docklands that would be fear.

"Why not a flashlight?"

Allegra cut her eyes to him, the corner of her lips twitching up into a smile. "Got a better use for batteries when I can get my hands on them."

"A lamp?"

"Electricity comes and goes."

Darius had noticed that last night, mere moments after they'd bedded down, just as he was wondering if he should get up again to switch off the flickering overhead neon. No need. The generator went offline all on its own, as if by magic.

He held out a hand. "Can I have my tie back?"

The change of subject seemed welcome. Allegra cocked her head back into the pillows. "You could just come and take it from me..." It was only then that Darius noticed that her smiles were all dimples — that in just the right light, with dawn limning her hair gold and her cinnamon lips peeled back as she laughed, she seemed almost carefree.

For the very first time since they'd met, Darius wondered what a woman like Allegra could possibly see in him. It wasn't the badge or the car. It certainly wasn't the job. Ten years ago, it might have been the body, but that was going, too, as time softened the planes of his belly and added padding to his once-strong legs.

There must have been something, though, because he refused to believe Allegra was only playing him. Those fears had been put to rest.

"That," Darius recalled, "is precisely how I ended up aborting my last attempt to leave your bed." He pointed this out with a pedant's scrupulousness even as he took a tentative step closer to the mattress. He watched as Allegra splayed her legs under the sheets, grinning broadly.

A sudden, shrilling noise pierced the sultry innuendo — Darius' handset, stirring to life.

"Saved by the bell," Allegra teased, rolling over onto her belly.

Darius scrambled to liberate his comm unit from his jacket and flicked it open to take the call. The only people who called him anymore were co-workers and superiors — both of whom were entitled to know where he was and why wasn't busting his ass to solve this case. His mother's nursing home left messages if he was late with the payments.

He could only hope he didn't sound as harried as he felt, as it dawned on him that the sun was already up and he hadn't even thought about getting down to the precinct.

By the sound of it, that was about to change very soon.

"I'll be right there," he said, hanging up.

Allegra tugged one end of the tie until the length of silk slid free from around her neck. "Trouble?"

"Yeah, that was Jasme." Darius was frozen, synapses firing in his brain without his body quite knowing how to follow through. "There's been another murder."

"Oh." Allegra's face fell. "So you won't be coming back to bed, then?"

Allegra was under his skin, in his blood. He couldn't smother the ardent need he felt for her, much less when she was making eyes at him from the mattress. Yet their momentary safe haven had been shattered. Just like that, the real world was creeping back in, demanding it be allowed to take precedence over Darius' worthless libido.

He cleared his throat. "Have you seen my pants?"

They dressed quickly, without playfulness or promises for what they might like to do later. It was understood, though neither one of them said it in so many words, that later might not be possible.

They had a killer to catch and a string of murders to solve. If Osker was to be believed, Allegra would be getting her long-awaited surgery in lieu of fifty pieces of silver. No more Bliss for her, no more reason to work for the APU or spend any more time with Darius.

He shoved the thought away, his heart heavy with the knowledge that what they had was ephemeral at best and career suicide at the worst.

Much to Darius' surprise, the Mustang was still parked outside the warehouse, unmolested, when Allegra drew back the latch and the two of them stepped out. The car wasn't even tagged with slurs. Darius hardly knew what to make of it.

Without the cover of darkness, the Docklands emerged from the fog more derelict and sad than menacing. Last night's glaring thugs and knife-wielding boys were nowhere to be seen. Against the odds, it seemed like he and Allegra might well escape any trouble.

"I take it that Aaron kid is a friend of yours," Darius said as the car rumbled to life. He couldn't turn it into a question for fear the answer might be closer to *no, he's actually my lover.* Jealousy was an ugly thing, but easier to give into than admit self-doubt.

He tested the brakes gently before he leaned on the accelerator, mostly to satisfy his paranoia. There were easier ways to kill cops. Besides, slashed brakes couldn't be resold on the black market.

Allegra's flinty gaze was hard to ignore. He wound up slanting a glance her way, wondering if the Bliss was still dulling her perceptiveness or if she was picking up on his doubt, his envy. Concentrating on driving them back into the city wasn't enough to distract Darius from that fundamental question — what could she see that he didn't?

"He's more of a little brother," Allegra said, glancing away. Darius recalled his own question, shame quick to claim the upper hand over his envy.

"Didn't look that young," he offered vaguely.

"And I don't look that old," Allegra countered, something in the cadence of her voice exchanging playful teasing for testy aggravation. "If you hadn't seen my file, you'd give me, what? Twenty-one, twenty-two?"

"Eighteen," Darius confessed, feeling not a little bit guilty at the thought of lusting after — of sleeping with — a mere girl. It made him feel like even more of a creep.

Allegra seemed to read his mind. "You have read my file, though, so you know that's bullshit. I won't lie and pretend it doesn't work out well for me on the streets, but I'm not a kid." She insisted on that, twisting around to watch Darius' profile for a long moment. He deliberately refused to meet her scrutiny—cowardice was a familiar sentiment in matters of the heart.

"I'm not," Allegra said. "You get that, right? I can take care of myself."

There was no profit in pointing out that she'd taken care of herself into a warehouse without utilities or that she routinely sold her body for drugs—or that she was being used by the APU and would probably be discarded as soon as Mallory Osker deemed her input unnecessary. She was a smart girl.

Darius gripped the steering wheel hard enough that his knuckles went from pink to stark white. "I know," he muttered. There was more injustice in dispelling the notion than there was in letting Allegra tell herself lies just to keep going.

They made little conversation for the rest of the drive. If Allegra noticed they weren't heading back to the precinct, she said nothing. The sight of APU patrol cars crowding a narrow avenue in the ritzy part of Arcadia had her drawing a sharp breath, but that was the extent of her surprise. They were maybe half a block from the park where she had gone to her knees for Darius—a lapse of judgment that didn't bear recalling now.

"What've we got?" Darius asked the uniformed officer at the scene. He already had the basics, courtesy of Jasme—an emergency call had been placed that morning around seven from the home of one Hedworth Levin.

Darius couldn't immediately decide which was the first name, or if the owner of the house was male or female. "Where's Levin now?" he asked instead, steering clear of troublesome pronouns.

The officer informed him that Hedworth Levin was already dead, as if that was news. "Garroted in his bedroom, looks like."

Jasme had caught the report first and seen enough similarities with their case to summon Darius to the scene. She wasn't wrong.

"You find any drugs?" They were being led inside, past the police cordon, with a few forensics techs glancing curiously at Allegra as she walked past in her neon-orange tights and fringed denim skirt.

"That's just it, sir." The officer handed Darius a pair of latex gloves, hesitating only briefly before providing another for Allegra.

"What is?"

There was no need for explanation. The bedroom in which Hedworth Levin had been found might have been as sumptuous as a French palace in its natural state, but the clutter got in the way. Boxes were piled high along the walls, branded with the PharmaCorps logos of every firm that had ever produced or sold Bliss in Arcadia.

There must have been enough pills and injectable ampoules to turn the whole city crazy.

"Interesting," Darius drawled for want of anything better to say. It wasn't just interesting — it was plainly illegal, a drug bust of epic proportions. "Who found him?"

It was Allegra who answered. "She did," she said, pointing to a sobbing young woman being questioned by another officer in the hall. Her maid's uniform was askew, hair frizzy around her pretty face. Makeup ran down her cheeks in inky tracks.

At first Darius thought she might have been a housekeeper, but one glance at Allegra told him differently.

"Daughter?" *No*, he thought, *too old for Mr. Levin*. The victim appeared to be in his thirties at most.

The officer who'd greeted them cleared his throat. "We've been having a hard time getting much out of her, but it seems she might have been, ah…employed by the victim." An eyebrow wiggle confirmed Darius' suspicions.

The Docklands didn't have a monopoly on prostitution — or, for that matter, fraud and drug dealing. Here was proof. He could only imagine how this would play out in the media if Osker didn't manage to bury the story fast enough.

"I'll want to talk to her," he told the officer, "but just for now, let my — partner take a crack at her, will you? Allegra?"

"Hmm?" She glanced up at him, bemused. The same expression was painted across the officer's fair, babyish face. "I'm sorry?"

Darius tried not to think of how Allegra had looked this morning, how she'd sounded when she moaned and cried out his name. "I want you to talk to the girl."

"Why?" Confusion struck first, then fear. Self-doubt. It didn't take an empath to read her sudden hostility.

He took Allegra gently by the shoulder and drew her away from the many people listening in on their conversation. "Because I'm asking you...and because," Darius added, regretting the words even as they left his mouth, "you two have something in common. You're..."

"In the same trade," Allegra finished for him. She was too smart for her own good. Her reaction was immediate and obvious, features shuttering into that old mask of apprehension and disdain that Darius had sincerely hoped never to see again.

Allegra played at being okay with what she did for a living, but she wasn't. It didn't take a cop to see the wasted potential, the sacrifices made to keep starvation and insanity at bay. When Allegra broke free of his hold, Darius did nothing to stop her.

"Is your partner a profiler, sir?"

The officer's question seemed totally guileless, but Darius didn't bother answering. "Walk me through what you know so far."

Crime scenes were a smorgasbord of details, most of which said something about the victim or the way he'd lived, but few of which were immediately useful to piecing together a coherent picture of what had ultimately cost a life.

The voluminous cartons of contraband were compelling evidence, though.

The cop introduced himself as Officer Anachie, and promptly explained that the victim had been strangled in his bed, likely while lying on his back. At least that was how Anachie and his partner had found Levin on their way in. Darius filed that observation under things to go over with Rhodes and enquired about alterations made to the crime scene since the body had been discovered.

"We didn't touch anything," Anachie said. "Other than check Levin's pulse to confirm that he was dead, everything is as we found it."

"What about his employee? Did she perhaps turn Levin over?" Darius glanced to the hall where Allegra was speaking in soft, unintelligible tones to the girl. The young woman couldn't have managed such a feat on her own, although adrenaline was as powerful as any drug.

"Ms. Kaelin."

"Hmm?"

"That's her name," said Anachie. "Raine Kaelin." He was checking his notes. "According to her statement, she said she came in, found Levin in bed and almost excused herself. They have a standing appointment on Thursday mornings…"

"Almost?"

Anachie nodded, his jowls resting heavily on his blue collar as he glanced back down at his PDA. "She said she noticed Levin's eyes were open."

The silk and damask covers had concealed the strangulation marks around his throat until she'd come closer to the bed. It must have been some surprise, particularly for a high-class escort who only took clients with deep pockets.

Crime was prevalent in all circles of Arcadian society, but in this part of town, it was never so vulgar.

Darius sighed. "What about the Bliss? Does she know anything about that?" The crates were hard to ignore, particularly when they clashed so tackily with the gold-leaf moldings on the ceiling and the mahogany furnishings of the room.

"Couldn't say, sir. Must've gone into shock. Maybe Detective Allegra will be able to get her talking?"

Detective, Darius thought, biting his tongue. He couldn't bring himself to make the correction.

He wasn't surprised when Allegra came through for him.

Darius would've loved to be a fly on the wall during the interview, but Allegra was finished within ten minutes and came over with hands thrust into her pockets—latex gloves and all—with a guarded expression. Her eyebrow ring gleamed every time a camera flashed.

"I'm done. What do you want to know?"

Questions came to Darius faster than he could ask them. What was the nature of Ms. Kaelin's relationship with the victim? Had she known him long? What was she doing in his house at seven in the morning?

Had she touched the body? Or noticed the Bliss cache in the bedroom?

"You already know he hired her for sex," Allegra drawled, sighing as though bored. "Didn't say how long she'd known him, but he hired her once a week, every week since a bit before his wife died. Seven o'clock on a Thursday was the beginning of her workday. That was part of the arrangement. This morning she only approached the bed because she thought it was weird that Levin wasn't talking when his eyes were obviously open."

One of the CSI techs must've closed them in the interim, because when Darius glanced to the bed, there was no round, blank stare to meet his. He turned back to Allegra. "Go on."

"She said Levin was something of a pack rat, but that he told her there was nothing illegal in what he did."

"And she believed him," Darius said, incredulous. This was just Ms. Kaelin trying to wash her hands of any accusations of collusion.

"Wouldn't you? Rich guy pays you lot of money to come by once a week and put on a uniform, you learn to trust the bullshit that comes out of his mouth. Or at least shut yours." Allegra's answer came from a place of vitriol and little mercy.

"Was it the truth?" Darius asked as they made their way back to the car. Allegra wasn't cleared for fieldwork and Ms. Kaelin had to be interviewed by someone with an actual badge before her words carried any weight.

Allegra slid into the passenger seat with an eye roll. "Some of it." The rumble of her voice was all bruised ego.

"Look," Darius started.

"Save it. She didn't lie about the crime scene, if that's what you're asking." Allegra pursed her lips. "Not like the other witnesses. You know, the ones doing honest work and being all pure and morally upright?"

Darius glared. "What's your problem?"

"Nothing. Just drive."

"Not until you tell me what the hell is —" The rebuke tapered off under the shrilling of his cell phone for the second time that morning.

The reflection of Allegra's sneer was perfectly visible in the car window. "You should get that."

"We're not done." One glance at the caller ID told Darius that he might be. He hit the answer button with a grimace. "Deputy Commissioner, what can I do for you…?" He tried to inject authority into his voice, but that sort of thing never seemed to do any good with Osker.

"Detective," she purred, "I hear there's been another murder." As far as greetings went, Darius privately thought that hers could use some work.

He pinched the bridge of his nose. "Unfortunately, yes. Hedworth Levin of —"

"Spare me the details. He could be a citizen of Timbuktu and it wouldn't make the least bit of difference. What I want to know is why there's another victim at all. Was I not clear enough the last time we spoke? I want this solved, the culprit brought to justice, and I want it done *yesterday*. You're being remarkably laissez-faire about Arcadia's one and only serial killer in over a decade. You understand the press has been asking questions?"

"Yes, ma'am."

Allegra was glancing his way. Darius fought for the appearance of calm. Anything more sincere was beyond his reach.

"And you understand their chief query is why the APU is incapable of doing its job?" This time, it wasn't really a question. Mallory Osker dipped her voice to a low and dangerous growl. "I assigned you extra resources, Detective. I even gave you free rein in how you choose to avail yourself of them. You have a dedicated partner and your job—your *only* job—is to solve this case. Let me be very blunt. This is either the last victim of the Bliss Slayer or the end of your career."

Her tone brooked no argument. It didn't invite his assurances. Darius swallowed hard. Osker had already hung up by the time he lowered the phone.

Allegra was biting her lip. "Was that—?"

"Yes." Darius slid his cell back into his jacket and turned the key in the ignition. "Yeah, it was." Osker's threat had been loud and clear. So, too, was the implicit observation that the deputy commissioner knew exactly where and with whom he'd been spending his time.

Bile rose in Darius' throat. He couldn't seem to swallow it back down again.

Chapter Thirteen

They were no closer to finding the Bliss Slayer at the end of the day than they had been that morning, but there was some progress being made as far as quietly ignoring each other over the spread of freshly collected crime scene photography. Even the coffee tasted stale, though that was probably because Allegra rather than Jasme had brewed it.

"I'm throwing in the towel," she announced after rereading the same line of the pathologist's report five times in a row without understanding a single word.

The victim wasn't going to be any less dead if she made it to the end of the report. Nor was this in any way Allegra's area of expertise.

Perhaps it was time she ceased pretending otherwise and went back to helping the APU in areas where she did have some input to give — witness tapes, family interviews. Hell, even watching the victims' home videos might do more good than playing detective at Darius' side.

He didn't seem to want her there, anyway. He'd been weird all day, but now he wasn't even listening. Self-doubt practically oozed from his pores. Allegra couldn't help wonder if it had something to do with their sleeping together last night and this morning. Mostly this morning.

She forced the thought out of her mind.

"I'm going to head home," she said, gesturing to the door. "If that's okay."

Darius nodded. "You need a ride?"

"No. Nah. I'm fine." Sure, she'd almost had a minor breakdown last night, but that was the absence of Bliss, not a regular thing. Normally, Allegra was just fine on her own two feet. She waved a hand. "I'll see you tomorrow."

"St. Michael's, eight o'clock sharp," Darius answered.

"Right. I'll be there." She didn't have a choice.

Journeying through the rows of now-empty desks reminded her of how little she wanted to be here. Darius had told her point-blank that there was no prize waiting at the end of the road, so why was she still pretending? Osker's lies were only as good as the idiot who believed them.

Allegra was almost at the door, her shoulders slumped and her sneakers dragging with every step, when she felt Darius come up behind her.

"Are you...? Are you sure you don't need me to drive you home?" he asked again. "It's not a big detour." As the crow flew, that was exactly right, but the Docklands were peopled with all sorts of creatures that only came out at night, eager to make trouble and stop traffic. If they caught whiff of a cop in their midst, there would be a free-for-all. Bad enough Aaron had figured out whom she was hanging out with these days.

The earnest glimmer in Darius' eyes wasn't enough to make her forget the real danger of attracting attention to herself.

"You've got work to do," she said. "A lot of work. I'll see you tomorrow."

Jasme waved from the break room and that was it. That was all there was to it—just a flash of disappointment chasing her out.

Cold air chilled Allegra's cheeks as she stepped into the eerily quiet Arcadian night.

She'd taken a pill this morning, but as she started toward the subway stop, Allegra patted her coat with an absentminded gesture. She liked having her stash on hand, just in case. Knowing she had dumped her pill bottle in hopes that clarity of mind would translate into a break in the case made her want to punch herself in the face.

Respite was not to be underestimated. If she stuck to the

meds, Darius could believe she was trustworthy—or at least as trustworthy as a slut ever got to be.

There it was—her smarting ego. Allegra spurred her feet as though she could run from it if she just walked a little faster, if she just pretended not to take a cop's words to heart. There was no denying that the careless, offhand remark had hit a nerve. It was harder to say why.

All Darius had done was point out that Allegra was a hooker, that she sold her body just like pretty Raine Kaelin. Most days she even pretended to be proud of it. If not for Mallory Osker and her mobster-like proposition, Allegra would be on the street corner with the other destitute young men and women right now, hoping to score her next hit. Aaron would be keeping her company, like in the old days.

She took the bullet train into the Docklands, a voyage made too short by the miracles of modern transportation to give her time to adjust to the transition. One minute she was in Arcadia, surveyed by CCTV and surrounded by people who fearlessly wore their jewelry out in the street, and the next she was back in her hometown, surrounded by vagabonds and feral dogs.

The smell of famine hit her first, then the lure of pestilence. She saw freshly painted graffiti announcing that this block had changed hands and now belonged to that gang while the next alley was the new fiefdom of this other up-and-coming small-time gangster. If the four horsemen of the apocalypse had been real, Allegra couldn't help feel they'd take one stroll through the Docklands and hightail it right back out.

Much as she might have wanted to do the same, she couldn't. This was home. This was where she belonged. Hookers and drug addicts and all the other unwanted city vermin crowded together in one cancerous district. It almost made her feel nostalgic.

Surprisingly—or not so surprisingly, considering—her lucky streak ran out some two blocks from the warehouse, to the tune of six massive thugs peeling out of the shadows like ghosts. "Oh, look what we got here, boys," drawled the one at the head of the pack. "White meat."

"Are you kidding me?" Allegra sighed. "I'm off the clock, dude. Get out of my way."

She might have been more impressed by the show of initiative if last Christmas these same guys hadn't taken turns to the tune of a nice, round million credits.

No one in the Docklands was better informed about peckers than the resident hookers. Six of the smallest pricks in all of Arcadia had gathered as close as lovers now, boxing Allegra in with leering smiles that fell well short of threatening. There wasn't a lot she could still lose to the sextet, not if they were hoping for another lucky Christmas this year. They didn't seem deterred when she said as much.

"Seriously?" Allegra grumbled. "You can't be that hard up. There's a whole street's worth of—"

"Oh, we're not here for your ass, bitch," said the self-appointed chief of that small band of miscreants. There were dozens like them in the Docklands, both pro and junior league, involved in everything from human trafficking — which wasn't all that profitable unless you had the balls to venture into APU territory — to drugs and ammo.

Guns were rare in the Docklands, though not in Arcadia, but people died from stab wounds just as easily.

A flash of silver caught Allegra's eye. It was the glint of a three-inch shiv blade on a five-inch ivory handle, and it was clutched in a burly fist.

More importantly, it was being waved in Allegra's face.

"What the hell," she muttered, some of her weariness dispelling to make room for mounting fear. "I've got no quarrel with you."

"Nah, you're all honest, cards on the table sort of chick, right? Is that right? Avey-babe…" The thug-in-chief pressed the knife tip against her cheek.

Allegra fought not to recoil, aware that five other guys were crowding around and behind her. They would grab her if she so much as breathed wrong. They could be mighty jumpy, for knife-wielding thugs. The thought came to her then that this didn't feel like any ordinary a shakedown.

It wasn't even an attempt to intimidate.

They're afraid, she mused, not entirely sure she wasn't mistaking wishful thinking for empathy at work.

Something more serious than the usual racket was at work here. Allegra felt a sliver of panic course down her spine as a gust of warm breath as foul as the harbor water wafted over her. It made for a strange, stomach-churning cacophony of tobacco and stale sweat and greed.

"I hear you've been keeping all kinds of high-class company. Ain't that right, boys? We've got ourselves a little snitch here."

Oh shit. They knew about Darius.

"An honest-to-gods police informant," the leader was saying, all didactic despite the whole four classes he'd gone through as a kid and his imperfect grip of what it meant to be knowledgeable.

Allegra didn't want to quibble at details when there was a knife in her face and a bunch of angry men circling around her like carrion eaters.

"You've got it all wrong," she wheezed. "I swear. I'm not what you think I am, I'm—" She almost said I'm on your side, but that was neither true, nor particularly credible, considering that the only guy on a thug's side was that thug. "I'm nobody."

"That," the man said, "I can agree with. And now you're about to become a dead nobody, 'case anyone else wants to go blabbing to the cops. Docklands is ours. APU don't have any power here and that's how we like it."

Allegra's heart leaped into her throat. "Let's not act rashly."

"Now you're getting second thoughts?" The man clicked his tongue. "Should've thought about that before you moved against us, bitch."

"I haven't!" Protests fell on deaf ears, as they always did when the popular vote was cast against a lone dissenter.

159

The man grinned, showing off the gap between his yellowed front teeth. "Going to make an example out of you..." There was nothing funny about that, in Allegra's opinion, and yet the thug seemed so damn pleased. In different circumstances, she might've been thrilled on his behalf, but when it was her life hanging in the balance, sympathy proved in short supply.

"Please, please don't do this —" Fear gripped her in her a chokehold as she felt hands coil around her wrists, aborting any attempt to break free. She should've tried to get away when she had the chance instead of trying to reason with these bastards. Now it was too late.

Hookers died all the time in the Docklands. Who'd miss her?

"I'm going to serve you up to your boy at the APU with croutons," the thug cackled. The knife trailed down Allegra's chest, cold and sharp like a razor against the wide shelf of her collarbones. "Think he'd like that?"

Allegra could taste bile in the back of her mouth. She had seen crime scene photography and had stood by Darius in a morgue without feeling this same visceral disgust, but what had been gloomy then was a flint now. Panic surged, spilling over. Her hands quaked in the white-knuckled grip that held her captive.

Another second and that son of a bitch was sure to follow through.

Gods, I'm going to die here —

A raw, white-hot flood of pain and panic swept through and out of Allegra like a tidal wave. She felt the malevolent, bloodthirsty echo of the thug's desire to wound and kill, the eager anticipation of his cronies — everything about the moment seemed heightened. Time itself stretched, seconds drawn out as if in the fall of the knife there were many minutes and every one was a weapon for Allegra's use.

Her knees began to give way — and yet she was still upright, held in hands that were become claws and eyes that had widened with fear. *Her* fear. She could suddenly see her own reflection in the glassy mirror of wide pupils, and it wasn't that of a peroxide blonde begging for her life.

Allegra saw amber flame, a conflagration blazing like liquid fire. She saw fear itself and it bore a human face. A piercing shriek blasted out as stretched and as strident as her lungs could expel the air inflating them. It was a wretched sound, choked off when Allegra ran out of breath.

Silence crept over the street.

When Allegra's vision focused once more, she found herself kneeling on the cold ground, limbs heavy and her head pounding like a drum. She swiped a sweat-damp palm over her eyes, found tears staining her cheeks.

What had just happened? And how?

The men who'd held her were no longer blotting out the faint glow of street lamps. Instead, they were prone on the cement around Allegra, a sextet of tattooed limbs twisted at unnatural angles. If not for their eyes still being open, Allegra might have said they were the world's oddest bunch of narcoleptics.

She staggered to her feet like a drunkard on stilts.

The alley seemed to flicker around her, concrete dipping like an inflatable mattress. A bouncy castle at a fair.

She ran as fast as she could, not seeing the gaunt, hungry faces of her fellow paupers, not caring that her feet were taking her away from the Docklands and the only home she'd ever known.

In the train car, Allegra held her breath and kept her head ducked for fear of anyone catching her eye and knowing what she'd done. That it had happened in the first place still hadn't sunk in. She could have checked the bodies before she ran off, but she already knew what she would find if she had.

Death carried a particular scent, an aura that an empath could feel a mile away.

She had killed those men without meaning to. Without thought.

The revolving rungs of the subway stop caught in her

clothes like grasping hands. Her own were shaking as she barreled through the gap.

A smattering of late night commuters shot her wary glances, but there were no APU patrolmen to stop her, only the cameras mounted high on the walls, little black spheres keeping an eye on any disturbance. Allegra had never been happier to crawl aboveground again, the air there crisp and cool.

She could feel her pounding heart echoing dully in her ears. This was the way she had come before, she remembered the freshly swept streets and the storefronts only now closing up business for the day.

Darius' flat was only a little farther. Allegra slipped into the building and up the stairs without thought. Police would throw her into a cell, but Darius wasn't like that.

Darius would know what to do.

She smacked her fists against the door with all her might. "Darius! I know you're in there." She knew no such thing—the curl of panic in her breast was all imagination and despair. She wasn't thinking straight. "Darius!" *Please*, she thought. *Please, please, open up*.

She staggered against the door, her scalp prickling, hair sopping with blood. At least she looked the part of a criminal. Her photograph wouldn't run in the paper unless she was run-of-the-mill unsavory.

"Can I help you?" a male voice asked behind her.

Allegra turned to find a neighbor standing in the doorway. He seemed simultaneously pissed off and wary as he scrutinized Allegra with an eye more anxious than aroused.

"I—yes." Allegra licked her lips. "The man who lives here—he's a police detective. Any chance you know if he's left again?"

The neighbor's gaze narrowed, suspicion palpable in his hesitation.

"Please," Allegra insisted, "it's important. It's about a case we're working on. I mean, that *he's* working. This could save lives."

That was overstating it a little. A bunch of dead Docklands thugs weren't worth the APU's resources, not unless Darius had mastered necromancy. There was really nothing for him to do.

"He came back a little earlier." The neighbor sighed. Allegra felt hope kindle in her chest. "But he left again maybe ten minutes ago. Banging his door at all hours, doesn't he know that some of us are trying to sleep here?"

So much for hope. "Don't suppose you know where he went?" Allegra asked warily. The precinct seemed the likeliest, but Allegra wasn't sure she could brave the APU and its horde of trained interrogators just now.

They would figure out she'd committed murder. Osker would come after her, toss her into prison and let her slowly go insane. One less thing to worry about.

The neighbor shook his head and made to close his door. "You know your ear's bleeding, right?"

"What?" There was, Allegra discovered, a trickle of syrupy, crimson blood leaking out of her ear and soaking into the collar of her lime-green shirt. Her stomach roiled. "Could I use your—" But the man was already gone, the sound of his door latching up tight as if to announce that he'd had his fill of dealing with stragglers.

Allegra staggered down the narrow steps and into the street. A patrol car was rounding the far corner, driving away. It would be back. She couldn't muster more than passing interest. The strength had sapped from her bones, apathy replacing the desperate tug of urgency as she turned back inside.

She leaned against the wall, patting her pockets for the vials Darius had slipped her after they parted ways at the precinct. Her fix for services rendered. Their shape had been a familiar source of discomfort against her left buttock— literally, a pain in the ass. It took Allegra a moment to recall that she'd tossed them.

She had no barrier between her terror and the satellite

dish of her so-called gift. She was exposed, vulnerable. It wasn't the first time. Back at the jewelry store, with Darius laid out like a sacrifice, the same overwhelming dread had slithered into her belly, consuming the parts of her that might have put honesty forth as a defense in the aftermath. Allegra knew what she'd done. This time she was just alone to shoulder that horrible burden.

Chapter Fourteen

It was already coming up on two a.m. by the time Darius left Mrs. L.'s. Earlier attempts had been met with lighthearted rebuke and not so humorous remonstrations. Did he think that old folks needed twelve-hour nights? Was he trying to say Mrs. L. was too old to have fun?

And, worst of all, was he bored of talking about Harlan?

To the latter, Darius could only offer staunch denial. He had gone to see her in hopes that she would accept his thanks. He didn't expect to be treated to a plate of corn on the cob followed by pork chops, green beans with sesame and a frankly embarrassingly large slice of chocolate cake.

It stretched belief, but oddly enough not one dish was poisoned. Darius was grateful. His olive branch was a withered, pathetic thing indeed. It wasn't worth dying for.

Taking the stairs of his apartment building in the aftermath of that feast had him wheezing like an asthmatic. He was glad when he finally hit the landing. The thought of sprawling into bed and getting a solid three hours of sleep beckoned to him like the Holy Grail.

That was when the sight of Allegra fully registered.

"Hi," she said, waving a hand. "You don't leave a key under the doormat. I, uh, I saw people do that in old vid-reels. But not you."

"It's a palm-print lock. What are you doing here?" Darius asked, still too shocked to know what to do with the fact that there was blood on Allegra's shirt and face. "Are you okay?"

She rolled her shoulders into a shrug. "I'm fine. Just I changed my mind about seeing you. Thought you'd be home, so I came over."

"I was out," Darius murmured.

"So I gathered. I thought I'd wait." Allegra pushed herself up to her feet, blonde hair sticking up in tufts at the back. "You got nice neighbors."

He couldn't tell if that was supposed to be sarcasm. Allegra was never particularly easy to decipher, and even less so when she was avoiding his eyes.

"Would you like to come in?"

She did meet his gaze then, if a little warily. "Yeah."

The blood on her shirt had dried. Darius couldn't tell if it was hers. Her stockings had a run in them, neon orange giving way to pale pink skin and an ugly, mottled bruise darkening the meat of her thigh.

"What happened?" Something had. He didn't need special powers to understand that much. "Allegra—"

"If you ask me if I'm okay again, I swear I'm going to beat you over the head with a chair," she threatened. "I told you. I'm fine. Had a minor altercation with an idiot on the train, that's all."

Darius didn't believe her, but getting into a spat at this hour didn't appeal. He let it go, doffed his coat and toed off his shoes. "You want something to drink?"

He didn't know Allegra to ever turn down free booze or free food, so he was a little surprised when she shook her head.

"Where were you tonight?" she asked, plopping down on the couch. "Visiting Ms. Kaelin at home?"

"What?"

Allegra took no note of his outrage. "I'm just wondering how far police protection extends, you know?" She was toying with a loose thread in her skirt, feet up on the coffee table and her smile shark-like. Were her eyes red from crying or Bliss? Darius couldn't tell.

He paused, feeling lost in his own home. "Are you asking me if I slept with a witness?"

"Would you lose your job if you did?"

166

"Yes." There was no doubt about that. The way things were going with this case, he was going to find himself on unemployment soon enough anyway.

But Allegra wasn't satisfied—she had to twist the knife in the wound. She glanced up at him through her lashes. "Would you lose your job if you slept with me?"

"There's no *if*. I already did that." And what was worse, he didn't regret it.

"Oh, good. You remember."

Darius frowned. "What are you talking about? Of course, I remember..." He hadn't been with anyone since Harlan, and though going to bed with Allegra was a grave professional mistake, he had enjoyed every moment.

"Funny. The way you've been treating me since says otherwise."

"Is that what this is about?" Darius gaped. He couldn't afford to dwell on the brush of Allegra's fingers through his thinning hair, much less the shape of her breasts or how she tasted when he put his mouth to her cunt.

There was too much at stake. Even Mrs. L. had figured out that something was afoot—and she had only met Allegra once.

He sighed, tried again. "I went to see Mrs. L., to thank her for being decent to you the other day."

She was beating an entirely different horse. "Did you tell her about me?"

"No."

Allegra stood, glaring at him with all her might. "Because I'm a whore?"

"Because Osker already owns my ass!" Darius shouted, at the end of his tether and fast tipping past the point of no return. He fell silent almost instantly when he realized what he'd done. "I'm sorry—I didn't mean to do that."

"You think yelling is going to scare me?" Allegra huffed a disbelieving breath. "Babe, I've had guys threaten to carve me up for snacks and make lampshades out of my skin. I'm not some fragile pet."

That was the furthest thing from Darius' thoughts. "I know that... Look, if the deputy commissioner fires me, I don't know what she'll do with you. If she'll reassign you to work with Jasme or —"

"Or what? Toss me back into the Docklands where she found me?"

"You're being oddly cavalier about that..."

Allegra shrugged. "I'm not scared of going back there."

It sounded almost like an ultimatum, but something in her tone, in the fixed, unblinking stare she turned on Darius, had him doubting her bravado.

"What about your surgery?" he asked, playing the last card he had in hand — the joker.

The sneer stretching Allegra's lips morphed into a shallow, rueful grin. "What about it? Come on, honey. We both know I'm not getting any treats. Osker's lying through her teeth."

"You knew?"

"You *told* me," Allegra said. "Last time I was here, when you were drugged out of your pretty little mind — don't you remember?" She hitched up her shoulders. "Don't fret. I'm over it."

"That was days ago."

Allegra nodded. "And you can't figure out why I'm still around."

Darius hadn't been chomping at the bit to ask in quite so many words, but yes, that was the extent of it. If she knew there was no carrot at the end of the ride, why was she still trudging along? Why was she still letting Darius drag her around crime scenes and boss her around?

Why had she allowed him into her life if she knew it was all for nothing?

"Because I want you," Allegra answered, as if it was the most obvious thing in the world. It didn't fully register until she was touching warm palms to his cheeks and saying, "I want you, you fucking idiot. I want you to take me to bed. Right now."

It might not have been the most romantic come-on Darius had ever heard, but coming from Allegra, it could've been a litany of slurs and he still would've complied. He heard the order in her request and did the only thing he could.

He slid a hand around her back and another around the knees and picked her up. His back wouldn't thank him in the morning, but it was worth it just to hear Allegra yelp as she was hefted off the ground. At least this time they would make it to the bed. *Progress*, Darius mused.

* * * *

Allegra slid her hands under the waistband of his boxers, clever fingers closing around his cock in a grip so tight that Darius had to close his eyes and suck in a breath to keep from coming.

"Too much?" she purred. "Want me to stop?"

Darius growled low in his throat. "No goddamn way." Two could play that game. He threaded his digits through her wispy blonde hair, cupping the back of her skull in his hand. Allegra was soft skin and goose pimples wherever he touched her. She took his breath away.

You're making a mistake, he tried to tell himself, but the admonition didn't stick.

She felt too good in his arms to let go. Even when she pulled back, a smirk twisting at her lips, Darius had to steel himself to keep from following suit. She wasn't stepping out of his reach, though, merely peeling off her shirt.

The whorls of ink on her skin were familiar by now. Darius still couldn't read them, and the urge to trace them with his fingers hadn't abated, but he knew them. The splotches of brown and purple bruises were another matter.

"Must have been some altercation you had," he grunted.

Allegra's expression shuttered, a blink-and-you'll-miss-it kind of hesitation, before the smile came back with a vengeance. "I took care of it. And now I want to take care of you. Got a problem with that?"

Darius watched her sink to her knees on the carpet, his breath catching at the sight of her peering up at him as if — as if she wanted to be there, kneeling for him. He palmed her cheek and shook his head. No, he didn't have a problem.

"Good," Allegra breathed and dipped her head.

She licked him from root to tip, her gaze never straying from his. There was a devilish glimmer in her eye as she wrapped her fist around him. "You felt so good the other night. When we fucked. Gods, I liked that... Did you like it?"

"Yes." The answer was torn from him on the cusp of a plea. He didn't want to rush her, but if she kept this up, he knew all too well he'd end up spending himself into her hand. Allegra must've known it, too, because she didn't keep up the teasing for long.

Her mouth was sinfully hot as she dipped her head and swallowed him down to about mid-shaft. Darius didn't dare breathe for fear of scaring her off — she kept telling him she could handle herself, but he couldn't help wish she wouldn't have to. He dug his toes into the floor. He didn't want to be like the other men she'd had.

There was nothing noble about it. He nearly came the second Allegra relaxed her throat and swallowed him down almost to the base of his cock.

"Fuck — Allegra," he gasped, struggling to remember why breathing was important. "Gods, how are you — oh fuck, that feels so good." Pure, meaningless drivel emptied his lungs of breath. It was too much to witness, to experience. He wasn't freakishly long or anything, but communal showers had never been a subject of unease for him. He was well endowed and yet Allegra made sucking him off seem effortless.

She was grinning smugly as she slid off with a wet, vulgar noise. A rosy flush stained her cheeks. "You all right? You sound like you're about to have a heart attack."

Darius sucked in a breath. "I damn well hope not." He hadn't felt so lightheaded making love in a long time. The edges of his vision had gone blurry. He welcomed the solid wall at his back, afraid his knees might give out if he wasn't careful. "You mind if I sit?"

"I'll take it as a compliment," Allegra told him with a cocky smirk. She rose gracefully, more gracefully than anything Darius could've managed in her stead, and let him pull her into a sloppy kiss.

She held it together longer than he had, but she wasn't made of stone, Darius knew that now. Self-preservation carried a hefty cost if it meant she had to make herself cold to a man's advances — especially those of a man she wanted to sleep with. Darius couldn't afford to think otherwise. He listened to her moan as her nipples grazed the smattering of hair on his chest, felt the slow roll of her hips against his.

They were both breathing hard when they broke away. Allegra's cocksure grin was nowhere to be seen. Her temptress routine seemed to have fallen by the wayside, leaving them equal in anticipation and arousal.

"No," Darius murmured as Allegra made to settle on her back on the bed. "Like this." He guided her gently to her stomach, stroking a palm between the wings of her shoulders as she settled into place. "I mean, if it's okay."

Allegra nodded into the pillow. "It's okay." She hesitated only briefly before reaching behind her and tugging him by the hand.

Darius followed easily. It didn't occur to him to resist any more than he intended to refuse her. He'd never been very good at seducing people. He liked to think he was a straightforward kind of guy, what you see is what you get. Perhaps if he'd been better at it, he would've known how to tell Allegra that he only wanted to return the pleasure she'd offered him.

He didn't want to say 'don't worry, I won't hurt you', because Allegra didn't seem to believe anyone could. She bore her bruises with pride.

"I don't do it like this much," Darius heard her say, distant, like she wasn't discussing sex, but some vague and unimportant rumor. "Have you got any slick?"

"I wasn't. I mean, we can do it that way, too," he said, increasingly flustered, "but I was hoping you'd settle for the more mundane?"

He'd had plenty of lubricant on hand as a married man, but it had been years, and though there were tubes stashed here and there, not impossible to find if Darius put his mind to it, they were probably past their expiration date. Harlan had taken Darius' sex drive with him when he left.

Darius hesitated. "Do you not want—?"

"I do." Allegra shrugged her shoulders. "Sorry, I jump to conclusions. It's been said." Apologies didn't suit her very well, but Darius could tell this one was sincere.

"As long as we're on the same page," he murmured, bending to kiss her nape.

He went slowly, stroking his hand down her flank and over the swell of her hip. The jut of her hipbone was a divot in his path, an erogenous spot that made her sigh then laugh. "Ticklish?" Darius asked, though it was obvious. She rolled her hips back onto his in encouragement, the soft skin of her buttocks lazily brushing Darius' hard cock.

"I like where this is going. Don't stop now."

"Didn't even cross my mind." But the request was harder to heed, because it meant hitching up one of Allegra's legs around his thighs. The sight of her sex all glistening and wet was almost more than he could stand. He had to stop and rally before he could go on.

He heard Allegra titter—the sound spurred him on.

"You're doing great," she encouraged as he stroked her slick cunt. "You're doing—oh, right there." She grasped a corner of the pillow in her fist, her mouth parting on a sigh. She seemed to like it best when he circled the opening of her vagina more than anything else, so he grew bolder, let one fingertip dip inside.

"Oh fuck, baby—"

"You like that? Is that good?"

Allegra laughed, canting her head into a harried nod.

She pinched her nipples with a trembling hand, as if in tandem with the slow, rhythmic thrust of his fingers inside her. For a few, breathless moments there was only the pressure of Allegra's inner muscles grasping his fingers tightly and the warmth of her buttocks against his shaft.

Then Allegra huffed out a laugh. "So last night...wasn't a one-off for you, huh?"

"Did you want it to be?"

"No," Allegra said. "You're pretty good at this."

"Don't be so surprised," Darius breathed, too choked to sound properly cocky. "This isn't my first rodeo."

Allegra chuckled, bucking a little into his hand. "Oh yeah? Bet you're a heartbreaker on your off hours, Officer..."

"*Detective*," he corrected, the pedantic note reduced to a warm exhale against Allegra's throat. It wasn't hard to stop himself from decorating her skin with any more bruises, however much she might have moaned with pleasure when he worried her flesh between his teeth.

"Yes, sir."

Darius worked another finger into her, just to hear her retort devolve into a breathless whimper. He took his time, though his cock was hard as steel against Allegra's thigh and waiting was no picnic. It fell to Allegra to tell him — to order, really — Darius to just get on with it.

The request was rewarded with a crook of fingers and a sharp thrust just there, against that soft, fleshy part of her just a couple of inches inside her cunt that had breath failing her and her limbs tensing up as though electrified.

"Darius, gods—"

"Ask me nicely."

"W-what?" Allegra couldn't seem to help the greedy tilt of her hips against Darius' fist. He didn't want her to.

"Ask me," he murmured, "nicely."

She did — insofar as 'fuck me, you son of a bitch' qualified as nice. Darius didn't quibble. He wanted this just as much as she did, maybe more, and nearly slipped inside her bare before he felt Allegra stop him with a surprisingly pointy elbow.

"There's a condom in my purse," she said, her voice rough with want.

"I've had all my shots—"

"But I haven't. Get the condom."

Darius didn't object again. It was Allegra's turn to fumble the foil wrapper before finally tearing it free along the dotted line. Darius couldn't say which one of them shuddered worse as she rolled it down Darius' cock. It didn't matter because moments later, Allegra was shifting to her belly and propping herself up on her knees.

"Like this, right?"

He nodded.

Allegra glanced at him over her shoulder, something mild and indulgent in her gaze. Did she know that Darius was barely holding on by his fingernails? That his heart seemed lodged somewhere in his throat and butterflies kept dancing in his belly?

It would've been easier if she stuck to calling him an idiot and son of a bitch. But no, Allegra had to prove generous and patient. And Darius had to let her in, always a fool for a pretty face.

He settled over her, their bodies aligned, and tilted his forehead against the speed bump notches of her vertebrae. He could feel Allegra pinning her toes against the sheets, the slip-slide of flesh against cheap synthetic fibers audible but ultimately unimportant. Darius arched his hips and Allegra bore down and just like that, they were suddenly, intimately joined.

Darius wrapped her in his arms. He moved at a glacially slow pace, savoring every moan and needy plea. He wanted to feel Allegra come around his dick once again, like he had back at the warehouse. He wanted to know that whatever pleasure he took in this was shared. He didn't have to wait long for the rising pitch of Allegra's moans. She seized his wrist in hers, grabbing hold as though onto a life raft.

The sharp sting of her fingernails was enough to spur

him on, every sloppy thrust bringing him a little closer to climax. "Come with me," he breathed into Allegra's ear. "Come on, I want to hear you…" He kissed her lobe, tasted metal and salt-sweat, couldn't tear himself away to check if Allegra was weeping.

He heard her cries tangle in her throat almost out of nowhere. Her body gripped him tightly, a wet clutch seizing around his cock, and he spent himself into the condom.

When he finally came down, his limbs were aching to the point of pain. With the very last of his strength, Darius pulled out and collapsed onto the mattress, where he wouldn't hurt Allegra. It wasn't long before he felt the clutch of hands against his flanks, and the hazy, confused echo of endearments being pressed into his hair.

There was only so much he could do to give a woman like Allegra shelter and comfort. Pleasure was easier to conjure into being.

The air in the bedroom smelled of sex and sweat, of their intermingled musk and Darius' gun oil—a strangely soothing amalgamation of their daytime partnership and the illicit pursuits Darius knew he ought to have been ashamed of.

"Will you stay?" he murmured, once he could speak again without his voice cracking.

Allegra kissed his sternum. "For a while."

It wasn't the forever Darius might've liked, but it would do. Exhaustion was catching up with him fast, paying him back for all those hours he'd wasted at the precinct when he should've been trying for at least one REM cycle.

"I'll make blueberry pancakes in the morning," he mumbled blearily, eyes already drooping shut. "I'll even run you a bath…" It spoke to how ill-equipped he was for a relationship that he could think of nothing else to offer.

She was kind enough to say nothing at all.

Chapter Fifteen

Allegra didn't sleep. She could feel contentment and pleasure practically radiate from Darius, but her own emotions were too fidgety for sleep. She couldn't seem to find a position that wouldn't make her ache, or pull at her hair. Darius didn't snore, but even his soft, deep breaths quickly grew grating.

Impossible to imagine that she had ever found comfort sleeping beside him. It wasn't her memory that was faulty, but the crawling in her veins. Somewhere in Darius' apartment building, someone was raging against a spouse who hadn't come home. A kid was afraid to close his eyes because the monsters under his bed weren't the scariest around.

Allegra swung her legs over the edge of the mattress and sank her toes into the plush carpet. She could clutch at her hair all she pleased. It wasn't thoughts that troubled her, but the thing that lived beyond them.

The wrathful being she could unleash if pushed to extremes.

She hadn't told Darius. By the time he'd appeared, the initial flare of shock and fear had burned itself out. There was only ash in its wake—well, that and guilt, because killing someone turned out to weigh heavily on the heart.

At least now I know it's true. I am *a danger to others.*

Hateful, egotistic Mallory Osker had been right from the beginning.

Allegra gingerly padded away from the bed. The things she had done, she could do again. Had Darius been just any odd lay, it wouldn't have mattered. He wasn't.

He was—she stole a guilty glance at the bed, watched the soft rise and fall of his chest—important. She had to get herself under control before he became her victim.

There was one way and one way only that she knew to make her body behave.

She searched his pants, first, then the battered trench coat in the other room. Turning the pockets inside out was no use. Other than some loose change, a piece of gum and a stubby pencil, she came up empty. Allegra made her way into the bathroom and repeated the process with his cabinets, going through the labels of every bottle she found in hopes that she would find one that even remotely suggested it might be the thing she needed.

Darius owned a treasure trove of sleeping aids that would've fetched a pretty penny on the black market, but none of them interested Allegra. Dejected, she trudged back into the living room. The street outside was dark, the hour so late she didn't think anyone would be around to spot her walking around in the nude. But one window in the building just across the street was lit with a faint yellowish light.

Mrs. Ley's window.

The thought came to Allegra that if anyone else on this block was likely to have Bliss on hand, it might be the mother of a man who'd suffered from the same condition Allegra was struggling with.

It was a long shot, but it was all she had. Darius would have to pardon her skipping away in the night.

* * * *

There was something about being greeted with gun in hand that Allegra didn't think she'd ever get used to. She pardoned it of Mrs. L., because the other woman scared her, but the urge to drop to the floor was still there, alive and well, at the sight of Alma.

"I thought I saw a light on," Allegra offered by way of

greeting. "I couldn't sleep."

"So you decided to bother me?" Mrs. Ley took one look at her in her bloodstained lime green T-shirt and torn tights and beckoned Allegra inside with a wrinkled hand. "Come on in, I made pink lemonade."

Allegra obeyed, smothering down twin waves of smug satisfaction and disapproval. They didn't belong to her. It was only natural, when the Bliss began to wear off, for the other shit to come crawling in. She dragged herself over the threshold, the best she could do.

"Mrs. L., I, um…"

"Well, don't just stand there," the old woman barked, "get in here."

She left Allegra to close the door, already tottering on her mecha-legs in the general direction of the kitchen. "Darius came by earlier. What brings you here? Round two?"

In more ways than one. Allegra winced. "I heard," she said instead. Any attempt to inject sarcasm into her answer only yielded a migraine. She rubbed a hand over her brow, trying to do away with the frown she couldn't seem to smooth out. "This is going to sound strange, but you don't happen to know if your son was on any medication before he — before Darius ended the relationship, do you?"

Mrs. L. didn't miss a beat. "Sure, I do. Boy used to tell me everything. And when he'd finish I'd read him a bedtime story and we'd braid each other's hair. You know how boys are with their mothers — they don't keep no secrets." She hobbled out of the kitchen with a pitcher and two glasses balanced awkwardly in her hands. Somehow she managed to avoid any spillage.

Allegra hovered at the edge of the living room. At least one of them could stand to behave normally. "Do you know if he was taking any Bliss?"

"Ain't that normal for someone with your disease?"

"It would be, yes." Before it was made illegal, anyway, and people like Allegra were carted off to costly surgical procedures that could well leave them lobotomized.

Miracles of modern medicine. She filled her lungs with breath, steeling herself for the stern talking-to she expected she'd be in for. "Do you have any of his meds left?"

Mrs. L. glared, narrowing her beady eyes. "What for?"

To stop me killing again, because I have no idea how I did it the first time.

"Couldn't sleep." Lying came easy to her, but not when she was faced with the likes of Mrs. L.

The old woman's icy blue gaze raked over her like a pair of searchlights. "It's started, has it?"

"What?"

"You know *what*, girl," Mrs. L. scoffed. "Don't give me that sullen stare. It don't work on me." She sighed, shaking her head as though Allegra presented a hopeless case. It shouldn't have come as news. "You'd best sit down and tell me what happened."

Was she that transparent? Darius hadn't noticed a thing. He'd been distracted.

"I don't— Nothing happened," Allegra said, trying to laugh away the question.

"Want me to give that boy of yours a call?"

A cold shiver slithered down Allegra's spine. She wouldn't—would she? A sidelong glance at Mrs. L. was enough to tell her that she shouldn't try to call the other woman's bluff. Between the two of them, Mrs. L. had nothing to lose. Hell, she might do it just out of spite, to keep Darius from finding any sort of happiness without her son.

That's why she's treating you to pink lemonade, is it? Allegra heard a voice crow at the back of her mind. It sounded disturbingly like Darius.

She sat down. "Please don't tell him." For one thing, he'd be forced to lock her up. It was the law—you killed someone, you went away for a long time, whatever deal you'd made with the higher-ups. Allegra didn't have enough money to buy herself a jury. Ever since she'd stopped working, she was surviving on other people's kindness. It wasn't until now that she realized how vulnerable that made her.

Mrs. L. was still shaking her head. "I should've thought you kids knew to steer clear of that horseshit by now."

"What shit? I don't understand —"

"The Bliss," Mrs. L. interjected. "Gods above, Darius sure knows how to pick them..." They weren't close, Darius had said, so her displeasure with his romantic partners came as a surprise.

Allegra arched an eyebrow, struggling to muster a smile. She could feel her heart juddering in her chest. "I'm not the first?"

For some indefinable reason, the thought made her ache like a blow to the belly.

"He was married, wasn't he? And my Harlan went down the same nasty path. You're a — what? Four? Five?"

"Seven."

Mrs. L.'s mouth fell open.

"Think this might be the first time I've seen you speechless," Allegra muttered, wishing she could hide. She was trying very hard not to give in to panic, but it was hard to do when even a woman who put on her insulated beekeeper suit to brave a midday scorchers and casually threatened people at gunpoint seemed wary. "I'm not dangerous." Not usually, anyway.

"My son was a three... Not enough for the brain-butchers. He wouldn't hear of treatment. Said his gift was of the gods."

It wasn't news. Some people, when they first discovered they could read emotions and decode the complexities of human behavior, thought they were touched by divinity. Then again, most were capable of selective reading.

Allegra was a different animal. A different kind of freak.

"What happened to him?" she heard herself ask. "Darius doesn't talk about him. I haven't seen any pictures in his apartment..." She knew she shouldn't have been looking. Marriages just ended sometimes. People moved on.

She didn't have pictures of her parents, either, their

faces lost to the fog of an imperfect memory, but she was Docklands-stock. Arcadia was supposed to treasure its past.

Mrs. L. pursed her lips, a stony expression slotting over her features like a carnival mask. "That bookcase over there. Top shelf," she said, and beckoned with a crooked, wrinkled finger to a leather-bound tome inscribed with gold. Allegra had to tilt her head to one shoulder to make out the words photo album in cursive. "As for what Harlan did... He ran out on his husband. Went crazy first."

"Because of the, um, because of his gift?" It had been a long time since Allegra had last feared herself. This evening seemed as good a time as any to pick up the slack.

Curiosity prompted her to rise, though, and liberate the album from the bookcase. She'd never actually touched one before. They only existed in vid-reels now. Most rich folk had moved to electronic frames and perpetually changing, randomized slideshows of their most meaningful memories.

Mrs. L. must've shared Darius' fondness for flammable paper. The apartment was small and crammed with mismatched furniture a couple of decades past its prime, all full of clutter that could easily go up in smoke.

"Because of his medication," she said. "Because of the Bliss."

"He got a bad batch?"

"There were no bad batches back then. Trade was legal. His doctor prescribed it, Harlan would get it in a pharmacy. Not like it is now." The tight-lipped smile Mrs. L. offered her was enough to tell Allegra just what she thought of her choices.

"It's just as necessary," Allegra countered. "Just because it went underground doesn't mean the rest of us need it any less..."

"You know that for a fact? My Harlan was just fine till he started taking those pills. I'm surprised Darius hasn't said a word about it to you. He's your dealer, isn't he?"

It didn't take schooling or a great deal of intellect

for Allegra to figure out what Mrs. L. made of their arrangement. "He's been very generous," she said, steering clear of outright confirmation. This of all things shouldn't have made her feel ashamed.

"The longer you're hooked up on that toxic stuff, the worse it'll be for you. Mark my words, it won't make you better."

"But it does," Allegra insisted. She could feel the thrum of indignation pulsing right beneath her skin morph into simmering rage. She recognized the sensation—it had been with her in the Docklands, when she'd lost her mind to the tune of six dead bodies.

Mrs. L. knew it, too, because she reached ever so tenderly for Alma's steel grip.

Allegra winced, darting to her feet. "I'm sorry. I'm not— I'm really sorry." Anything more eloquent was outside the realm of possibility. "Maybe I should talk to Darius." He'd fix her up, but he would want to know why.

One way or another, it seemed the end of the line would always be prison.

A knock on the door curtailed whatever brisk reproof Mrs. L. intended to offer—Allegra knew her too well by now to expect coddling.

"Were you expecting someone else?"

Mrs. L. shook her head. "It might be your boy Darius. Stay here." It was an order Allegra couldn't imagine challenging. They were on the fourth floor. Escaping out of the window would be suicide.

Mrs. L. tottered into the foyer, gun in hand. Heard her call out, "Who is it?"

A female voice answered. "A friend of Allegra's. She'll want to talk to me."

Allegra balked. "Don't open the door," she pleaded. She recognized that voice.

It meant she had already lost.

They're going to cart me away into lock-up, I'll never see Darius again. Never know what it's like to live like my own person.

She was hyperventilating before she knew it, doubled over with the photo album sprawled out on the floor at her feet. Two men were smiling blithely at her from one glossy still. One of them she recognized as Darius — younger and holding himself very straight in his tux, but still familiar. The other man had his arm around Darius' shoulders. He was smiling too, showing off two rows of perfectly straight teeth.

He must've been the husband. *Harlan.*

Allegra couldn't even muster envy. She started when she felt a hand on her shoulder, touch sending a clear stab of glee right between her ribs, like an arrow striking true.

"Oh, what a pretty pair," Deputy Commissioner Osker cooed. "I do like the look of them together, don't you?"

Allegra opened her mouth to ask what Osker was doing in Mrs. L.'s apartment, but her hostess waved her to silence.

"Drink your lemonade," Mrs. Ley advised curtly. "You'll feel better." Allegra could've read her pity with her eyes closed. With them open, she noticed that Mrs. L.'s slate-tinted eyes had drifted to the photograph of Darius and his husband. Her son.

Osker straightened first, releasing her with a squeeze of clawed fingers. "We should talk."

"So talk." *'Cause I sure as hell have nothing to say.*

"I was in the area and I thought you might like to know that your little problem in the Docklands has been taken care of," Osker said. She was wearing one of her militaristic pantsuits, her hair pinned back into a severe ponytail. Allegra didn't believe her for a second.

She tilted back, sprawling again the backrest of the couch with false bluster. "What problem?"

"Oh, very good. Lying to police? Always turns out well for small-time crooks. Although," Osker added, narrowing her eyes, "you're not so small-time anymore, are you? I hope to see some return on my investment soon, Ms. Avenson. My patience is wearing thin."

"Sorry about that," Allegra shot back, nothing in her tone

suggesting contrition. "I could have told you myself you'd end up disappointed. I'm not a detective —"

Osker gripped her chin in a very cold hand. "No, you're so much more."

"Think she got the message," Mrs. L. cut in balefully. She tapped Alma against her metal leg brace.

"You think that's wise? Threatening an officer of the law —"

Mrs. L. snorted a laugh. "I'm eighty-five years old, lady. What can you do to me that my health hasn't already? Girl heard what you had to say. No use beating a dead horse."

For a long, protracted moment, Allegra witnessed what had to be the strangest face-off she'd ever seen. Osker backed down first, retrieving her hand with a sneer. "I'll see you tomorrow."

"Bright-eyed and bushy-tailed," Allegra gritted out. Holding her tongue had never been her strongest suit. "I told you not to let her in," she snarled once the door had banged shut in Mallory Osker's wake.

Mrs. L. arched a pencil-thin eyebrow, the wrinkles on her forehead creasing like parchment. "Because I need your permission, child? Think your secret's out," she added, setting the pistol aside. "Could mean trouble."

"She won't tell Darius."

"You sure about that?"

Allegra wasn't sure about many things — herself, Darius, what Mrs. L. had told her about the Bliss all included — but she knew she was right about this. "She needs me."

She wasn't sure she'd convinced Mrs. L., but the older woman mercifully let it go. "Pick that up," Mrs. L. said, pointing the gnarled clutch of a hand to the album sprawled on the floor. "There ain't nothing in this place worth much, only them pictures."

For once, Allegra did as she was told.

The sight of Darius grinning toothily at the camera had her insides doing back-flips in her belly. It didn't even matter that he had a stranger's arm slung around shoulders, careless pleasure writ across their faces. Harlan had inherited his mother's blue eyes.

Mrs. L. had mentioned she and Darius didn't talk anymore. Here, right before Allegra's eyes, was the reason why.

"What happened to him?" Allegra asked. She felt a surge of grief from Mrs. L., a burst of feeling so strong it left her breathless. She choked up and couldn't say if it was residual or second hand. She couldn't say which emotion was thoroughly hers anymore.

This was what it meant to live without Bliss.

"Same thing that's happening to you." Mrs. L. held her gaze. "He always knew when I was upset—even when he was still a little baby. He'd react to his Dada's moods like they were his own. Flip of a switch and I'd know we were in for a night of shouting at each other. When the old man went and got himself another wife, we were better off. My boy found Leon, and I had peace and quiet. Reckoned we were set for life." She turned her head. "They tell you not to tempt the gods…"

"What happened?" Allegra pressed. The man in the pictures seemed clear-eyed and happy. He might have been sixteen. Was the joy on his face only skin-deep? Allegra wondered if there were any photos of her left anywhere, if she could go back and study her own childhood image for signs of what was to come.

She couldn't help feel like the only people keeping a record of her these days worked for the APU.

Mrs. L. sighed. "He found Bliss. Double doses, at first. Then triple. Then he'd go through a bottle in a week. Mood swings started getting worse. You couldn't talk to him without getting an honest-to-god migraine. Lost his job, started making money on the sly—gods know how."

"He became an addict," Allegra scoffed, "that's not—"

"He got violent with Darius, child. Those boys were friends long before they were anything else. They knew everything about each other. When my son went—" She caught herself, cleared phlegm from her throat. "When he got himself into trouble and quit his job, I thought Leon would do something about it. I suppose I didn't realize how much he was hurting. Words were said. We're both stubborn old mules, so it's been hard getting 'round to an apology."

Allegra bit her lip. "So you don't blame Darius."

"I wish I did. Might make it easier. But gods' honest truth is that my boy made his own choices. Bad ones, yes, but they were his. Best thing I can do is hope he's all right wherever he is right now." She fixed Allegra with her sharp, steely eyes. "You mark my words—it's the Bliss that did for him, not his gift. Not what you've got."

Allegra thought about the sextet in the Docklands, thought about the blood leaking from her ear like a warning. About Mallory Osker having her tailed as though she'd known all along it would eventually come to this.

If Bliss wasn't just a mildly addictive inhibitor, what else could it be used to accomplish? And by whom?

"I have to talk to Darius," Allegra said, apprehension slotting into her bones like a familiar ache. "I think… I think I know who the Slayer is."

She made to stand, but the room chose to join her, tipping over dangerously with the change of altitude. Allegra wobbled in place, sucking in air that didn't seem to reach her lungs. Mrs. L. was struggling to stand, too, her lips shaping words Allegra couldn't make out over the ringing in her eardrums.

She lurched as her knees gave out, tipping forth into the arms of oblivion. The world narrowed to a single disc of light, until that too died out.

Chapter Sixteen

"This still doesn't add up," Darius said, reclining in his desk chair. It was a last-ditch attempt and it left him pulling out his hair by the roots.

With Jasme's help, they had mapped out the murders geographically, then cross-referenced every witness, friend, family member or acquaintance the victims had in common. There were a few hits, but the evidence was largely circumstantial. Mr. Lucan, the Greys' housekeeper, happened to know the second victim's driver. Raine Kaelin's aunt had attended the same primary school as Mr. Weiss' accountant.

The links they'd found were as far from relevant as they were from interesting on a human level. It was another dead end.

Darius scrubbed a hand over his face. He felt tired, but going home the once hadn't helped, so he wasn't trying that again no matter how hard Jasme implied, cajoled or outright told him to call it a night.

"You look like death warmed over," she protested when he sent to her refill his coffee mug. "I'm afraid you'll start decomposing soon and then I'll be running after you, picking up the pieces."

Darius rolled his eyes. "That's not actually possible." Besides, he'd woken up to an empty bed. He didn't want to head back to the apartment.

"Are you a pathologist now?"

"I have one on speed dial."

Jasme squinted at him, her gaze flinty with disbelief. "For real?"

It would have been a very interesting use of his phonebook if that was the case, but Darius was forced to admit he didn't. "Annoy me and I'll just make you call Rhodes."

"It's, like, three in the morning." Jasme mock-yawned, flopping down into a plastic chair. In truth, it was closer to five. "I'm pretty sure he's still in bed. As—"

"—I should be, yes. You've said already. Be more original."

"Is that what you pay me for?"

"Technically *I* don't pay you anything," Darius pointed out. "You work for the city of Arcadia and its fine, tax-paying citizens." And whatever donors decided to sponsor the APU directly to get exemptions.

Jasme nodded. "I'm sure they mind very much that their cops don't have any real comedic chops. I know when I was growing up I kept wishing the law would be more like a Brady Bunch episode."

Darius glanced over at her, frowning incredulously. "You know what that is?"

"I've seen reruns," Jasme explained. "Excerpts, anyway. Are you here to quiz me on my knowledge of archaic vid-reels or solve crime?" She was grinning behind her mug.

"I'm not getting very far on the crime solving." His head felt heavy, eyelids drooping, but he knew that if he went home he'd only be lying in bed, staring up at the ceiling and imagining the files he could peruse while at the office. Imagining Allegra in his arms, all warm and soft—never pliant, but he liked that about her, too.

There was an answer in here somewhere. Every piece of evidence had been collected, every testimony checked and double-checked. They'd even had an empath weigh in for gods' sakes!

"And there it is," Jasme cried.

Darius startled. "There's what?"

"I was waiting how long it would take you to think about Allegra. Fifteen minutes. Congrats, boss, I think that's a new record."

For a rookie cop, she must have felt very secure in Darius' ability to distinguish playful ribbing from disrespect. Either that or Jasme simply didn't care. She was a clever young woman embarking on a career that didn't pay very well and presented considerable risk. It wasn't entirely outside the realm of possibility that she had decided to pursue other avenues for professional growth.

It didn't stop Darius from shooting her a glare. "If you've got something to say, say it."

Jasme shrugged unconvincingly. "She's nice?"

"Yes," Darius agreed almost mechanically. "Is that all?"

"And she's hot."

This time, Darius said nothing. He was sure that his expression gave him away. Impossible not to think that Allegra looked like a drowned cat when she was all decked up in those ridiculous shirts, her hair sticking out like a mop, but when she'd lain naked in Darius' bed she'd been more beautiful to him than any woman, ever.

If he closed his eyes, Darius could still see the way moonlight had painted her body in hues of blue and silver, the way she'd shivered as they'd rocked together.

He couldn't afford to think about that now.

"Sir, don't take this the wrong way, but I have to ask…" Jasme bit her lip. "Do you trust Allegra's input?" Like Darius, she had read the file and knew all about Allegra's history.

"Prostitution and possession of narcotics is nothing compared—"

"I know," Jasme interjected, hastily brushing an unruly strand of auburn hair behind her ear. "I just meant that— she's a high-powered empath, boss. I've never heard of another level seven walking free. And she can still talk and function like a normal person."

The wording stung. "Of course she's normal," Darius heard himself say, defending Allegra even though it was probably the last thing she wanted from him.

There was nothing wrong with her, she just happened to

be blessed with a particularly strong intuition.

Jasme nodded. "Sure, but my point is—"

"That she should be a drooling, sedated mess locked up in some government facility somewhere?"

Osker might have tiptoed around that sad reality and given Allegra reason to suspect that the worst thing she had coming was a minimum jail sentence in a low-security prison. Darius hadn't had the heart to correct the threat, but Jasme wasn't wrong. A level seven empath was a prize he couldn't imagine a business-savvy type like Osker simply releasing into the wild.

"I don't know why she's so well-adjusted," he said, sighing. "She pops Bliss like candy. I've seen her... But she's not *hopeless* without it."

"You've seen her off the meds?"

Darius nodded. He wouldn't give details, but he could admit to standing beside a level seven empath when she wasn't drugged to the high heavens and living to tell the tale. "She's fully conscious, you know. Coherent. Maybe a little slurred, but Veland looks worse after a few beers than Allegra did when she went off the Bliss."

"Were there other symptoms?" Jasme pressed. "You know, depression, erratic mood swings?"

Darius was glad she didn't ask about any promiscuous episodes. Bliss was a common party drug for non-empaths. It heightened arousal, awakened the senses—and most importantly, it lowered inhibitions. He tried not to think about Allegra coupling sex for money with access to the pills.

At the end of the day, it wasn't so different from their non-relationship.

"What's with the twenty questions?" Darius deflected. "What are you asking me here?" And more importantly, why? He didn't think Jasme was in the deputy commissioner's pocket, but stranger things had happened.

He watched as Jasme hopped out of her seat.

"Something I was reading earlier... This research thing

on Bliss withdrawal symptoms and what happens when an empath stops using. It's supposed to be pretty gruesome." She rifled through her tablet as she spoke, fingers skimming down the touch screen keyboard before Darius could stop her. "Here, I've got it — 'known symptoms of DT from Bliss include nausea, paranoid delusions, volatile moods and possible violent episodes. The user is often overwhelmed by a heightened acuity to the collective's emotional shifts. In high-level empaths, this can degenerate into self-harm or violence against others'."

Jasme glanced up.

"What is it? I left my mind-reading powers in my other trousers."

"Projection," Jasme clarified. There was a level of confidence in her voice that Darius didn't often hear.

He felt the wispy hairs on his forearms stand at attention. The last time he heard the word in conjunction with chronic empathy, Bliss had been a legal drug, marketed to people like Harlan. "You got your hands on serious research into outward projection of Acute Empatheia Nervosa?" Darius asked, lowering his voice. It was all he could do not to glance around the bullpen. The walls had ears around here.

"No, but —"

"Then you shouldn't trust every bullshit article you see online. Let's get back to the case."

Jasme scoffed. "This *is* the case. We're collaborating with a woman who should be barely functional even when she's on medication and here you are telling me she's perfectly functional without it."

"You're twisting my words," Darius protested sharply. He didn't know how else to manage his guilt. "I didn't say perfectly functional, she's definitely overwhelmed... Just not to the point of going, you know, crazy." He remembered the warmth of Allegra's body against his, her soft voice whispering promises of pleasures untold if only he gave in. She hadn't been too overwhelmed for that.

"I didn't read about the projection of Acute Empatheia

Nervosa online," Jasme said, more quietly.

"What?"

"I read it in your file."

Darius gave that a moment to sink in. Jasme made to speak again, but he stopped her short. "We're going to come back to how that's even possible in a minute," he bit out coldly. "What exactly is it you think you know, Jasme? Speak up, now's not the time to be shy."

She might have been an extraordinarily clever girl, but this was a mistake and she seemed to realize it. Darius watched her throat work as she gathered her wits. "Boss, when you were questioned in connection with your husband's disappearance eight years ago, you mentioned a series of incidents that made you believe he was – for lack of a better word – manipulating your behavior. As you believed empaths are able to do."

Like a cat, she landed right back on her feet again, leaving Darius to grapple with the slippery, shorter end of the stick. Maybe there was hope for a future Deputy Commissioner Sarli just yet.

"What's the question?" Darius pressed her.

To her credit, Jasme didn't flinch from the shut-mouth tone. "*Do* you believe it's possible for empaths to influence a person's state of being?"

"There's no evidence to support that assertion. Anyone who says differently is either a crackpot or a conspiracy theorist – which are often the same thing."

Jasme said nothing. She was waiting for an actual answer. It would've been easier to oblige if not for the lump in Darius' throat. He tried to swallow past it.

"I don't have any proof, but like you said, I was married to an empath." He still was, legally speaking. "I know what I felt when we fought, when we – did other things. He'd been taking Bliss for a while, back when it wasn't called Bliss and the PharmaCorps didn't hoard their supplies like gold. Every time he'd go off the meds, there would be incidents. We experimented with the limits of his abilities when he was in the mood for it, but when he was conscious of what he was doing nothing seemed to happen."

"It had to be involuntary," Jasme echoed.

"Something like that. And now if we're done prying into my personal life…"

Jasme bulldozed past his attempt at shutting down the conversation. "Did you ever wonder why the PharmaCorps ever stopped manufacturing Bliss? I mean, the recipe's still out there, floating around, and the need for some kind of inhibitor hasn't decreased in the past decade."

"I assume it's because surgery has proven more effective." It was also more expensive and forced empaths to register on committee-approved lists in order to be eligible. There was no mystery. PharmaCorps had stopped offering the drug to avoid competition with a more expensive product.

Jasme wasn't listening. A faraway look had entered her eyes and she was biting her bottom lip. She had never seemed more like a kid—a trick of light Darius blamed entirely on his aging eyes. "What if it was the other way around?" she murmured.

"What if what was the other way around?" Darius asked, unable to follow.

"What if the PharmaCorps pulled Bliss off the shelves *because* the drug inhibits the disease and they wanted to exacerbate it?"

Darius shook his head. "But that hasn't been the case. We've still got people using, only now it's the black market version that someone's cooking up in their kitchen."

"Which is coming from where? Mars?"

PharmaCorps warehouses, Darius had always assumed.

He wasn't sure, he didn't run the narcotics beat and didn't want to know who had gotten his ex-husband hooked on the illegal stuff, anyway. If not for the street drug, more kids would be on the lists and groups lobbying for equal access to the procedure would have a better chance of getting things done.

He needed to believe that.

The expression transmuting Jasme's features told him there was another, more obvious possibility that he hadn't considered. "What is it?" he asked, not sure he really wanted to know. "We're drifting a little far from—"

"We're really not, boss." Jasme swept back her hair and turned her tablet around so he could see the screen. "Acute Empatheia Nervosa causes behavioral alterations if left untreated, right? Read the next line."

Darius squinted at the screen, thinking that he could probably get Jasme reassigned somewhere nice when he was finally fired. Perhaps Veland might want someone to bother him. He was always complaining about lacking resources.

At Jasme's instigation, he read.

"'Some chemical interactions can exacerbate symptoms. Such chemicals include'—I'm not going to read that, I can't pronounce it—'properties paradoxically found in the street drug known as...Bliss.'"

Darius felt the blood drain from his face.

"Bliss was never meant to be an *antidote*," Jasme said, hushed and urgent, trying to convince him. "It's—I don't know what you'd call it—hair of the dog?"

Darius reached for the tablet. "Where did you find this?"

"Hedworth Levin's personal cache." This time, Jasme' smile was not self-satisfied half as much as it was keen. "The plot thickens, right? Do you need me to—?"

"Yes," said Darius.

Sure enough, Mr. Levin had apparently gotten his enterprising hands on a study that argued that prolonged exposure to Bliss had the power to awaken and develop Acute Empatheia Nervosa in those who already suffered from a predisposition to the disease.

Jasme was already on the holoscreen, pulling up every victim's medical records. "None of them were diagnosed with AEN at birth," she said, her hands flying over the keyboard buttons, "except Trina Grey."

"How did we not see that before?"

194

"She was marked as a level one," Jasme answered, shrugging. "Don't look so shocked, apparently I'm a level one. Do you know what that means? It means I'm just that much grumpier when I'm PMSing."

"Thanks for that."

"You're welcome." Jasme didn't even glance away from the screen. "Hey, boss?"

"Hmm?"

"Did something happen with you and Allegra?"

"That part where I derailed your questions earlier? That was a sign I didn't want you pestering me for an answer." And not answering now was only going to make Jasme more curious. *Gods protect me from clever children.*

Jasme grinned. "She's nice."

"Which would be valuable information if we were talking about a dog," Darius scoffed, "but Allegra Avenson is a very powerful empath. And if we're right, she's something of a national treasure…" Allegra had been taking Bliss for years. She'd taken it that first night, when she had come to see Darius. She had been drugged and volatile and horny — and Darius had taken advantage.

The thought was a cold shower. Darius had screwed her against the front door, unable to contain a sudden wave of arousal that had simply come out of nowhere. Allegra hadn't been off her meds. She'd been high on Bliss.

"Boss?"

Blinking, Darius refocused his attention on his partner. It couldn't be that simple — could it? "I just remembered something Allegra said about everyone lying." She'd sounded so sure, too, though there was no evidence to support the claim. "She said that every single one of our witnesses was lying about the way they'd found the victims."

Everyone, Allegra had said, from Ms. Weiss, to Lucan, and maybe even Raine Kaelin, was spinning tales. Motive and means didn't follow. Unless — Darius felt as though someone had pulled the rug from under his feet. He was free-falling, tumbling blind.

"Did Levin's report say anything about Bliss as a form of mind control?"

"Of users?" Jasme asked, rolling her chair to grab the tablet for another look. "I don't recall any—"

"No, I mean of others. For example, the people around them?" If Allegra had projected desire onto Darius that night, could someone who was very sad, possibly even suicidal, project despair onto another person? Could they force someone to commit murder?

The penny dropped. "Suicide by proxy," Darius said, already on his feet.

"Holy— Wait, where're you going?"

"I'm going to interview the Greys' housekeeper again. He should be at work already." The whole family had relocated to a resort until they were finished mourning, but Lucan was the tireless sort. He took great pride in not missing a single day of work in his life. "You stay on this thing. And get Ms. Weiss in as soon as possible. If I'm right, we're going to need to shake them down a little."

Jasme frowned. "Why? Boss, I don't understand. What's going on?"

His trench coat flapping open, Darius was already jogging through the labyrinth of empty desks in the bullpen. "I think I know who the murderers are," he called over his shoulder.

He trusted Jasme to put the pieces of the puzzle together.

The precinct doors slid open before him, admitting the crisp evening breeze. There was only a faint whiff of sulfur in the air, like a particularly cloying *amuse-bouche* that most definitely didn't remind Darius of Allegra's abandoned warehouse in the Docklands.

Chapter Seventeen

Allegra's head was swimming as she pulled herself upright on the floral chintz sofa. There was a bitter desert in her mouth, the remnants of Mrs. L.'s spiked lemonade long erased. She swallowed in a dry throat, ran a hand over her face and nearly smacked herself in the mouth in the process.

It was proving hard to gauge distances.

"You're off your meds," Mrs. L. growled uncharitably from an armchair at her right. The end of a cigarette glowed gold and amber between her fingertips, marking the precursor to a long, misty exhale.

Allegra nearly jumped halfway to the ceiling, startled by the sound of her voice.

"I'm—what?" What was she still doing here? She remembered running to Darius' apartment and scaring his neighbors, definitely recalled sleeping with him—but wasn't sure how she had wound up taking shelter in Mrs. Ley's living room again.

Had there been another scorcher?

She glanced through the windows beyond the window boxes, discovered that the sky was barely beginning to brighten in the east. Dawn was slowly making its way into Arcadia.

It was almost morning. So what the hell was going on?

Allegra pinched the bridge of her nose. Her thoughts were like threads she couldn't seem to seize between slippery fingers, her vision foggy. She only barely made out movement on her right as the imperturbable Mrs. L. staggered to her feet.

"You passed out 'bout an hour ago," she explained wryly. "Nearly had me calling the police before I realized that'd probably make things harder on you. You want a drink?"

"Think that's what got me in trouble the first time," Allegra drawled. "You're unsafe at any speed, Mrs. L. What was in that stuff, anyway?"

Mrs. L. ignored her. "Quit whining and get up. We're driving to the precinct."

A flood of weariness hit Allegra, settling like cement in her shoes. "Why?"

"You did something illegal, sweat pea. Don't think I went and forgot that just 'cause I'm senile. Up you go." For an octogenarian, Mrs. L. proved remarkably spry in getting to her feet.

She would have nudged and prodded Allegra until she followed suit were it not for Allegra obliging before she could get the chance.

"We'll get Darius on your side," Mrs. L. said. "Don't you worry."

"Somehow I don't think he'll be very excited to hear I, uh... To find out that I—" *Killed six people.* Allegra couldn't get it out, but the memory was there, etched in vague shades of gray and muted misery, about as harmless as an ice pick wrapped in silk. It was probably just her brain trying to keep trauma at bay—self-preservation at its finest.

Failure to remember every step she'd taken between running home and leveling half a dozen men didn't make her crime any less grave or any less real, whatever Osker had said.

Allegra remembered the moment when her fear had gotten the better of her, when it had become a weapon. She hadn't known something like that was even conceivable, much less as a concealed weapon at her fingertips. And she remembered something else, too—Mallory Osker had been here. But why? Allegra staggered to her feet, running a trembling hand over chapped lips. It was a good idea to get Darius involved. He could spring her for Bliss, at least, and stem some of the ugly itching Allegra could feel blooming under her skin.

For the prison thing, there was nothing, no reprieve or clemency. Darius would do what he had to do and Allegra would take it like a big girl. She scratched at the inside of her wrist, wincing when her nails scored red welts into the skin.

"I don't feel right," she told Mrs. L. "Feels like my skin's too tight."

"That's the pills for you." There was no mercy in Mrs. L.'s voice, no compassion.

She snorted when Allegra made to get behind the wheel of her battered yellow Volkswagen. "What do you think you're doing, kid? I'm not letting you drive me off a bridge. Back seat—and don't you forget the seat belt."

"You're kidding." It didn't look like she was kidding.

Allegra dallied uselessly on the sidewalk for another half second before scooting dejectedly into the passenger seat. Between a senior citizen who was half machine and a junkie hurting, quite literally, for her next dose, Arcadia's pedestrians would be lucky to make it out alive.

The early hour played in their favor. There was barely any foot traffic at the crossings, and the few cars they encountered dashed past and out of sight before Mrs. L. could pull any risky maneuvers.

Allegra still winced, still gritted her teeth. It might have been just the withdrawal making it worse, or anticipation getting the better of her were it not for Mrs. L.'s athletic braking.

They parked just outside the precinct—sideways, with the two front wheels on the sidewalk.

"I don't see his car," Allegra said, staggering to her feet. She was sweating through her bloodstained shirt even though the night was cold and dark and full of whispers.

Mrs. L. snorted. "Maybe he took the bus. You go in."

"Aren't you coming with me?"

"I've seen my fair share of police," Mrs. L. shot back,

cantankerous even in this. "I'll wait a while, 'case Leon ain't around."

That was kind of her, Allegra thought, but kindness didn't alter the path she was making her walk. "I can still turn myself in."

"But you won't."

"But I won't." Not to anyone who wasn't Darius. At least with him, there would be a friendly face to walk her into jail.

"Hey," Mrs. L. called from inside the car. "Do you remember what you said before you fainted?"

Allegra frowned. "No…" She steadied herself against the hood of the car. "Was it important?"

She watched Mrs. L. purse her thin, chapped lips. "Find that boy." It was sound advice, but not the answer she'd been hoping for.

She tried not to let fear get the better of her as she stepped through the sliding doors of the APU headquarters. Too much time spent in the Docklands meant anxiety whenever she came face to face with the law. That the night watchman ensconced behind chicken wire and Plexiglas was dozing when she walked in did nothing to ease the jack-rabbiting pace of Allegra's heart.

"Uh, excuse me…" Allegra tapped the glass for want of any other way to get the guard's attention. "Sir?"

"Allegra!" Jasme called out, her tangled hair visible as she rounded the corner. "I thought that was you I saw on the security cameras. What're you doing here?"

The watchman's voice warbled, distorted, through the speakers. "You know this one?"

"Yeah," Jasme said. "I'll vouch for her."

Bad idea. The inner door slid open, durasteel and reinforced glass giving way to Jasme's tepid smile. Anxiety thrummed in her bones like radioactive energy.

Allegra staggered a little under the force of it. *Focus. You only have so much time before you forget which way is up.* "Is, uh, is Darius around?"

Jasme shook her head. "He was, but he left a little while ago. Said he'd cracked the case." Something in her voice told Allegra that she wasn't entirely at ease with that development. Her lips pressed together tightly as she waved Allegra to her desk. "You want to sit down? You don't look too hot. I swear, you just missed him…"

"Yeah, that keeps happening," Allegra drawled, but her attempt at a smirk fell well short of the mark.

Her head was hurting again, vision going blurry as she dropped into a chair. There was so much stuff in the precinct—residual frustration crawled over the furniture like swarms of flesh-eating ants, hollow despair wafted in eddies of smoke around her head.

Allegra covered her face with her hands. A paper bag would've done just as well.

She felt a hand touch her shoulder—and, with it, knowledge. The fear of not being taken seriously vibrated in Jasme's heart, but she was a confident kid, she'd pulled through after her parents died and she wasn't afraid to speak her mind if she felt it could help. Some might have said she was pushy and foul-mouthed, they could fuck off because Jasme might not have had parents to steer her true, but she had drive and no one held a monopoly on truth and— Allegra jerked as if slapped.

"Don't touch me," she choked.

Jasme had retreated back a step, hands held aloft in surrender. "Oh! You're dry, aren't you?"

No use denying it when the signs were written all across her face. The longer she sat there, the more she could feel Darius like a ghostly presence.

"Did Darius leave something for me?" Allegra asked and swallowed hard. She didn't know how to ask if Jasme knew that Darius supplied Allegra with drugs.

They were inside the APU headquarters, surrounded by cameras and the pregnant, infectious disdain that policemen and women like Jasme reserved for people in her position. One misstep and it could be game over.

Jasme said nothing, only reached into a pressure-locked drawer and produced a small plastic vial. She deposited the offending, illegal container on the table rather than set it into Allegra's waiting palm and stalked off into the break room.

Plausible deniability, Allegra realized, though whether it would stand up in a court of law, she couldn't say.

Skull pounding with the echo of her self-doubt, Allegra watched Jasme go. She waited a beat, then filched the Bliss off the desk and quietly popped the cap off with her thumb. There were five pills inside the vial, round and pink like rose petals, but rather than scoop one up as she was supposed to, Allegra upended the bottle into her mouth and did her best to gulp down the entirety of its contents. It took a little effort — the pills caught in her dry throat like peanuts.

She nearly choked on the disintegrating, crumbling capsules with their waxy, chemical flavor. It could be the height of irony, a junkie killed by their poison of choice. Any other day and Allegra might have obliged.

Not tonight. Allegra had swallowed worse things by virtue of her profession. Bliss would at least iron the jagged shards of clarity she could feel stabbing against her retinas, dust out the cobwebs.

"Here." Jasme held out a glass of water. She was back and Allegra hadn't even heard her footsteps across the sticky tile. She must have been more out of it than she'd thought.

"Thanks."

They sat in silence for a while, interrupted only by the sound of Allegra's greedy gulps, her unsubtle belch. She finished the water, breathing hard. "About Darius—"

"He left maybe ten, twenty minutes before I saw you on the monitors."

Allegra nodded. "And you're worried."

"Picked that up, did you?"

Like most all people who discovered the extent of Allegra's abilities when left unchecked, Jasme sounded less than pleased with this new development. A pity, because

Allegra had taken a liking to her in the short time they'd been collaborating.

"I think it might be my fault."

"How do you figure that?"

Tread carefully. Allegra grimaced. "If I say it's intuition, would you believe me?"

"Why wouldn't I? Plus, I'm pretty sure *I* wound him up," Jasme said, sighing. It wasn't quite an answer, but it was better than an outright dismissal. "He went off without backup. Could be that's not going to cause an issue, but Darius seems to think he's impervious to the risks of fieldwork." *And this,* she seemed to want to add, *despite recent events proving the contrary.*

Guilt followed on the heels of that uncharitable assessment, an endless, rolling wave of self-reproach that likely drew its source from events much further back in Jasme's past than Darius' latest bout of negligence. Allegra blinked, forcing the cumbersome sentiment aside with both hands. "Where did he go?"

"The Greys'," Jasme answered guilelessly. "We were working on finding a common link between the cases — other than the Bliss and the method of the crime, there doesn't seem to be one, as you know. So I started telling him about this report I found among Levin's personal effects that said Bliss can sometimes exacerbate more aggressive strains of Acute Empatheia Nervosa…"

"Wait, that's a real thing?" *Could Mrs. Ley be right?*

There had been rumors, back when a diagnosis was first offered, and more than a handful of pastors had come out in favor of ostracizing the sinners — because they had to be, no devout person could be thus afflicted — who pried into people's heads to reveal their secrets. Fortunately, the majority of parishioners were sane enough to give the government clerics the cold shoulder they deserved. Empaths like Allegra had only narrowly escaped mandatory commitment into mental institutions.

She didn't know what to do with the possibility that those

people might have been right in their forewarnings.

To think Darius believed them shone a light on their more fraught dealings. Suddenly he wasn't just a guy going through paranoia after fucking a hooker, he was one of *them* – a standard-bearer for the 'lock them up and throw away the key' brigade.

Allegra closed her eyes and opened them again. She was tumbling down the rabbit hole here. She needed an anchor.

She found it in Jasme's shrug, the shallow curve of her shoulders as they creaked from too many late nights followed by ridiculously early mornings. "To be honest," Jasme said, running a hand through the shaggy mane of her tangled, auburn hair, "I have no idea. Levin's report seemed to suggest so, and then I had to dredge up Darius' past… Now he's gone to see the Greys again and he told me to call in all our other persons of interest – and I don't know why, but I've got a really bad feeling."

Allegra shared it, like a crawling in the pit of her stomach. "Jasme, what exactly was the theory you were working with? That the victims, what? Killed themselves?"

"No, more like they strong-armed other people into doing it. Assisted suicide, if you will. Maybe not intentionally." Jasme grimaced. "At least that's what Darius seemed to think. I swear, sometimes I wish I could be like you and read minds."

Now there's a thought. "Trust me," Allegra said, "you don't."

She thought back to every testimony she'd reviewed, all those voices tight with grief, gazes furtive and red-rimmed. Lucan's testimony had become practically hostile when Darius inferred Trina Grey had been anything less than a saint. Weiss had proven overprotective of her dead nephew and answered questions with a thin veneer of suspicion, as if fearing entrapment.

Even Raine Kaelin, the hooker who'd found their last victim, had treated Allegra's questions with distrust. They were all so different and they were all plagued by so many competing emotions that Allegra hadn't been able to pluck out a single shared thread to untangle their motives.

All they really had in common was the Bliss.

"I guess," Jasme added quietly, as if following along with Allegra's racing thoughts, "Darius thinks we're not looking at an Angel of Death as such...but rather at people whose addiction *literally* killed them." She shrugged. "They were all high, that much we know for sure. And if the PharmaCorps buried research that suggests Bliss can be weaponized, then..."

Allegra swallowed hard, stretching herself out as far as she could through the shapeless, volatile shadows of the city, the invisible membrane that she could always feel pulsating around her when she wasn't high. Five million heartbeats, chorusing like the clash of cymbals. And somewhere at the heart of the clamor, the man who had once accused her of planting desire into his unwilling body.

"Call his cell," Allegra breathed.

"Why?"

"Because Darius is right." And what was more, he was in terrible danger.

Chapter Eighteen

"Mr. and Mrs. Grey are not in," Lucan said when he found Darius on his front step. It was said graciously enough, but the armor of proper etiquette couldn't conceal his confusion.

A house visit from an APU Detective, especially at this hour, was unusual. Darius hadn't even called ahead.

"Their daughters, too…"

"That's all right," Darius assured him. "It's you I wanted to see. May I come in?" He stopped short of nudging the door open all the way, but the message was clear.

After a moment's hesitation, the housekeeper obliged. "I was about to close up the house," he confessed, trying for apologetic and coming across as uncertain, even worried.

I'm starting to sound like Allegra. Darius eyed his fretting host with little sympathy.

"Can't this wait until the morning?"

A small, reluctant smile crept onto Darius' lips. "I'll only be a minute, I think. I'm going to talk for a bit and then you'll come to the precinct with me to make a statement."

"*Another?*" Lucan sounded justifiably exasperated. He had been called in twice already yet the police had been no help in providing answers, never mind catching Ms. Grey's murderer—a fact loudly and frequently deplored in the press, as the deputy commissioner enjoyed reminding Darius.

"This will be a different kind of statement."

Lucan eased the door shut behind Darius, perking up. "You've found Trina's murderer?"

"I think so. May I?" Darius gestured to a chair in the

atrium and sat down just as quickly. He hadn't slept more than a handful of hours in two days, only partly by volition. He was running on fumes.

The house was too dark for him to make out much more than the details closest at hand. A silver chandelier drooped from the ceiling, unlit at the moment, and the baroque imitation furniture seemed reserved for decorative purposes. The marble floors had been buffed clean, shining like glass underfoot, to say nothing of the ornate staircase that led the way up into what must have been the family's private domain.

As housekeeper, Lucan had his hands full.

"This is a nice place. You must feel lucky to work here."

"I do, Detective. I really don't understand what this is about. I was under the impression that you—"

Darius held up a hand. "You're in a hurry, I understand. I only ask if you're content with your position because Ms. Grey's death could cast a shadow on your future opportunities. No one likes to be reminded of death, especially in this town."

Lucan grew very still, the wrinkled crease around his eyes drawing sharp. "I have faith that my future employers won't hold this tragedy against me. But the question isn't relevant at the moment. I'm needed here."

"Indeed. You're very close to the Greys—but your favorite was the late Ms. Grey, correct?"

The heft of the housekeeper's gaze could have melted the polar icecaps had there been any ice left at either one. "I don't—yes, I suppose she was. I appreciated Trina's spirit. She was taken from us much too soon…"

"She was suffering from severe depression," Darius deadpanned. "And you knew. Did she ask you help hide her condition? Is that why you said nothing of her drug habit?"

"She didn't have a drug habit."

"We found the pills." Bottles and bottles, all obtained without prescription and concealed less than artfully

207

among her lingerie. Trina Grey had been no Bliss addict, true, but she had played fast and loose with her mental health for some time. "Did you procure the amphetamines on her behalf?"

Lucan fumed. "I don't know anything about that." He sounded sincere, if aggravated, but he wasn't denying the possibility that Trina Grey might have suffered from an excess of zeal as far as her academic performance was concerned.

"Did you have a sexual relationship with Ms. Grey?"

"Are you mad?" His outrage echoed around the foyer like a ricocheting bullet. "How dare you—" Lucan clenched his fists, as if he was barely restraining the desire to rearrange Darius' face. "Get out!"

It was a guilty kind of screech—a telltale sign that Darius was on the right path.

He levered forward, leaning over his own knees with palms pressed together in a loose hold. Almost forty and he still didn't know how to shy away from a brawl. "You were always there for her, weren't you? You listened when she told you about her ambitions and her fears, you tried to offer counsel. No one else had the time."

"I'm old enough to be her father!" Lucan protested, livid.

"Were," Darius corrected. It was like setting up a controlled detonation, but as long as there was only smoke in his eyes, he could cope with the deafening noise. "It's not uncommon. Probably better for her to latch on to you than anyone else…"

"You're sick."

Darius ignored the accusation. "Was that how you started procuring Bliss for her? Did she ask you or did you do it out of the goodness of your heart? Come now, Lucan, the cat's out of the bag. Don't pretend you didn't know that Trina was having trouble. You wanted to help, but you didn't want her taking amphetamines. They're a gateway drug, right? So you found a dealer who sold the next best thing. *Bliss*. You handed her a loaded gun!"

"I didn't—"

"Stop lying!"

It happened so quickly. One moment Darius was shouting back and the next, Lucan had him by the lapels and he was wrestling Darius out of his seat, shouting, "I didn't know it was Bliss!" The whites of his eyes caught the faint glare of light streaming through the atrium windows. He seemed horrified and horrific at the same time, a man at the end of his tether. But it was too late—the confession had already passed his lips. "I-I didn't know... She said her friends bought from that dealer. She told me it would be stims."

"But it wasn't." Darius felt the hands folded tight in his trench coat unwind and release.

Staggering, Lucan lurched out of the way, pressing his back to the wall. "No."

"And you didn't know she'd take the whole stash. How many pills was it? Ten, twenty?" There was no answer from Lucan, and the exact quantity was only tangentially relevant. "It *was* suicide," Darius said, softer now. "Trina Grey took her own life. You were just a means to an end."

The housekeeper said nothing. It couldn't have been easy. He had watched the Grey children grow from dolls to graduation robes, every day keeping their manse running like a well-oiled machine. When the youngest Ms. Grey had fallen off the wagon, he'd done the only thing he could—he had tried to help. Here was the result.

Perhaps there was an easing of the spirit in having the truth come out. Darius sighed. "There never was a Bliss Slayer, in this or any of the other cases. Just accidents and suicides. And collateral damage."

Lucan laughed, suddenly and hoarsely, the sound roaring from somewhere deep in his chest and erupting with more grief than Darius had ever seen the man express until now. He opened his mouth to ask what was so funny but was interrupted by the shrill ringing of his phone.

Jasme's picture flashed on screen, her auburn bangs all but covering her keen eyes.

"Oh, come now, Detective... You know as well as I do," Lucan said, "that Trina didn't die from an overdose. That she was *strangled*." Darius was too busy wrestling with his phone to note the wary condescension that slithered into Lucan's voice. By the time he caught on, it was already too late.

Momentum carried Darius into the nearest wall and from there to the floor, the back of his head striking the tile hard as he landed. Disorientation followed with exquisite swiftness. Vision swimming, Darius put up an arm to cover his head — experience dictated that an assailant usually went for the face, wrongly believing that it was the easiest way to a kill. Lucan was no different, although he had the foresight to grab Darius by the jaw and neck and slam him back into the floor for a second and third time rather than maul him with his fists. It was an effective strategy.

Pain exploded through Darius' nervous system, momentarily paralyzing him where he lay. He recognized the alarming sensation of being trapped in his own body from the jewelry store.

This is what you get for playing action hero, old man.

When he figured out how to move again, Lucan had him by the throat, both hands locked in a vise-grip and resolutely engaged in cutting off his air supply.

Darius struck out with an elbow, then his fist, then his other fist. The longer he delayed, gasping, the more disoriented he would become, so it was imperative to dislodge the other man quickly.

On the fourth hit, Lucan's nose cracked audibly. He cried out as he fell to the side and Darius found he could breathe again. The urge to cough rattled his body, making it that much harder to regain control of his limbs. By the time he struggled to his feet, he had lost sight of his assailant.

The shadows in the foyer didn't help. Darius steadied herself against a side table, the potted orchid artfully displayed upon it teetering slightly.

He needed to call for backup — that much was obvious. He

intended to, but his phone wasn't in his hand anymore. Nor was it in his pocket. It must have fallen when Lucan was trying to split open his skull. *Okay, no big.* That meant no backup. It meant he was in this alone, unless Jasme decided to crash the party unannounced.

Darius squinted into the shadows. There was blood on the floor, evidence that when his fist had collided with Lucan's nose, he had struck true. That was the last time he got to be smug about hitting the guy, though, because on his next breath he found Lucan lunging for him, face transfigured by the blood that stained his cheeks and chin and leaked out of his mouth in a grotesque outpouring.

The nose was one thing, Darius realized, but apparently he'd knocked out a couple of teeth, too. His knuckles ached when he tried to clench his hands into fists again.

It didn't matter, he didn't get the chance to strike out twice.

Lucan must've found a vase somewhere and he lobbed it at Darius with a hoarse, defiant cry. The earthenware caught Darius' arm and the side of his face as it shattered. More compromisingly, it sent Darius tripping over his own feet and into a gold-leaf mirror that cracked as it dropped onto Darius' head. Shards skittered around the floor and caught under his shoes. Something warm and tangy sluiced down his face, but there wasn't much pain. He was less hobbled by impact than by his own clumsiness.

Age and a desk job meant he'd lost whatever spryness he'd had as a young man. It showed when Lucan came for him again, armed with a piece of glass no bigger than Darius' palm. Stubborn self-preservation had him striking out with a foot just in time to pop Lucan's kneecap – a good hit, though with little practical application. Adrenaline had taken Lucan past the point of pain. He lunged for Darius again, snarling and stabbing the air like a wild thing.

The trench coat came in handy as their bodies collided in a haphazard heap. It protected Darius from most of the damage of the sharp, jagged mirror fragments. There was nothing to be done about the shard still clutched in Lucan's bleeding hand. Darius watched it slide ever closer to his jugular. He tried to offer resistance, straining with every breath. It was no good. His strength was leached. He couldn't fend off the assault.

He was going to die here. *Oh gods.*

A sudden blast of white light speared the darkness.

Lucan glanced, rabbit-quick, to the source of that unnatural glare.

Darius didn't think, he liberated a hand and scrabbled for the nearest weapon—a shard of porcelain no bigger than his fist. He closed his fingers around it tightly.

With an exhausted, desperate surge of effort, Darius drove the piece of debris into Lucan's throat. Blood gushed tepid and slick onto his face and hands, stinging where it dripped into his eyes, but Darius hardly noticed. A tidal wave of wood splinters ricocheted from the door as it gave way to an APU durasteel ram.

The eerie glow of SWAT-manned flashlights found him laid out on the floor, panting under a dead man's still-warm body.

* * * *

Veland's bedside manner sucked, but Darius submitted with far greater ease to his ministrations than he had to the paramedics'. Maybe it was a sense of kinship—Veland had come crashing through the door in a cardigan and slacks, looking for all the world as if he'd been called in while having a barbecue in his back yard—or maybe it was the fact that Veland accompanied scrubbing the blood off Darius' face with a steady stream of vaguely berating questions.

"The hell were you thinking going out into the field without your partner? This isn't the Wild West. Why do we bother throwing rookies at you if you're just going to leave them behind when it counts? Gods-damned—" And on it went for a while in that vein, until Darius finally found an opening.

"She called it in, didn't she? Jasme?"

Veland nodded gruffly. "Must've had a sixth sense about your sorry ass. Said we had a man down. Units answered from all the way across town."

Despite the sting of his busted lip, Darius found himself trying to smile. "I'm touched."

Veland's reaction was immediate. "She didn't say it was *you*, asshole. If I'd known, I would've stopped for coffee and a bagel... Ah, here's your fairy godmother now."

No sooner had he finished speaking that Darius saw Jasme zig-zagging between parked cars toward the ambulance. She wasn't alone. Bleached-blonde hair standing on end, Allegra was trying to keep up with Jasme's quick footwork. Every second had her falling behind a little farther, perhaps intentionally. Where had she come from?

It was then that Darius saw the battered yellow Volkswagen Beetle on the other side of the street, its solar panels dusty and the inside drenched in shadow. He didn't have to see the plates to know who it belonged to.

"Boss!" Jasme threw her arms around his neck. "I thought you were dead..."

"Some of us were hoping," Veland snorted, retreating to the side.

Darius flipped him off with a bandaged hand. "Think Jasme's trying to finish the job." She let go, but not before play-punching his shoulder with a loose fist. "Thanks," Darius told her, and meant it more than pride allowed him to say.

His young partner smiled crookedly. "I had help."

Hands thrust into her pockets, Allegra stood some distance away, her lips stained cinnamon-dark and her eyes red. Had she been crying or— Darius curbed the thought. She must have gone by the precinct to get her fix and found Jasme there, fretting.

It had been a coincidence, a stroke of luck.

213

"Thank you," Darius told her, trying to sound official and reserved, more like a wounded detective than a doped-up, clingy boyfriend who'd thought that he'd never see his beloved again.

The paramedics had pumped him full of painkillers, which excused the nonsense washing up in the wake of his latest adrenaline rush.

Allegra hitched up her shoulders. "Anytime."

Darius returned her grin instinctively. *Gods, I wish I could hold you right now.*

There was a flurry of flashes and microphones being thrust over the police barrier as they wheeled Lucan's body out. The black bag he'd been thrust into made it impossible to see his face, but by morning the media would likely have a full profile and the whisper sheets would be denouncing him for a traitor as well as a would-be cop killer.

"That him?" Jasme asked quietly.

Darius nodded, but it was Veland who answered. "Good riddance. One less freak on the streets. Now we can go back to fining drivers who park illegally and tracking down patrons who don't leave a tip. Arcadians will sleep easy knowing the Bliss Slayer's been caught."

"What?" Darius felt his breath catch. "But that wasn't—"

Veland arched an eyebrow. "Tell it to the cameras. The deputy commissioner's already released a statement. I hear she's already booked on the morning shows." He fished his jumper off the stretcher and arranged it on his shoulders like a cashmere cape. It made him look ridiculous, but Darius didn't have any breath left for laughter.

Lucan had acted out of fear, to protect Trina Grey's memory and his own livelihood, but he wasn't a serial killer, let alone one who hunted Bliss addicts all across Arcadia. Darius opened his mouth to say as much, but Veland was leaving and Jasme was busy checking her tablet for online chatter and he realized with some dismay that there was nothing he could tell them they didn't already know.

A hand caught Darius'. It was Allegra, surreptitiously

standing beside him with an unreadable expression on her ashen face.

"You okay?" Darius whispered, squeezing her fingers.

Allegra met his eyes searchingly, but said nothing.

"I know you had something to do with the fact that I'm still here. I'm grateful," Darius said. "It's not the first time. I'll make it up to you somehow."

The demurral was swift. "Don't be stupid. It was Jasme who put it all together when you didn't pick up your cell. Always have to go make things more complicated than they are..." Allegra put on a good show, but Darius wasn't fooled.

"I'm beginning to know your tells," he pointed out in a low voice. "Admit it. You're a little bit relieved. I bet I know why."

Allegra licked her lips. "You do, do you?"

"We closed our case. That means you get to have your surgery." The deputy commissioner had promised and, for all that she was slippery as a snake, Darius intended to hold her to her word.

He gave Allegra's hand another squeeze, lazily stroking his thumb over her bony knuckles. "You'll get to see what it's like being one of us normals. Excited?"

Allegra smiled wryly. "You know it."

It might have been the painkillers or a trick of the flashing, blue-red police lights, but Darius could've sworn that Allegra was blinking away tears.

Chapter Nineteen

Darius scrubbed a hand through his shower-damp hair. "One of these days we'll make it to bed, won't we?"

"One of these days," Allegra agreed, grinning with half a mouth. She was wearing his shirt with her scuffed sneakers — because the tile was cold and his slippers were like scuba diving paddles — and for once she liked the way she looked under the glow of unflattering neon spotlights.

Her roots were growing in, dark where the rest of her hair was silver-blonde. The dark circles under her eyes had begun to fade, too, subject to sleeping like the dead in a plastic chair at Darius' bedside when they took him in for tests and again later, at home, while he napped on the couch. It was there that she had joined him a little under an hour ago, her clothes scattered across his living room floor like dead skin.

She'd read every quiver of arousal and apprehension to cross his mind as he went from slumber to wide awake. Exhaustion had quickly given way to interest and they had made love like two people who were too tired to put much effort into it. Darius was still bruised from his latest bout of heroics, his skin marred with mottled splotches of color where he'd enjoyed a face full of broken glass. His wounds had yet to heal, but they would. He'd jumped when Allegra pressed her lips to the marks.

"Does it hurt?" Allegra had asked, pulling back.

"No. I keep expecting it to, but — no." His eyes soft, he'd combed his fingers through her hair. "This must be what it's like when you're on your meds."

The thought came to her as she turned off the sink tap that

Bliss had once been the very thing Darius most dreaded about her. Now it was legitimate medication and no one doubted her need for it.

"Darius," Allegra started, but there was no time. Darius slid arms around her hips, his strong, hirsute chest pressing against the wings of her shoulders.

He murmured, "Hmm?" but the glide of fingers across the V of her pelvis told Allegra he wasn't really interested in conversation. That was probably for the best. After what he'd been through, the doctors said he needed rest and relaxation. News that he'd been deceived wouldn't meet the mark.

Allegra sighed. "You're getting me all wet," she muttered, aiming for playful nagging. She could do that now. Darius had all but said he wanted her around. And if she was getting her surgery, then maybe it could work out between them.

Maybe they had a shot.

"I like you wet," Darius whispered into the shell of her ear. He met her gaze in the mirror, some strange, unfamiliar sentiment hovering his eyes, just outside of Allegra's ability to decode. "I like *you*," he said, more quietly than before.

"Honey, you're so drugged up you'd probably like a corgi just as much…" Allowing for any other possibility was a dangerous thing. She couldn't afford to let herself get tangled in that web, so she took Darius' hand and pressed it down between her thighs by way of distraction. "This is more in line with what I had in mind."

She wasn't sixteen anymore. Being *liked* didn't count for much, but she could feel Darius' cock against her tailbone, a solid, warm weight. He was aroused—not hard, not yet, but getting there quickly enough. He wasn't alone.

Sex worked well for them. For Allegra. All she needed to do was lean her hips into Darius' talented touch and let him take her away as steadied herself against the sink. The brush of his lips against her nape was incendiary, sending streams of liquid fire down her spine. It delighted her. It turned her on.

She was glad to feel Darius dispose of his towel. It was skin on skin after that, with only his wrinkled shirt to separate them. The scent of him was everywhere, a constant that Allegra could cling to as she splayed her legs a little wider in invitation. Darius caught on fast. It wasn't long before she felt him press a finger into her body, quickly followed by a second when she demanded it.

"You're so tight," he breathed into her ear.

"You love it," Allegra shot back, because bruises and a near-death experience didn't mean he got to have the last word.

Darius drew the lobe of her ear between his lips, flicking his tongue against the sensitive nub of flesh as if he knew it would make Allegra moan—maybe he'd been paying attention. "I do," he said, all devilish smirk and slow, tender strokes working to undo her defenses where she stood.

Don't say stuff like that, Allegra almost admonished. Nothing offensive in it, but she could feel intensely how sincere he was. He meant it. Painkillers could make him talkative, could take away the agony of getting pummeled with a porcelain vase, but they couldn't mutate mere lust into something else.

Allegra closed her eyes in a vain attempt at simply pretending she hadn't heard him the first time. If she didn't acknowledge it, it wasn't there—just like the monsters under the bed or the men she'd killed, one way or another.

It was the height of the absurd, but even as her morbid thoughts settled, Allegra could sense her orgasm within reach. She tightened her grip around the sink, fists white-knuckled with effort as her body squeezed down on Darius' fingers. She wanted his cock, his mouth—she never wanted him to stop what he was doing. Somehow, he had figured out that grinding the heel of his palm in time with the steady thrust of his fingers into her pussy was the way to get her off.

Clever boy, Allegra thought, only distantly aware that

she was moaning his name, begging for Darius to let her come, as though his permission ever entered the equation. She was so much more than *just* an empath. She was — she could do things that would make Darius' hair stand on end if he knew. *I could tear down your whole world*, Allegra mused, clinging to his forearm when nothing else could hold her upright.

Darius didn't let her down. He tightened his hold around her waist, gasping hotly against her ear when Allegra ignited under his sweet, merciless torture.

She couldn't say how long he held her like that. It might have been seconds, an hour. In the end, Allegra simply turned in his arms and let him hoist her legs up around his hips, like that first night when Darius really should've trusted his instincts. It wasn't his fault. Allegra had dragged him into this and now she was too scared to let him go.

They fell into bed sweat-soaked and boneless. Allegra, on her third orgasm of the afternoon, couldn't stop clinging.

"You okay?" Darius mumbled against her nape, one heavy arm draped across her midriff. He was too sharp for his own good. Didn't he know that Allegra was trouble?

"Yeah. Just thinking."

It was the wrong answer to give. Darius pinned an elbow against the pillows, levering up to watch her with soft black eyes. If she'd left, cut loose when she had the chance the night of the massacre, she would've regretted this sight. The gentle tug of Darius' fingers through her tangled blonde hair wasn't bad either.

"What about?" he asked, like she'd known he would.

"How this works," Allegra said, deflecting. "Where we go from here... You're back on active duty starting next week, right?" The APU didn't believe in giving its officers any sort of real vacation, not even when they netted a serial murderer to everyone's satisfaction.

Darius nodded. "Which gives us another two days of doing whatever we want — four, if you count the weekend."

Four days to herself, in his company. Allegra could hardly

imagine the possibilities. "Will we be getting out of bed in this mini-break scenario of yours?"

"Now that we've found our way into bed, you want to get out?" Darius snorted, eyes wide with mock indignation. Allegra swatted his shoulder in retribution, but gently, because he was hurt. He still winced with a pointed "Ow."

"Want me to kiss it better?" Allegra asked, smirking. She didn't wait for his okay before she slid one leg over his hips and lifted herself into place. "I think I like this view…" It wasn't a matter of flattery. Darius had a nice body — not for a man his age, not for a cop who routinely got his ass kicked whenever he ventured out from behind his desk. He was hirsute and pleasantly fleshy, his nipples dark, but more importantly, he was sexy to Allegra. Heat pooled in her belly as she ran her fingers through the soft curls on his chest. She liked watching him flush pink when she spread her labia over his stiff length.

His sharp intake of breath went straight to her clit like a zing of electricity.

"Don't tell me this hurts, too," she teased, feeling a wave of need course through her and not knowing if it was her own. Not minding, for once.

"Maybe you should kiss it better," Darius said, voice strained with effort, "just to make sure."

Allegra grinned. "I had something better in mind…" Part of spending so much time in the hospital listening to Darius breathe under heavy sedation meant reading all those pamphlets about sexually transmitted diseases and why it was so important to vaccinate. She rose up on her knees, hips flexing as she steadied Darius' stiff length with her hand. "I put the shot on Osker's tab," Allegra confessed, sensing the cocktail of bemusement and arousal that Darius was battling with. "You don't think she'll mind, do you?"

He laughed, which was answer enough, but it wasn't until his broad palms settled at her hips that Allegra sank down on his cock, taking him bare as she hadn't done with any man, for many years.

They started slowly, like they had on the couch and again just now in the washroom, but it didn't last. Allegra's body couldn't muster another orgasm, but she could easily share in Darius' pleasure as he moved inside her. She rode him hard, anticipating his needs as though they were her own. In a sense, they were.

"Stop thinking," Darius pleaded as they kissed.

Allegra nodded, grinding down to give him the release she knew he craved, but what she meant was *I can't*. It wasn't something she could explain, it could only be experienced. She only knew she didn't regret her condition so much in that moment, as Darius spent himself with a hoarse cry, his lips silently shaping her name. As if in sympathy, her aching pussy tightened around him, inner muscles clenching and releasing, working her into a breathless frenzy. She came so hard that for long moments after, Allegra could barely hear herself think as blood rushed against her eardrums.

For a brief, glorious moment, she caught a clear glimpse of what a life with Darius might be like—not perfect, not ideal, but better than she could have imagined. Certainly better than she deserved. They could have something almost normal in this austere, impersonal apartment. It could be theirs.

She knew what she had to do.

* * * *

Crisp white bed sheets, a paper gown that didn't close all the way in the back and myriad cannulas protruding from under the electric blanket draped across her body all made it hard not to feel as if she was one with Dr. Rhodes' lifeless friends—laid out on a slab, about to be sliced open.

Allegra dragged in a low, shuddering breath. The instructions had been clear—no food or drink for twelve hours before the surgery, no matter how dry her throat felt. Outside her window—she had a room with a view, gods only knew how Darius had swung that—morning was creeping along steadily through scraggly tree branches. A swallow darted between the yellowed leaves, its eyes too small for Allegra to know if it glanced her way.

She did feel hunger and animal fear, but those could well be her own sentiments.

The breathtaking wave of affection that intruded was not.

She started at the sound of the door creaking open. "Ms. Avenson?" the nurse said. "You have a visitor."

Darius stepped through the gap without her say-so, bulldozing right over any compunctions Allegra might've had about being laid up in bed like an invalid. Affection vibrated like a strummed cord.

Relief, too, but not without a faint thread of uncertainty.

"Look what the cat dragged in..."

"Hey," Darius grumbled, "be nice. I brought flowers." He seemed a little sheepish with the roses in his hands, but Allegra knew that what he felt was apprehension. He was worried for her.

"That's sweet." Allegra smiled. "You shouldn't come any closer. I haven't had any Bliss for about seventy-two hours." Another pre-op requirement.

She swallowed past her own selfish guilt, focused on the white-hot burn of indignation instead. Darius had never been easier to read, but she didn't want to end up projecting what she was experiencing by accident.

"I mean it," Allegra insisted. "The only reason I'm not climbing the walls is that they've fixed me up with some really good stuff." She raised one wrist beneath the covers to show off the IV taped to the inside of her forearm.

"Ah, so you are high out of your mind."

"Just not with the thing I should be taking. What are you doing?" Allegra's eyes widened a little. Darius had crossed the room to stand at her side, a long line of chamois trench coat and pale skin. Even the roses smelled of cinnamon. "I'm not kidding."

The memory of what she had done to those thugs in the Docklands stuck out. The APU might have granted

222

her a pardon on account of there being no bodies—the disappearing act itself the doing of Osker's cronies—but Allegra knew her own strength now. She didn't want Darius getting hurt.

That's all there is to it, Allegra told herself. Not as if she spent the long, lonely hours daydreaming about his mouth or what it might be like to go out on a date with him, like they did in the old vid-reels. Not like she cared.

"I'm not kidding either," Darius said, grinning. He brushed his palm over Allegra's knuckles. She couldn't help leach his warmth and comfort any more than she could miss the unspoken *I'm going to be right here when you wake up.*

She had to bite back a whimper, momentarily—blissfully—overwhelmed.

Darius had only closed his eyes briefly, but when he opened them again, his grin remained. "Done reading my mind?"

"Not much in there," Allegra shot back. "Didn't take long."

How could he be so flippant about this? It felt like only yesterday Allegra had woken up in APU custody, apprehended for trafficking Bliss—which she hadn't, whatever Osker might've said—and threatened with jail time if she didn't help Darius catch a serial killer.

The stick would've been enough, but Allegra needed this long-promised carrot too much to refuse the deal.

She wanted to free her hand and tell Darius to get the hell out. That it was his turn. The words stuck in her throat like honey. In the end, what came out was more along the lines of, "You know, I think you're supposed to bring the flowers after."

"Yeah?" Darius glanced speculatively at the red blossoms he'd set down on the sliding table at Allegra's right. "I'll keep that in mind for my next visit."

"You don't have to." Allegra had never been good with relationships. Her profession had something to do with her dismal track record, sure, but the truth was that her—affliction didn't make it easy to attract lovers.

People fled when it became clear she could read their intent. Darius knew that better than most. So why was he still here?

Allegra looked him over, wishing she could find a trickle of obligation or guilt or lust that compelled him to act so damnably chivalrous. There was none.

"It'll be okay," Darius said, inexplicably confident.

If Allegra bristled, it was done more for old times' sake than out of genuine offense. "What? I know it'll be okay—what's that supposed to mean?"

"It means..." Darius drew a deep breath. His hand hadn't yet moved from Allegra's, so every flash of protectiveness and care ricocheted through her like a stray bullet.

Eventually, it was Allegra who extricated her palm in an effort to give him some privacy.

Darius didn't stop her. "It means you're going to have surgery and then you'll come home with me and we'll... make this work. Somehow."

"Make what work?" Sure, they'd fucked. Allegra remembered that pretty clearly. Their time together had been memorable for more than its lack of price tag, yet to go from a stress-relieving romp—or five—to -sharing an apartment seemed like a pretty big step.

Doubt twitched at the corners of Darius' lips. "Us."

Allegra hadn't realized there was an *us*, hadn't allowed herself to consider the possibility with any great degree of seriousness. It was stray hope, a fantasy. Nothing more. She almost said as much, but the expression on Darius' face became tight with wounded pride. For a man like him to even consider giving Allegra more than a passing glance was pretty rare. To imagine him waiting—Allegra couldn't. She grappled with the impossible, tried to see herself as desirable to a man like Darius.

"I'm still a junkie from the Docklands," she pointed out. "My paperwork, my record... Surgery won't change any of that that." She'd stop being an empath and therefore privy to Darius' every mood swing, but she would still be persona non grata for the rest of Arcadia. Her collaboration with the APU would have reached an end, too, without her abilities to justify the free pass.

"I know," Darius said.

"I'll have trouble finding work," Allegra pointed out stubbornly. "I've never lived like a normal person, so I don't know how I'm going to cope with—"

Darius shook his head, stopping her short. "You are normal. You're just...more."

"And in a few hours, I'm going to be less," she snapped, more furious with herself for yearning than with him for lying. It was one the thing she'd always dreamed of — peace and quiet, no other sentiments loitering under her skin except her own. It was a sweet thought.

At last she would be able to divorce herself from other people's anger, from their worries. The smallest flash of second-hand hatred would no longer take seed in her chest or spawn anxiety that kept her up night after night.

"You'll still be you," Darius insisted. "And I'm going to be right here waiting when you wake up."

This had always been the trouble with Darius. He said what he felt. He wasn't one person in his head and another when he interacted with the world. It made it hard to remember why Allegra was so reluctant to give their relationship a shot.

She could recognize dread, she just had trouble accepting it as her own.

"Us, huh?" Allegra tested the word on her tongue. "I like the sound of that."

"Yeah?"

The door creaked open, distracting Allegra from the sharp slant of Darius' grin. One of the nurses appeared in the doorway. "Sir, I'm going to have to ask you to leave. We need to prep Ms. Avenson for the OR."

"Time to face the music," Darius teased, and bent over

the bed to brush a chaste kiss at the corner of Allegra's lips. His own were chapped and tasted faintly of caffeine. "I'll see you later."

"You will," Allegra agreed, trying for a smirk.

He disappeared around the corner with shoulders stiff and his hands in his pockets, a man bent on willing the Fates to see eye to eye.

The nurse pushed another few cc's of whatever delicious compound they had on tap and told Allegra to relax. Indifference rolled off her in waves, despite the professional, thin-lipped smile. Perhaps she thought Darius was Allegra's sugar daddy?

"I'll be right back to wheel you in, Ms. Avenson."

"Take your time," Allegra slurred. She felt as if she was floating. Her head lolled against the pillows. She glanced out of the window again, hoping to see the blackbirds bounding from branch to branch in the olive tree, but the glare of sunlight was too bright against the pane and Allegra couldn't make them out.

Vision blurring, she tried to look back to the nurse, to ask about the birds. How come no one was making them into stew in this part of Arcadia? The question promptly tangled in her throat.

The nurse was gone, but at the foot of the bed stood a frightfully familiar figure – Mallory Osker, in the flesh.

"What're you – ?" Doing here.

"Visiting an asset," Osker answered softly. "The woman who caught the Bliss Slayer... Your name should be in the papers, you know."

No, it shouldn't. Allegra had no desire to attract attention to herself, least of all when her contribution had only been made possible by her disease.

Osker seemed to read her mind. "Of course," she added, "then we'd have to tell the general public that Acute Empatheia Nervosa is more than just a chronic illness. Can you imagine the panic if people knew your kind can alter the way we feel?"

Panic rose in Allegra's chest. Every other word out of Osker's mouth was a threat, but this time there was something else. Pieces of what Allegra had been able to pick up from Jasme and Darius following Lucan's death finally slotted into place, like keys sliding into a lock. Overdose was the method by which all four victims had expired, but there must have been a reason why strangulation was identified as the cause of death.

Osker's razor-sharp smirk held the answer. And, suddenly, Allegra understood. It was a red herring, easily planted with the help of an obliging pathologist—which also explained Jamal Reid's DNA being found under Trina Grey's fingernails, the better to make it seem like there was a single murderer on the loose, corrupting then killing Arcadia's young debutantes. For a while, that must've been enough, but the real killer needed to dispose of one more—so Efrenn Weiss paid the price.

Hedworth Levin had followed, taking with him any chance that the PharmaCorps business model could be exposed. The victims—so disparate, so seemingly random—were a perfect mixture of dangerous political ambition, anarchic cultism and up-and-coming extortion.

PharmaCorps stood to lose much more if any of them opened their mouths.

Only Trina Grey stood apart from the rest. And with her murderer's death making him the perfect scapegoat for all the victims, it meant that no one would ever dig into how the other three had been killed.

Allegra felt as though she'd been punched, but she couldn't stop, she had to chase the rabbit hole to the end. Obviously, the Bliss trade would go on just like before, behind the scenes, in the dark alleyways of the Docklands and the ritzy ballrooms of Arcadia's most lavish fortress-mansions.

Who better to orchestrate it all than someone like Mallory Osker? Pride leached from her and into Allegra like water through soil.

She had played the public from the very beginning, covering up any PharmaCorps wrongdoing, all while making herself and her department appear like heroes — and she had done it masterfully enough that no one would ever doubt her. Allegra tried to reach for the call button as surreptitiously as she could, but her body was still, unmoving. The drugs were doing their work.

"Don't trouble yourself, Ms. Avenson." The deputy commissioner was still smiling. It was the expression sharks wore before they took a bite of human flesh. "Arcadia thanks you for all your hard work. We'll talk again." She patted Allegra's ankle with an icy hand, the strokes rather like a hammer falling again and again onto fragile bone.

Allegra tried to flinch, but couldn't. The awful glint of Osker's black eyes blurred overhead.

Only her voice remained clear, like a single, echoing metronome in a black void, saying, "We have so much to do, you and I..."

Allegra was alone in the room when the nurses finally came to wheel her out. Perhaps she had been alone all along. She tried to force out a warning to Darius, but not only did the wispy glow of his aura seem distant and removed, Allegra couldn't even reach out to touch her fingers to its frayed, shimmering tendrils.

She felt ice creep slowly around her, numbing her body from the toes up as the darkness of an unnatural sleep took her under. She thought of Darius. She clung to his light, before that, too, dimmed and gave way to shadow.

Chapter Twenty

Darius made his way through *Portraits*, *Letz* and six past issues of *The Arcadia Times* — all lambasting the APU for their ineptitude in apprehending the Bliss Slayer — before one of the ward nurses suggested that he go home and sleep.

"She won't be out of the OR for another two hours, dear."

"I know." He'd gone over the details of the procedure with the staff before Allegra was interned. He had done his homework.

The nurse sighed, pinching her lips into a commiserative pucker. "Time won't pass any quicker if you practice taking the shape of that chair."

Darius knew that, too, and still he made no move to rise. If the plastic chairs in the waiting room were designed to hurt, then he would happily cultivate his masochistic streak. He squirmed a little, the folds of his trench coat rustling as he balanced on hip and elbow.

Two hours was nothing. It was a stakeout with fizzy, carbonated drinks and cheap takeout. He'd suffered plenty of those throughout his career, and for far less payoff.

The nurse sighed and stalked off, her shoes squeaking with every step. He tried not to think about Mrs. L. Or her son.

The digital clock above the nurses station marked the hour. Minutes ticked by like pulse beats, the green LEDs flashing on and off with every passing second. It had a hypnotic effect. Darius felt his eyelids droop, the world going soft and fuzzy around the edges. His vision pinholed gradually, not at all like the swift curtain call of a blackout.

He woke when his chin became too heavy for his wrist.

The wall clock read midnight. Allegra would be out of surgery by now. She would be back in the room, if it all had gone according to the blueprint. Dread pitched violently in his stomach.

The waiting room had cleared of visitors and fretting family members. Cleaning bots whirred quietly along the floor, sweeping up the day's offal. Darius rubbed a hand over his face, fingers scraping through a smattering of rough stubble. He rose creakily.

The nurses station was manned by a bored-looking orderly in green scrubs. The man glanced up at Darius' approach.

"Hi. Um, is Ms. Avenson—"

"Family or spouse?" the orderly asked abruptly.

"Neither, I'm her…" Boyfriend? Jailer? Darius was too old for the former and too exhausted to sham the latter. "Well, I'm her—"

"Darius?"

Allegra's shadow stretched long and willowy over the checkered tile. The woman herself stood perfectly straight-backed in the doorway of her private ward, blinking in the harsh neon glow.

Maybe it was the amount of 3D ads Darius had flicked through before he fell asleep, or maybe it was just the inanity of his addled mind, but he found himself thinking she looked like a mannequin. She might as well have descended to earth from behind the dull gleam of a shop window.

'Beauty convalesces' or 'sanatorium chic' could be the tag line.

She embodied the quintessential horror flick specter, all washed-out pallor and sunken eyes. The bandages that covered her head from nape to brow were impossible to miss.

"What," she murmured, "no flowers this time?"

Darius would've thought he was hallucinating if not for the orderly's audible inhale, his sputtering indignation.

"You—you can't be up! Get back to bed—"

Allegra ignored him. Darius followed her example. Two strides were enough to carry him to her side. Once there, he didn't dare touch her for fear that she would vanish before his eyes.

"What are you doing? How...?"

She'd always been a little on the pallid side, but this was extreme, even for a Docklands rat. Her eyes appeared punched in, lips the hue of the whitewashed walls.

"You should be sleeping off the anesthesia," Darius pointed out softly. He was close enough to kiss her. He didn't dare. She looked exceptionally breakable today.

"It wore off."

"Already?"

Allegra rolled her shoulders. "Guess they didn't want me loitering around for long."

The orderly fetched up beside them, two red spots coloring the apples of his cheeks. "Ma'am, I really must insist—"

"Yes, all right," Darius interjected. "Let's get you back to bed."

He pressed a timid hand to Allegra's spine, the crinkly hospital gown catching under his fingers. He flinched before she could.

"Sorry, I shouldn't—"

"It's fine." Allegra smiled with half a mouth, her gaze distant, foggy. "It's all right now, remember? The surgery made it safe to touch."

"It is?"

The surly orderly was still standing by, ready to employ more forceful means if persuasion alone didn't yield results. He made to follow them into the room.

Darius blocked his passage. "Give us a moment?"

"Visiting hours are over."

"Please? I won't be long." He didn't flash his badge, tempting as it was, because the APU had only so much bargaining power—and Allegra would need to be treated even after Darius left the premises. He didn't want his impatience to reflect badly on her.

The orderly sighed. "Five minutes."

"Thank you."

Allegra had already crawled back into bed when Darius eased the door shut. He caught her swinging her legs back and forth, brow furrowed as if she was trying to untangle some great mystery.

The flowers he'd brought her earlier drooped in a waterless vase on the windowsill.

"What's wrong?" Darius asked, heart in his throat.

"It's quiet."

"It's the middle of the night," he answered. It took him a moment to understand what Allegra meant. "Oh. Do you mean…?"

She nodded. "Guess it worked." Her voice shook. Twenty-odd years of listening in on other people's mood swings and now she was alone with her own. No more need for Bliss.

No more guessing Darius' mind before he could figure it out for himself.

A hundred hours' worth of waiting couldn't prepare him for the burst of astonished laughter that snarled in Allegra's throat. *That's what joy sounds like.*

Darius took her hands in both of his and pressed chapped lips to her bony knuckles.

"Why are you crying?" Allegra asked, swiping a thumb through the salt streaks on his cheek.

He hadn't noticed he was until she said it. Then he couldn't scrub the evidence away fast enough. He was a grown man. He had no business sniveling. "I wasn't. I'm not."

"I don't mind you crying."

Darius believed her, but guilt stuck his lips together. He couldn't say 'I worried I wouldn't see you again. I was afraid something would happen during the surgery'. "How do you feel?" he asked instead, because that was far more important.

"Strange."

'It's quiet', she'd said, sheepishly.

"Does it hurt?" He was reluctant to touch her bandages for fear of causing her pain. But Allegra shook her head. Her fine blonde hair had been sheared off completely, leaving her skull bare. Patches of skin were visible around the dressings, gleaming pink and shiny like healed burns.

"Think I'm going to keep the *look*," Allegra quipped. "Make it a fashion statement."

"Could work."

"Yeah?" She tightened her grip around his hands, but her hold was lax, easy to break. A clinically induced blackout—plus doctors puttering around in her brain—had inevitably sapped her strength. It was a miracle she could stand unaided, let alone have full use of her limbs and speak like she'd just gone in for a nap. She barely even slurred.

"Yeah," Darius echoed dumbly, feeling like a teenager all over again. The knot in his throat had everything and nothing at all to do with diffidence. For the first time in years, he could see himself finding religion.

* * * *

The neurosurgeon swung by in the morning, while Allegra wolfed down an unappetizing breakfast of avocado gelatin and protein sticks. Darius was on his third cup of coffee. He bounded to his feet like a coiled spring in the presence of Medical Authority.

"What's this I hear about you strolling up and down the ward?" intoned the doctor. He was a reedy, pencil-thin figure with hooded eyes. For some reason he put Darius in mind of a stork—it might have been the coffee. "You're defying every prognosis, Ms. Avenson."

"That's me," Allegra deadpanned. "Overachieving wherever I go..."

"The op went all right? No hitches?" Darius asked, overlooking her banter. *There were no problems?* Like anyone with an uplink, he'd read the crackpot doomsayer sites and

233

studied the evidence. His take on Allegra's condition was as unscientific as it was emotionally loaded.

He remembered full well the records from the Levin crime scene.

Much to his relief, the doctor nodded. "Like a pleasure cruise."

"And the recovery?"

The doctor waved his tablet toward Allegra. "That depends on the patient. You may feel some general soreness. Migraines are to be expected. I'll prescribe you some heavy-duty painkillers to relieve any lingering discomfort—"

"No." Allegra swallowed past a mouthful of green gelatin. "No pills."

"Would you prefer a patch?"

She shook her bandaged head. "I'll take the migraines."

"They may be more debilitating than you think. Your system is—"

"I don't care." Allegra's voice turned icy with intransigence. Docklands kids were nothing if not resilient.

"Strong *and* brave," the doctor chuckled. "You're a lucky man, Detective."

Was it that obvious? Darius caught himself smiling guiltily and mumbled something vaguely acquiescing.

He could feel Allegra's gaze on him when they were left alone. Perhaps that was why he felt the urge to needle her. "Is this part of the new and improved you? You're going to be a martyr?"

Allegra scoffed into her plastic pot. "Fuck you very much. I didn't go under the knife so I could start popping another brand of pills." Her fears were well founded, especially considering what their investigation had dug up—evidence now swept into some APU oubliette, never to be seen again.

"We forgot to ask when you can go home," Darius said, skirting the topic. He was quick to back down from a quarrel he knew he couldn't win.

"Guess that's whenever they throw me out…"

"Could be sooner, unless you're attached to your

breakfast."

Allegra flicked a quizzical frown his way.

"They may agree to discharge you into my care," Darius went on. He didn't have the guts to offer to take her to his apartment. It was another landmine to avoid. Yet if he could read Allegra, then Allegra could surely read him, gifted or not.

He met her gaze. "It's just a suggestion. We talked about it before you went in…"

"Yeah, that was a nice pep talk. Thanks."

"I meant every word." *Even if you didn't.*

He'd hoarded his hopes like a magpie, until he could bear them no more. They'd spilled out like counterfeit coins. Allegra had sized them up with a critical eye long before she had narcotics on her side to make her wary.

The furrow between her eyebrows was less than reassuring.

"You want to make *this* work," Allegra clarified, gesturing at the space between them with a plastic spoon.

"Yes."

"And you want me to bunk at your apartment for a while."

Darius nodded. "However long you need." Was that strange? Allegra had a way of fogging things up, like the whole world went a little out of focus when she was near.

"No Jell-O at your place?"

"My fridge is completely barren." Not exactly a point in his favor, but Allegra wouldn't be fooled if he claimed to be Suzie Homemaker all of a sudden.

He was what he was — an overworked, middle-aged washout stuck in a high-risk, dead-end job. But he'd been better with Allegra. And part of him suspected that she felt the same.

"Okay."

Darius arched an eyebrow. He wasn't going to make the mistake of assuming he knew Allegra's intentions again. The last time had been almost fatal.

"You get to argue with the doc, though. I'm bedridden."
Allegra flashed him a grin. "You better be sure you want
this."

I am. I'm very sure.

"I make no promises," Darius shot back. On impulse, he
leaned in and brushed his lips against hers. It was their
first real kiss post-surgery, and it was more timid than any
they'd shared before.

Allegra was still smiling when he pulled back, her eyes
soft with relief. Contact no longer sparked bursts of intuition
she shouldn't have been able to have in the first place. It
was no longer a doorway into madness. Darius kissed her
again just to prove it.

This time Allegra parted her lips to his and traced the sharp
edge of his teeth with her tongue. Her innate playfulness
was still there, buried in a shallow grave beneath layers of
trepidation and slow to decant. Darius would take great
pleasure in coaxing it to the surface. They had all the time
in the world to relearn each other, and no obstacles to stand
in their way.

"Oh, go away. I'm not making out with you in a hospital
bed," Allegra snorted, turning her head fractionally.

Darius pressed a kiss to her cheek. "Aren't you prudish...?"
He hadn't forgotten that night in the park, or the one in
Allegra's humble squat. He didn't force the issue. For once
their foot-dragging aligned perfectly. "I'll track down the
doc, see what needs to be done to turn you loose."

He could already imagine carrying Allegra over the
threshold and setting her onto the sunken couch in his
apartment. In his mind's eye, he conjured up pillows and
steaming mugs, a soft cashmere throw to cover her legs—
all the comforts of a real home, normally absent in his. He
would have to make do.

Allegra patted his stubbled cheek. "This isn't a dream,
right?"

"No." Darius started to laugh. *You dream about me?* The
years just peeled off where romance was concerned, didn't

they? He made a mental note to find a mirror, see if the gray in his hair was darkening to black again.

"When I was under..." Allegra trailed off.

"You dreamed?"

She nodded. "Weird stuff. I thought I saw Osker of all people..."

"Well, if you swing that way." Darius dutifully accepted the jab against his ribs. It was earned.

Allegra dismissed him with a wave of the hand, her wrist tag flashing. "You said something about springing me?"

"Right. Your mouth is—distracting."

"Heard that one before."

Darius geared up to rib her some more, but promptly realized that what sounded like a joke to his genteel ears was probably plain fact for Allegra. It was easy to forget that she'd had a life before him, that Osker hadn't conjured her into existence when she dragged her into the precinct.

He swallowed his retort. "I won't be long." Allegra's arched eyebrow drove home how pathetic it was to make promises at every turn. She wasn't wrong. But now that he had her safe and sound, Darius was all the more terrified of losing her.

There's a pill for that.

He asked for the neurosurgeon at the nurses station and was told to wait while last night's irritable orderly put in a call. There was no rushing him. At least Darius could see Allegra's closed door if he bent his back a little, if he craned his neck. Maybe in an hour or so, they could put the hospital behind them and move onto the next chapter of their lives. Whatever that was.

"This is strange," the orderly muttered under his breath.

"What is?"

Darius got a scowl for his nosiness, but an answer slowly unspooled from the orderly's mouth. "Dr. Choi isn't answering his comm."

"Why is that weird? Maybe he's with a patient..." Or scrubbing in. Darius had watched enough medical dramas in his day to have a vague, lurid picture of what went on behind OR doors. Even with bots in place and lasers to replace scalpels, human touch was still vital, if only to reassure the patients.

The orderly tried again, letting the call go through five times before he lost patience. Darius watched him wheel his swivel chair to the nearest red phone.

"Security, I need eyes on Dr. Choi..."

"It's not that urgent," Darius started. He was eager to take Allegra home, but not so eager that he wanted to make the doctor's life difficult.

The orderly paid him no heed. He gave Dr. Choi's last known whereabouts to the unseen security staff and rang off.

"If someone else is available—all I want is to know when Ms. Avenson can be discharged." Hospitals gave Darius the creeps when he was the one laid up in bed. When it was someone else—someone he cared about—he felt helpless.

"I'll send someone in."

Darius sighed. "Thanks." He dragged himself to the nearest coffee machine and scanned his credit chip before he could think better of it. He thought about getting Allegra a cup, but the murky brew was hospital fare and she was still medicated from last night's surgery. Darius decided against it.

He was barely halfway to the room when a trio of uniformed PrivaSec goons bolted past him. "Hey, watch it!" Coffee yawed dangerously in his plastic cup, nearly sloshing over the rim.

The men barely glanced his way. They were in a hurry.

Someone had probably tried to make off with a stethoscope.

He let himself into Allegra's room with a grumbling sigh, a string of complaints perched on the tip of his tongue. That was where they died when he cast a glance to the bed.

Allegra's face was turned away from him, but judging by the steady rise and fall of her ribcage, she was asleep.

238

Between her unearthly pallor and the crown of gold light spilling through the slats in the window blinds, she almost looked angelic.

Darius pulled up a chair and dropped heavily at her bedside, intent on watching over her. He could be a better watchdog than nursemaid. He just needed to rest his eyes for a few moments.

He barely had the foresight to set his cup down on the floor before he dozed off.

* * * *

"Darius." His name in Allegra's mouth was all sibilant consonants and soft vowels. "Darius, wake up." The clasp of a hand on his shoulder was slightly less gentle. Allegra pulled no punches as she shook him out of the fog of sleep.

He blinked in the sight of her with rheumy eyes. "Wasn't asleep."

Allegra pressed her lips into a taut line. "Yeah, right. What happened out there? I thought you said you were going to find the doc?"

"I was." Darius scrubbed a hand over his face. His stubble was steadily becoming a beard. A couple of days more and he'd look like the legions of homeless who peopled the Docklands. Except more unwashed. "I did…" He seized one thread of his frazzled thoughts and pulled, unraveling the yarn. "Right. They couldn't find him, said they'd send someone else. I'll go ask again…"

"Okay."

Darius recognized that tone. It would've stung worse if Allegra weren't laid up with a thick band of gauze around her head. "I *am* getting you out of here. I swear. They don't have any reason to keep you." And the APU had promised to pay only for surgery, not whatever aftercare Allegra might need.

Osker was a shrewd businesswoman.

His stomach gurgled as he made his way out of the room,

into hallways that were becoming increasingly familiar. Something was different this time, though. PrivaSec uniforms were stationed at either end of the hall, their chiseled faces impassive.

Then Darius saw the blue-red strobe of police lights streaming through the far window. He approached slowly, wary of what he'd find.

The hospital was shaped like a horseshoe, two wings bound together by glass-walled tunnels that repelled UVs and allowed natural light to stream through all the livelong day. Below, a labyrinthine network of perfectly manicured hedges gave way to silk-smooth footpaths and moving walkways.

On Darius' first visit, the entrance of the hospital had been barren and Zen, like something out of a catalog. Now it was swarming with police officers and reporters, news vans all but bottlenecking the street. Some five floors above on the other limb of the horseshoe, a window gaped open. White, gauzy curtains fluttered in the evening breeze.

Darius made his way to the nurses station. "Is Dr. Choi available?"

A flinch was all the hint he needed to guess the victim's name.

He returned to the room empty-handed. Allegra fixed him with a wary gaze. "Nothing?"

"Let's get you dressed."

She arched her eyebrows even higher, jaw dropping. "They said I could leave just like that? No post-op check-up, no—"

"Do you want to stick around for more Jell-O?"

Allegra shook her head. She needed his help pulling on her shirt, but she managed underwear and pants on her own.

"I'm a terrible influence, aren't I?"

Darius scoffed. "I was breaking rules before you were born." Which, in retrospect, had never worked out so well for him. *Times change.* He wasn't about to let Allegra linger in an administrative crack while the system picked through the red tape at snail's pace.

The impassive PrivaSec goons by the elevators stopped them with a rote "Sir, ma'am, I'm afraid—"

"APU business," Darius interjected. "Do I need to call your superiors?"

That put a damper on the firm but polite spiel. "May I see your badge?"

Darius handed it over, all the while trying not to feel as if he was trading on something precious. His principles hadn't kept him warm when his marriage fell apart, so why should they be a comfort now? Allegra leaned against his side, either weak with effort or else seeking his hand. He gave it without a second thought, twining their fingers together like that would keep the Fates from snatching Allegra out of his grasp.

The PrivaSec employee held out the badge. "Have a good night, sir."

I could've been like you. It was a heady, dangerous thought. Darius shoved it aside as he guided Allegra into the elevator.

She rounded on him as soon as the doors slid shut. A scowl twisted at her cinnamon-stained lips. The effects of Bliss took time to fade. "Now do you want to tell me what's going on?"

"Dr. Choi took the short way down." Darius swallowed hard. "He's dead." It wasn't an uncommon occurrence in Arcadia. People were complex, imperfect machines. All the accomplishments in the world couldn't keep inner gears and pulleys from clogging up with rot.

The Bliss Slayer-that-wasn't had proved as much.

Allegra recoiled as if punched. "Oh," she breathed, her hand still clutched firmly in Darius' grasp.

"It's not our problem." He winced when Allegra fixed him with a disbelieving stare. "Well, it's not." *We risked everything once. I almost died.*

I almost lost you.

They had earned the right to be selfish. Let someone else

save the day for a change. Osker would take the credit anyway, spinning the story like web to bolster her latest pet project while the rest of them fought over scraps.

The elevator eased to a stop in the underground garage. The gallon of coffee in Darius' gut resettled.

"We'll have someone come to check your stitches at home."

"Won't that set you back a pretty penny? House calls aren't cheap…" Allegra slid into the passenger seat with slow, deliberate movements. Darius didn't dare ask if she was in pain or if she was simply cautious. He didn't want to tread on her nerves.

"No more than keeping you here."

It was a lie, but Allegra wouldn't be able to tell anymore. Her genetic lie-detector trick was a thing of the past.

Darius pretended he didn't feel a flash of remorse as he keyed the engine. "You're going to have to let me take care of you for a change," he added, trying to sweeten the pill. "I *want* to."

Allegra sighed. "I know. I'll…try." Her voice was very low, almost drowned out by the purring of the engine.

She didn't react as they pulled out of the parking lot, rolling over the speed bumps in the road at a glacial pace. She didn't even care to see the kaleidoscope of artificial light bathing the front lawn of the hospital.

It was for the best. Darius spied the deputy commissioner at the heart of an impromptu press conference, the queen bee surrounded by her minions. She looked in her element in front of the cameras. Darius saw her lips move, but couldn't make out what she was saying. He didn't turn on the car radio to find out.

They had earned a little peace.

HELENA MAEVE

SHADOW PLAY

BEST
KEPT
LIES

CAPTIVITY IS A DANGEROUS THING
AND GRIGORY ALREADY OPERATES UNDER A CLOUD OF SUSPICION

Best Kept Lies

Excerpt

Chapter One

"You're a son of a bitch, you know that?"

The crackle of red vinyl dragged across Grigory's nerves, yet when he glanced up it was with a placid smile. No use antagonizing such a valuable asset.

Nathaniel wrinkled his nose at the cloud of stale cigarette smoke that rose from the bench seat as he sat down. He didn't comment on the setting. He had more important things on his mind.

"Was it your people?"

Someday, Grigory mused, they would look back on this and laugh. Assuming they lived long enough for hindsight to lend a touch of humor to their clandestine meetings.

"Don't you want to take your coat off first?" he inquired. "Make yourself comfortable?"

Nathaniel raised his eyebrows. He'd never come out and

say 'cut the crap'—crap being par for the course in their industry—but it was written in the disbelieving lines of his face.

"I won't be staying. They're expecting me back at the embassy in twenty minutes."

"Then you shouldn't waste time asking questions you know I cannot answer." Slowly, Grigory raised his coffee cup to his lips and returned his gaze to the flat-screen suspended above the bar.

There was something vaguely offensive about a café in Rome displaying every feature of a New Jersey watering hole. Before Grigory could give it much thought, the 'Breaking News' logo flashed on screen.

Ten Downing Street seemed both larger and grayer on TV. The prime minister fared no better beneath the flicker and flash of tabloid cameras. Burly men in stretchy dark suits flanked him like hailers. With little finesse, they bustled him into the back seat of a shiny Mercedes as reporters shouted questions from behind the barricades.

The BBC feed lingered on that one last glimpse of Prime Minister Craft before he disappeared behind tinted glass.

He wore the face of a man on his way to the gallows. Her Majesty hardly warranted the sulk.

A blonde head blocked Grigory's view.

"Good morning," greeted the perky waitress, her English beautifully accented. "What will you have?"

She wore a pale coral shirt that matched the sign outside the café and a pair of cut-off shorts. From her apron dangled a hand-scribbled name tag that read *Letitia*.

"Nothing," replied Nathaniel. Then, for Grigory's sake, he repeated, "I'm not staying."

"Chicken burger," Grigory said, ignoring him. "And guacamole."

"Would you like a beer with that?"

Grigory beamed. "Why not? Make that two."

Punctuating their order with a flick of the pen, the waitress fluttered her lashes and turned on her heel. Her ponytail swung as she sauntered toward the kitchen. She couldn't have been older than eighteen.

Watching her made Grigory feel impossibly old. Eighteen had been sweating over his university entrance exams and staring wistfully out of the window as neighborhood boys staggered out of their beds simply to trawl down to the public pool. Eighteen had been the certitude that if he hadn't got into Lomosonov University, his life would have been over.

Eighteen was an eternity ago.

"You know I don't care for Italian beer," Nathaniel muttered under his breath.

"Who says I ordered it for *you*?"

Nathaniel's stiff upper lip became a flat horizontal line. Like pretty, blonde Letitia, he struck Grigory as too green for the world. At least no one expected Letitia to deal in state secrets.

He allowed himself a sigh. "Your prime minister chooses the wrong call girl to unburden himself to and it *must* be the SVR's long reach twisting her arm?" If he clucked his tongue, it wasn't to dismiss the possibility but to chide Nathaniel for jumping to such a far-fetched conclusion.

It was a sad reality all across the globe that politicians were not to be trusted — especially when they pledged their loyalty to secret spy agencies first.

"Believe me, this comes as much as a surprise to us as it does you."

Young and inexperienced as he was, Nathaniel didn't take the bait. "Did you just ask me to believe a spy?"

"Intelligence officer," Grigory corrected. He couldn't resist pedantry when he had the upper hand.

Nathaniel stabbed a fingertip into the table. "*Someone* bloody well leaked this to the press. My superiors are furious. If it *was* your people, they should know this is being treated as a hostile op. What's the Russian word? *Dezinformatsiya*?"

"It's not false, though, is it?" Grigory helped himself to

another sip of coffee. Bitterness paired well with the stink of statecraft. "Propaganda seems more apt."

"The words 'Russian-backed coup' might have been bandied about the office..."

"There's a little Shakespeare in all of us."

Nathaniel went from barely restrained to combustible in a matter of seconds. "Damn it, Grig!"

It was just as well the café was largely empty and they'd sat far enough in the back that no casual passersby could see him seize Grigory's forearm in a vise-tight grip.

"This means internal investigation. Probes into every department... What do you think'll happen when they assign me a shadow, huh? If I'm found out, you can kiss your privileged access goodbye."

And the same goes for your career, your freedom – perhaps even your life. The British were no more tolerant of treason than Grigory's comrades.

"You won't be."

Nathaniel released his arm, falling back against the red vinyl of the booth. "You don't know that! Apparently you don't know *anything*." Agitation bubbled beneath his uneven tan, but the brief spike of fury had passed. He raked both hands through his hair and blew out a shuddering breath. His fingers shook when he made to straighten his skinny blue tie. "I want to talk to your handler."

"That's not possible."

"*Make* it possible. I've cooperated, I've jumped through every bloody hoop... Now it's your turn. I leave Rome in forty-eight hours. Set up a meet before then or I come clean to my superiors."

Grigory barely resisted the urge to rub his temples. He could feel the headache building behind his eyes, the throbbing of his pulse like a hydraulic piston.

This part of the conversation would have to be omitted from the report. He'd put too much work into smoothing things over after Nathaniel's maladroit recruitment to lose him on a threat uttered in the heat of the moment.

Managing informants was two parts hand-holding to one part drilling. Enlisting talent was simply the first step in obtaining valuable information.

"Nathan, be reasonable…"

The swish of soft cotton slacks was all the answer he received.

Nathaniel stalked out of the café without so much as a glance over his shoulder. The door swung slowly shut in his wake.

Reason was not on today's menu.

"Here are your drinks… Oh!" The waitress blinked fast, as though struggling to compute the sight of an empty seat across from Grigory. "Should…I take this one back?" she asked, waving the spare beer.

Grigory shook his head. "You can leave it. Thank you."

"Your friend seemed upset," Letitia ventured. Impossible to discern if she did it out of innate friendliness or if it was all part of the American flavor of the joint.

The alternative—that she was an undercover agent fishing for information—would've dogged Grigory in the early days. Paranoia was just another distraction.

Letitia sighed wistfully. "He should've tried the wings. Instant pick-me-up."

"That he should have…" Grigory glanced at his watch. He had another hour before his next rendezvous. "But you know what? I think I could use a plate myself."

The waitress's delighted grin almost took the sting out of his abysmal morning.

* * * * *

Streaks of white clouds pocked the midday sky by the time Grigory left the burger joint with a stomach full of bread buns and broiled meat. The taste of fearsomely spicy barbecue sauce lingered in his mouth, though he had done his best to wash it down with light beer. He walked slowly down the crooked, narrow streets, his body as sluggish as a snake's after a good meal.

This part of Rome was as much tourist-trap as it was a pedestrian wet dream. With no cars allowed, the fiercest roadside terror was the pigeons. Little rotund bodies defied the laws of physics as they swooped and scattered before Grigory in a rustle of gray wings. The feathery curtain revealed souvenir shops and overpriced eateries — mostly pizzerias and gelato sellers with Italian-sounding names, front windows showing off the *tricolore*.

No American-inspired hole-in-the-wall here. No smiling waitresses, either. The few servers Grigory spotted stood outside their place of employment with aprons knotted around their waists and cigarettes perched between two fingers. They seemed authentic in their thorough contempt for the world.

A boxy gray bus was pulling up to the stop at the end of the street just as Grigory rounded the corner. He sped his steps and the double doors sealed behind him. He shot the driver a smile as he scanned his RFID ticket against the yellow sensor.

Owing to its electric engine, the bus didn't jounce quite as much as its gas-powered siblings. Still, the potholes in the pavement were unavoidable.

Grigory listed this way and that, gripping the backrests for balance. He found a seat at the back of the bus and dropped down heavily, strength seeped from him as though by osmosis.

The bus was mostly empty at this hour, even on a tourist line. The gentle sway of overworked suspensions rocked him into an unpleasant sort of semi-awareness. He registered the bustle of passengers climbing on, climbing off, heard the hum of voices all around him, but the details eluded him. If asked whether the teenage pair three rows in front were Swedish or German, he would've been unable to say.

His thoughts veered, predictably, to Nathaniel's prickly ultimatum.

It was a bad time to be making demands on the SVR. It was a worse time to be issuing threats. Too many new faces in the Kremlin made for a chaotic foreign strategy. For all that Grigory knew, they *had been* the ones to out Prime Minister Craft in a fit of pique.

A so-called strategic war in Ukraine had been set in motion for the same reason.

"If we are, it was Moscow's decision," Zorin told him, her tone dismissive when Grigory shared his concerns with her.

He'd leapt from his seat three stops into his journey and stepped off the bus just outside the Teatro dell' Opera.

Crowds of tourists milled around under the European flag, some armed with long-lens cameras, others with smartphones or guidebooks—seldom both. Grigory was used to weaving between them with a strange sort of fondness. He'd been like them once—so sure of his world, so eager to trust.

Peering down at the swarm from the window of a barbershop that smelled of peppermint and sage, he felt only impatience.

"Jennings wants a chat."

Zorin looked up from the teapot she was maneuvering with expert care. "With me?" Her thick, blonde eyebrows nearly met in the middle when she frowned. "You told him that's not possible."

"He wasn't inclined to listen. This business with Craft..."

"I see." Zorin slid his cup along the table and folded long-fingered hands above her own.

She was often economical with words, but her protracted silences slithered under Grigory's skin.

"He's a little insecure," he explained.

"So reassure him." It's your job, she seemed to be saying.

"It might be best if I embrace my role as bad cop. Besides," Grigory added as he sat on the scuffed leather couch, "you have a gentler touch."

Zorin's mouth twitched. Before Grigory could tell if she was amused or offended, she had already smoothed her pale, angular features into a blank mask.

"When?"

"He leaves in two days."

"I know," Zorin scoffed.

Not amused, then.

Annoyance dripped from her voice. "When do you want this rendezvous to take place?"

"Day after tomorrow." Grigory had spent the ride to the barbershop on Via Firenze thinking up viable locations. He'd had a feeling Zorin would want solutions to the problems he presented. "Nine o'clock. I have tickets to *La Traviata*."

"Italian opera," Zorin scoffed into her tea. "A little on the nose, don't you think?"

Grigory shrugged. "I enjoy it."

"You would."

He concentrated on taking a slow sip of tea, the scalding brew blistering his throat as it trickled down. The barbershop had fewer ears than other Rezidentura-approved sites, but that still didn't make it secure.

Zorin must have been more irritated than he'd realized to take such a cheap shot.

"Oh, live a little, Zhenka..." Grigory stood and reached into his jacket. He couldn't resist a smirk as Zorin stiffened, training kicking in.

"You don't like your tea?"

"Too much sugar," he lied. The glossy ticket struck the table with a dull whack. "The black number with no back should do it. You know, the one the general likes?" He answered her glower with a crisp smile.

More books from
Helena Maeve

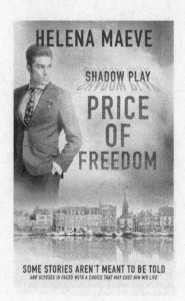

Book two in the Shadow Play series

Some stories just aren't meant to be told.

More books from
Helena Maeve

Surface Tension
Twice Upon
a Blue Moon

He's a man of
many secrets...

Helena
Maeve

Book one in the Surface Tension series

*Some affairs are like playing with fire, but knowing you'll
get burned is no reason to throw the game.*

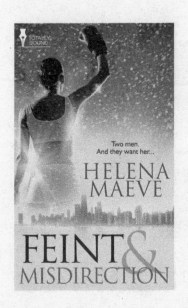

Two men.
And they want her...

HELENA
MAEVE

FEINT&
MISDIRECTION

*Imogen Dao is going to punch her way through this
championship even if it means losing the men in her life.*

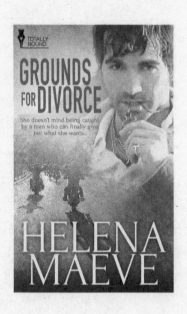

Kayla is convinced she's had her fill of bad boys when her boyfriend's debts catapult her into a stranger's arms.

About the Author

Helena Maeve

Helena Maeve has always been a globe trotter with a fondness for adventure, but only recently has she started putting to paper the many stories she's collected in her excursions. When she isn't writing erotic romance novels, she can usually be found in an airport or on a plane, furiously penning in her trusty little notebook.

Helena Maeve loves to hear from readers. You can find contact information, website details and an author profile page at https://www.totallybound.com/

Home of Erotic Romance